A MARRIED WOMAN

"Why isn't your husband with you? Where is he, Faith?"

She felt ashamed. "I don't know. He left me for another woman. He said he was going to California. I haven't heard from him in over two years."

"Do you still love him?"

"Still love him?" she echoed with a note of surprise. A bitter laugh rose in her throat. "No. No, I don't still love George."

With only a slight pressure, he turned her toward him. He lifted her chin with his index finger, forcing her to look up. He stared into her eyes with an unwavering gaze, looking down deep inside her. It felt as if he could see into the deepest secrets of her soul.

"You're safe here," he said at last.

He pulled her close and lowered his head with an agonizing slowness. The chill she'd felt only a short time before was forgotten, replaced by a languid heat that radiated through her the moment their lips touched. The kiss was infinitely sweet, immeasurably tender, and far too brief.

Books by Robin Lee Hatcher

Liberty Blue
Chances Are

Published by HarperPaperbacks

Chances Are

 ROBIN LEE HATCHER

HarperPaperbacks
A Division of HarperCollins*Publishers*

This is a work of fiction. The characters, incidents, and
dialogues are products of the author's imagination and are
not to be construed as real. Any resemblance to actual events
or persons, living or dead, is entirely coincidental.

HarperPaperbacks *A Division of* HarperCollins*Publishers*
                  10 East 53rd Street, New York, N.Y. 10022

Copyright © 1996 by Robin Lee Hatcher
All rights reserved. No part of this book may be used or
reproduced in any manner whatsoever without written
permission of the publisher, except in the case of brief
quotations embodied in critical articles and reviews. For
information address HarperCollins*Publishers*,
10 East 53rd Street, New York, N.Y. 10022.

Cover illustration by Jim Griffin

First printing: May 1996

Printed in the United States of America

HarperPaperbacks, HarperMonogram, and colophon are
trademarks of HarperCollins*Publishers*

❖ 10 9 8 7 6 5 4 3 2 1

To Christine. Chances are—this book wouldn't have happened without you.
To my family, all of them—Mom, daughters, grand-kids, brother, sister, nieces, nephews, aunts, cousins, in-laws, etc.—who have always, without fail, been there when I've needed them.
And finally, to Jerry, as always and for always.

All the world's a stage,
And all the men and women merely players.

—*As You Like It,* II.vii

Chances Are

1

Dead Horse, Wyoming
June 1886

     The physician shook his head as he slowly straightened and raised gray eyes to meet Faith's anxious gaze. "It's not good, Mrs. Butler," he said, his tone gentle and solicitous.

Faith Butler glanced down at her daughter, lying so still on the bed, and her heart twisted with grief and fear. Becca's skin was so pale, it was nearly transparent. Even her lips were colorless. Her frail body—small, even for a five-year-old—seemed to cause barely a wrinkle in the blanket that covered her. As she touched the child's brow, brushing limp strands of hair away from Becca's face, Faith felt apprehension slice through her.

"I believe it's her heart," Dr. Telford continued. "You say she was diagnosed as having rheumatic fever some time ago?"

Looking up again, Faith nodded, the lump in her throat making it too difficult to speak.

The doctor removed his glasses and rubbed his eyes with the thumb and index finger of his right hand. "Did you understand rheumatic fever is a chronic disease, Mrs. Butler?" He met her gaze again, not waiting for a reply. "Of course, I'm not an expert on diseases of the heart, but I believe, if your daughter is able to rest and get the proper care, she may recover from this episode. It will take a great deal of time and care, and you mustn't delude yourself into believing that she'll ever be strong."

Faith's own heart felt as if it would give out just listening to him. Becca couldn't die. She had to get well. She simply had to.

Dr. Telford continued grimly, "You must understand this, Mrs. Butler. If you put your daughter back into that wagon, she won't live out the week. She can't take any more jouncing around on rough roads. She must have complete rest and decent nourishment. She hasn't the constitution for such a vagabond existence."

Faith sank onto the chair beside the bed, fighting despair. "But what am I to do? The stage is how I make my living. Acting is all I know. If the company must go on without me . . ." Her voice trailed off into painful silence.

When sorrows come, they come not single spies,
But in battalions.

"Well," he said with a note of disdain, "if you must go on, there's a home in Cheyenne for orphan children. I suppose my daughter-in-law might agree to keep the child until she's well enough to send to the orphanage."

"No!" Faith shot back to her feet. "I'm not deserting my daughter." She stiffened her back and lifted her chin. "I'll stay here as long as it's necessary. I'll do whatever I must to take care of Becca."

The doctor cleared his throat. "That's very commendable, Mrs. Butler."

For an actress, she could almost hear him thinking. No doubt he also wondered if there actually was a Mr. Butler.

Unfortunately, there was. At least, she thought so.

She shoved away thoughts of George and the hurt and anger that came with them. She hadn't time to indulge herself in those emotions. Or in self-pity, either. She had to take care of Becca and Alex.

Mentally Faith added up the money she had tucked away during this most recent tour. There wasn't much, and Raymond Drew, the company manager, wasn't likely to part with any of her wages if she left the troupe without notice, especially out here in the middle of nowhere.

She shoved away thoughts of Raymond Drew as quickly as she had those of her absent spouse. She would deal with Raymond later.

"Dr. Telford, perhaps you could suggest where I might find work here in Dead Horse and where we might stay until Becca is able to travel?"

He raised an eyebrow. "I'm afraid there aren't many opportunities for employment here, Mrs. Butler. As you could see when you came into town, there's little left of Dead Horse these days. The stagecoach quit coming through nearly two years ago. The bank closed its doors six months after that. Folks've been moving out ever since. It's a wonder this hotel's still open. Wouldn't be if my son didn't believe the railroad would come north through this valley like they've been talking about." He scratched his temple. "About all that's left hereabouts are the cattle ranches and those are few and far between. Of course, women are scarce, too. If you're looking for a husband, you might find a cowboy or a rancher who is—"

"I have a husband," Faith replied tightly.

"Well, then, I don't know what there might be for you. The general store isn't hiring. The Golds have their six children to help them." He squinted as he gave the matter more thought, then he said, "I suppose Stretch Barns over at the saloon might have work for you."

"A saloon?" Her heart sank. She'd performed plays in plenty of saloons over the years. She'd seen what the work was like for women who had to dress up in revealing costumes and serve drinks to already drunken patrons. At least on stage she'd been protected from pawing hands and other unwelcome advances. "Isn't there *anything* else?"

The doctor seemed to hear the note of desperation in her voice. He reached out and patted her shoulder, his attitude suddenly changed. "It just might be you could get work up at the Rutledge place. Can't be sure, of course. I heard their cook quit earlier this spring. Don't know that Mr. Rutledge has hired anybody new yet. Even if he has, he's got that big house up there on the hill and a large crew working cattle for him on his range. Maybe he needs himself a housekeeper, too. There'd sure be plenty of room for you and your children. I know the ranch foreman. Parker McCall. He's an honest, hardworking fellow. I imagine he'd put in a good word for you, if I asked him to." He gave his graying head a shake. "Never have met Mr.

Rutledge myself. Don't know anyone in town who has. But I hear the cow hands like working for Parker. I think you'd do all right there."

A housekeeper or a cook. She could manage that. Not that she'd had much experience with keeping a house. She'd lived her entire life out of a trunk—traveling in wagons, staying in hotels, living in tiny rooms above theaters for a week or two at a time. As for her cooking . . . well, it left something to be desired, but at least she had some experience. She could make coffee over a campfire, and she could fry most foods without burning them. Surely she could cook well enough to satisfy a bunch of hungry cowboys.

And, after all, it wouldn't be for long. Only until Becca was well enough to travel. Then they could all go back east and Faith could find work with one of the theater companies in New York.

Of course, if she had been able to find work in New York City, she would be there now instead of in a wide spot in the road appropriately called Dead Horse. But she refused to consider the truth of that even for a moment. She also refused to think about what would happen if this Mr. Rutledge refused to hire her.

She closed her eyes, shutting out all doubts. She couldn't afford the luxury of giving in to fear. Becca and Alex needed her, and Faith would never fail her children. They'd already been let down too often in their brief lives. She would do anything—scrub floors, take in ironing, sew dresses—to take care of them. If she had to, if it was her only choice, she would even serve drinks in a saloon.

'Tis true that we are in great danger;
The greater therefore should our courage be.

Taking Shakespeare's lines to heart, Faith drew in a deep breath, opened her eyes, and asked, "How do I find Mr. Rutledge?"

"I've got a patient to see up at the Jagged R tomorrow. I'll take you along if you'd like." He picked up his black leather bag and crossed to the door, then glanced over his shoulder at her. "I'll be by first thing in the morning to check on your little girl. My daughter-in-law, Nancy, will come to stay with her while we're gone."

"I'm most grateful, Dr. Telford."

He left, but before the door could close behind him, Alex slipped through the opening.

"How's Becca?" her son asked, concern creasing his young brow. He was trying hard to be strong for his mother, and Faith fought new tears as she observed his bravado. He was only seven, but every so often she caught glimpses of the young man he would soon become.

Oh, God, what will I do if—

Faith sank onto the chair a second time and motioned for Alex to join her there. When he did, she put her arm around his back, pulling him close against her side. Then she took hold of Becca's hand and looked down at the girl.

"Becca's going to be all right," she whispered, making herself believe it. "She just needs rest. We're going to stay here for a while."

"I'll help take care of her, Ma."

Faith gave her son a squeeze. "I know you will. You've always been a big help to me." She kissed his cheek. "Would you tell Mr. Drew that I need to talk to him?"

Alex nodded, then hurried out to do as she'd asked.

After the door had closed again, Faith leaned forward and placed a kiss on her daughter's feverish forehead. "I won't fail you, Rebecca Ann," she whispered, her voice breaking with barely controlled emotions. "We'll get through this. I promise."

They'd already come through so much, she and the children. Surely they would get through this, too. They had to. Alex and Becca were all the family she had in the world. They were everything to her. Everything.

You mustn't die, Becca. You must get well. There is still so much for you to see and do.

Faith loved both of her children equally, but she'd always worried more about Becca. Rebecca Ann Butler had nearly died at birth, and her health had always been somewhat fragile. But she was perfect in every other way. As an infant, she'd rarely fussed, always smiling and cooing, never any trouble to care for. Even as a toddler she'd been well behaved, obeying her older brother, both of them sitting quietly behind the scenes during rehearsals and performances.

Becca had to live. She had to live and grow up to be all that Faith had imagined she would be. She had to grow up and be happy and have the things Faith wanted for her, the things Faith had once wanted for herself—a home with a white picket fence, a husband to love and cherish her, and so very much more.

Faith stared down at her daughter. "We're going to be all right," she whispered as she smoothed the blanket, tucking it beneath Becca's arms. "I promise you. We're going to be all right. We're going to—"

Her words were interrupted by another knock. She called out permission to enter, and the door opened to reveal Raymond Drew.

"How's she doing?" the company manager asked as he entered, nodding toward the bed.

"She's sleeping." Faith moistened her lips. "The doctor said Becca can't travel again until she's better. It's going to take time. Weeks. Maybe months. The children and I will have to stay in Dead Horse."

"Stay *here?* Great Scott! And do what, Faith? We've got a show in Cheyenne next week. You can get another doctor to have a look at her once we're there. This one doesn't know anything. What kind of doctor can he be if he's living in this godforsaken place? He probably doesn't know what's wrong with her any more than I do. He's nothing more than a quack if you ask me."

"Look at her, Raymond. You don't have to be a doctor to know he's right. It will kill Becca if I put her back in that wagon. If we were in Green River City and I could take her by rail . . ." She shook her head and met his gaze with a determined look of her own. "You'll have to go on without me."

"And just where do you suggest I find an actress to replace you? We have a contract, Faith Butler, and I mean to hold you to it."

She drew back, feeling as if he'd slapped her. Softly she said, "She's my child, Raymond. What would you have me do?"

He swore and spun away. "All right then. Stay here, if that's what you want. Christine can do your part as well as her own until I find someone else." He jerked open the door. "Just don't come looking to me for another job when you're ready to work again. You're not that good, you know." He disappeared into the hall, muttering something about actresses and hell.

Faith slept little during the night that followed. Each time she drifted off, she awakened with a start only moments later, fear strangling her.

What if Mr. Rutledge wouldn't give her work? She'd already told Raymond to leave her behind. The troupe would be gone by morning, and then it would be too late to change her mind. What would she do if she couldn't get work? What would happen to Becca and Alex then? Would she save Becca's life only to watch both of her children starve?

By morning, there were dark circles of worry beneath Faith's eyes and her body ached with a weariness that went beyond just the physical. One look in the mirror told her it wasn't likely Mr. Rutledge would want to hire her. She didn't look strong enough to lift a frying pan, let alone run a household.

She took her time dressing, putting on her best gown and arranging her hair with care. But despite her preparations, it was without a shred of optimism that she left the hotel with Dr. Telford. If not for her desperate circumstances, nothing could have taken her away from her daughter's bedside that morning, for she was certain the journey would end up a futile one.

As they left town, the doctor pointed south and said, "That's where we're headed. That's the Jagged R Ranch."

A three-story house sat on a high bluff, about five miles or so outside of Dead Horse. It seemed severely isolated, completely cut off from the rest of the world and the small town below. A terrible loneliness swept over her as she stared up at it.

What sort of man sought such solitude? she wondered, a shudder of trepidation racing along her spine.

They drew near the top of the bluff, and Faith realized the Rutledge house was larger than she'd at first thought. It was painted gray, all of the windows framed by charcoal-colored casings. There were numerous outbuildings, some large, some small. There was also a corral holding about a dozen horses, all of them sturdy, well-fed animals.

As they came into the yard, the front door opened and a man stepped out onto the front porch. He tipped his hat back on his head and leaned against the post as he waited for the buggy to stop.

"Is that him?" Faith asked the doctor.

"No. That's McCall, the ranch foreman."

She was disappointed. There was something kind and friendly about Mr. McCall's leathered face and the half smile tipping the corners of his mouth.

"Howdy, Rick. What brings you out this way?" The foreman's dark eyes slipped to Faith as he stepped down from the porch.

"I'm here to take out Gertie's stitches." The doctor inclined his head toward his passenger. "This is Faith Butler. Mrs. Butler, Parker McCall."

Faith nodded. "How do you do, Mr. McCall?"

"I do right fine, ma'am."

Rick Telford continued, "She'd like a word with Mr. Rutledge."

Parker raised an eyebrow, his smile disappearing. "See Mr. Rutledge?" He rubbed his chin. "The boss don't receive company. You know that, Rick."

"But I *must* see him," Faith blurted, afraid he would turn her away before she had a chance to even meet Mr. Rutledge, let alone ask for a job. Then, embarrassed by her frantic outburst, she clenched her hands in her lap, drew herself up straight, and said with as much dignity as she could muster, "Mr. McCall, I've come to seek employment. I have two children to support, and we are unable at present to travel elsewhere to look for work. The good doctor has given me to understand Mr. Rutledge may be in need of a housekeeper. I should like to apply for the position. And I can cook, too," she added hastily.

Parker McCall glanced at Rick Telford. "A house-keeper?" He was silent a moment, then his gaze returned to Faith. "Might not be a bad idea at that." A moment later he grinned. "In fact, I think it's a mighty fine idea. You just come on with me, Mrs. Butler."

Nervously Faith took hold of Parker's proffered hand and stepped down from the buggy.

"I think Gertie's in the barn," the foreman called over his shoulder as he led Faith away.

Upon entering the house, Faith found herself cloaked in a dim gray light. The windows in each room had been shrouded by heavy draperies, shutting out the sunlight so abundant in a Wyoming summer. She wondered if someone had recently passed away, then thought not. There was a permanence about it all that made her shudder with dread. An ominous feeling pervaded the air, and she wanted nothing more than to turn and leave.

Cowards die many times before their deaths. . . .

Parker stopped and rapped on a door.

"Yes?" a deep voice called from the other side.

"Got a minute, Drake?" Parker didn't wait for a reply. He simply turned the knob and opened the door, drawing Faith with him as he entered the room. "This little lady is Faith Butler. She'd like a word with you." He gave her elbow a squeeze, then stepped back into the hallway and closed the door.

The room was bathed in shades of gray and black, but Faith could tell she was in a library. The walls were lined with shelves and shelves of books. As in the other rooms, the windows here were hidden behind thick fabric. The only light came from a lamp, turned low, on the desk. Beyond it, she made out the form of a man, seated on a chair, pushed back out of reach of the lamplight.

"What is it you want?" he asked angrily. He rose from the chair, and his shadow appeared exceedingly tall and threatening, as threatening as the timbre of his voice.

Her mouth went dry, and she feared her knees would buckle. She wished she could see his face. If she could just make eye contact with him, perhaps . . . "Well?"

Don't get stage fright now. Remember why you came.

"Speak up, madam, or get out."

She drew in a quick breath. "Mr. Rutledge, I've come to your ranch to seek employment as your housekeeper."

"I have no need of a housekeeper."

"But *I* have need of a job." She stepped forward, determination driving out fear, if only temporarily. "Mr. Rutledge, my little girl is very sick. The doctor says if I try to travel with her, she could die. She *will* die. I must find work and a place to live until she is well again. Please, sir, I'm desperate. I'm not asking for charity. I'll work as hard as anyone else on your ranch."

A long silence followed. Then Drake Rutledge stepped around the desk, coming toward her with intimidating strides. His sheer height made her want to draw back from him, but she held her ground as he came to a halt mere inches away.

"I don't believe you belong here," he said in a low, resentful voice.

She tilted her head, staring up at him.

His shoulders were broad and powerful. She could see that he wore a suit, as if dressed to go out for an evening. His hair was dark—black, she imagined—and long, reaching his shoulders. His face, bathed in shadow upon shadow, seemed harsh and frightening. In the anemic lamplight that fought against the darkness, she saw that he wore a patch over his right eye.

Like a pirate. She subdued an instinctive shiver.

For a long time neither spoke, neither moved. Faith's heart pounded a riotous beat in her chest. Never in her life had she felt such rage as that which emanated from this man. It was like a white-hot fire, singeing her skin.

Finally he took a step back from her. "I think it's time for you to go, Mrs. Butler."

"But . . . but what about the job? You haven't told me if you'll hire me as your housekeeper."

He leaned forward. "Do you *want* to work for me, madam?"

She managed to hold her ground once again, not drawing away as she wanted. "No," she answered honestly, her voice quivering. "But I have no other choice. I'll not let my daughter die for lack of a roof over her head or food on the table. And I don't want my children living over a saloon, which seems to be my only other choice." Suddenly all her courage evaporated, allowing desperation to overwhelm her. Tears flooded her eyes as she extended a hand in supplication, nearly touching his chest. "Please, Mr. Rutledge. Becca's only five years old. Please help us."

There was another lengthy silence, then he cursed softly and stepped around her, heading across the room. "Tell Parker to give you and your children a couple of rooms on the third floor." He yanked open the door. "And stay out of my way, Mrs. Butler, for as long as you're here."

Then he was gone.

Faith drew in a deep breath and let it out slowly, scarcely able to comprehend what had just happened. She'd achieved that for which she'd come. She'd found a place to live and a way to support her children until Becca was well again.

But it was the dark, angry man who remained in her thoughts as she left the library and walked toward the front of the house. When her fingers alighted on the doorknob, she paused and glanced behind her, halfway expecting to find Drake Rutledge standing in the shadows, watching her.

'A was a man! take him for all in all,
I shall not look upon his like again.

But she *would* look upon him again, and instinct told her he was *not* like any other man she'd ever known. She felt another shiver, this one of apprehension for what the next few weeks might bring.

From the landing on the second floor, Drake listened to the closing of the front door. Then he moved to the window overlooking the yard and surreptitiously moved the draperies aside so he could peer down.

Faith Butler appeared a moment later, out from beneath the porch awning. She stopped when she reached the buggy and looked back at the house.

Her hair was red, the color of hot coals before they turn white. Red without a hint of orange, bright in the morning sunlight. Her bustled gown was striped in shades of gold and brown. She was small and perfectly shaped.

And she was beautiful.

His fingers tightened on the draperies.

He'd known she was beautiful, even in the dimly lit library. Even her fragrance—soft, tantalizing, womanly—had been exquisite. But he hadn't known the extent of her loveliness until this moment.

What in the name of heaven and earth had possessed him to tell her she could stay at the Jagged R? He didn't need a housekeeper, and he certainly didn't need a woman in his house, causing him grief. Experience had taught him that women, particularly beautiful women, were responsible for most of the grief in the world.

Yet there'd been something about the way Faith Butler had stood before him—afraid, but not fleeing—that had kept him from sending her away. There'd been something courageous in her stance that had given him reason to pause. But it had been the quiet note of discouragement in her voice that had been his downfall.

Just then, Rick Telford, Dead Horse's doctor, strode into view, coming from the direction of the barn. Although they'd never met, Drake recognized Rick from his previous visits to the ranch. Drake wondered what blame the doctor shared for bringing the woman to this ranch.

With scarcely a word to Faith, Rick helped her into the buggy, then climbed up beside her, took the reins in his hands, and slapped the leather straps against the horse's rump. The buggy jerked forward, quickly carrying the beautiful woman with the fiery red hair out of sight.

Drake swore again as the draperies fell into place, closing out the light and leaving him in familiar gloom.

She won't stay long, he reminded himself as he turned and walked away from the window.

He would see that she didn't.

Faith's heart was still racing as she turned the knob and opened the door to her hotel room.

Nancy Telford rose from a chair, looking none too happy. "Well, finally you've returned," she said as she reached for the basket holding her embroidery work.

"How is Becca?"

"Never a peep out of her."

Even with Nancy's words of assurance, Faith wasn't satisfied until she crossed to the bed and touched her daughter's cheek. Relief flooded her as she felt the coolness of Becca's skin. The fever had broken. Turning, she said, "Thank you for staying with her, Mrs. Telford. I don't know what I would have done if—"

Nancy made a sound of dismissal, waving away Faith's thanks with a flick of her wrist.

Faith smiled. "Mr. Rutledge gave me a job."

The other woman's eyes widened. "I don't believe it."

"Neither do I, but it's true." Her smile broadened.

"You actually *met* him?"

"Yes, I met him." She removed her hat pin, then lifted off the small straw bonnet, setting it on a nearby dresser.

Nancy stepped forward, her face alight with anticipation. "Well? What was he like? Tell me everything."

Angry, Faith thought. He was very angry.

But she kept the comment to herself, not wanting to betray the mysterious man who'd agreed to help her by giving her a place to live. "I'm not sure, really. He's a very . . . *private* sort of man. Not the least bit talkative. Our meeting was quite brief."

"I've always believed he must be running from the law. Why else would he hide up there in that house and never come into town? Mark my words. He's probably a murderer. You'll be sorry you ever went up there. No one but a fool would have taken my father-in-law's suggestion. No doubt you'll all die in your beds at the hands of a madman." With a toss of her head, she swept from the room.

Faith stared after Nancy, the woman's parting words echoing in the silence. *No doubt you'll all die in your beds at the hands of a madman.* Faith remembered the subdued rage that had been present in the Rutledge library and wondered if Nancy Telford might be right. Had she made a mistake? Was she taking her children into danger?

She turned to her daughter and leaned over to brush wisps of strawberry blond hair back from Becca's forehead. Just as she did so, the girl's eyes fluttered open.

Faith's heart tightened, then soared. "Becca, darling?" She sat on the side of the bed.

"I'm thirsty, Mama."

Quickly Faith poured water from a nearby pitcher into a glass and held it to her daughter's lips, supporting the girl's head with her other hand. Becca took a few sips, then closed her eyes again, slipping back into sleep as quickly as she'd awakened moments before.

"We're not going to travel anymore, Rebecca Ann. Not until you're completely well again. Mama has taken a job as a housekeeper in a big, beautiful house.

No more theaters or hotel rooms. Just lots of fresh air and sunshine." Suddenly she thought of the tall, shadowed man who was her new employer. "Mrs. Telford is wrong about Mr. Rutledge, Becca. I think he must have a very kind heart to help us this way. A very kind heart indeed."

Drake Rutledge rarely found sleep until the wee hours of morning. For years he'd spent his nights prowling the house or sitting on the porch as the hours marched toward dawn. There had always been comfort and peace in the darkness.

But tonight he didn't feel comforted or peaceful. He felt hollow, tense, and he knew what was coming. He tried to summon anger, rage, bitter fury—old, familiar feelings, trustworthy companions—but even those failed him tonight.

Standing at the edge of the porch, he stared down at the tiny lights of Dead Horse. Moonlight reflected off the ribbon of river that cut a swath across the valley floor. It was a serene scene, one he'd gazed down upon countless times in the years since he'd purchased this house on the bluff. One he'd been satisfied to view from a distance—and alone.

But I have no other choice. . . . Please help us. He heard her voice, sweet and frightened. He saw her face, beautiful and uncertain.

He cursed himself for listening, for allowing himself to respond. Faith Butler would bring only grief to the Jagged R Ranch. He should never have said she could come here to live. He should send Parker into Dead Horse right now to tell the woman he'd changed his mind. He didn't want her here. He didn't want any woman here.

And he knew why.

With a soft curse, he stepped off the porch and headed for the corral. He had to get away. He had to escape the memories that were pushing in, crowding him.

In a matter of minutes he had his gelding saddled and bridled and was mounted. He turned the pinto away from the river valley, heading out onto the sweeping plains. He gave the horse his head, trusting the animal's night vision far more than his own. Soon they were speeding across the range. The wind—cool and bracing—whipped against his face. It was a mad gallop to outrace things better forgotten. Horse and rider followed a familiar path, for it was a race they had run before.

It was a race they had never won.

2

Several days later, as the team of horses followed the road out of town and up to the Rutledge ranch, Faith sat in the back of Joseph Gold's wagon, cradling Becca's head in her lap and trying not to think about what she might face in the days ahead. Dr. Telford—who had insisted she call him Rick, as everyone else did—drove the borrowed wagon slowly, for which Faith was grateful. It didn't matter that he had said Becca was improved enough to make the trip. She was still frightened by every bump in the road, each jar of the wagon wheels, remembering only too well what harm the doctor had warned travel could cause.

Alex didn't share his mother's trepidation about the short journey. After too many days of confinement, he was eager to reach the ranch. He was full of questions about where they were going to live and would he be able to ride any horses and would he meet any real cowboys.

"Will we see any Indians?" he asked next, obviously hoping his mother would answer in the affirmative.

"I don't know, Alex."

Not satisfied, he addressed the man beside him. "Will we see any Indians, Dr. Telford?"

Rick muttered some sort of reply that Faith couldn't quite hear.

Becca opened her eyes. "Mama?"

"Yes, darling?"

"*Will* there be any Indians?"

Faith smiled as she stroked her daughter's forehead, comforted that Becca's fever had not returned. "I don't think so. And if there are, I'm quite certain they'll do us no harm. You remember seeing Buffalo Bill's Wild West Show, don't you?"

Becca nodded.

"Those Indians didn't really hurt anyone. It was all just for fun, remember?"

Her little girl nodded again.

"Then there's nothing to be afraid of, is there?"

Becca shook her head and closed her eyes.

Faith wished she could be reassured as easily. Not about wild Indians, but about her new employer. She'd tried not to think about Drake Rutledge in the days since he'd agreed she and her children could come to his ranch to live. She'd tried and failed. It had been impossible to erase his dark image from her mind. Impossible to avoid the questions that plagued her.

What did her future hold for her, working as his housekeeper? Would she be able to cook and clean to his satisfaction? Would he turn them out before Becca was well again? Worse yet, could Nancy Telford's dire prediction be true? Would they all die in their beds at the hand of a murderer? Was Faith making a horrible mistake?

She clenched her hands into fists, then opened them as she let out a deep breath, trying hard to relax. She reminded herself that she'd had no other choice. Each day the Butlers had remained in the hotel, their small savings had dwindled further. Faith had eaten little, giving what food she'd purchased to her children, fearing what would happen if she ran out of money before the doctor agreed Becca could be moved.

Now, Faith gazed up at the gray house on the ridge and subdued a shiver. *It's only for a short time. When Becca's well, we can leave. We won't be there for long.*

"'When I was at home,'" she quoted softly, "'I was in a better place, but travelers must be content.'"

"What's that, Mrs. Butler?" Rick asked, interrupting her musings.

She met the doctor's eyes, surprised that he'd heard her. "Just a line from a play."

"Shakespeare?"

"Yes."

"My wife always liked Shakespeare's plays." A frown furrowed his brow as he turned his attention back to the road before him. "I never cared for them much myself. Too difficult to understand the way they spoke, if you ask me." He paused, then added, "Esther loved it, though."

There was something in his final words—a melancholy tone—that told Faith he wished he'd not spoken. She swallowed her reply but welcomed the sudden flood of memories his comment had stirred to life.

To Faith, William Shakespeare had almost been a

member of the family. From early childhood she'd memorized his plays, come to know his characters as if they were her friends. In truth they'd been her only friends, for she'd known few other children.

After her parents—both Shakespearean actors—were divorced, Faith had followed her father around the country. She'd been raised backstage, in hotel rooms, in wagons, and on trains. She'd had her first role at the age of ten and had been performing ever since.

Perhaps my whole life has been just one long performance. Perhaps none of it has been real.

She frowned at the uncomfortable thought and quickly rejected it. Her life was as real as anyone's. She'd always admired great actresses like Sarah Bernhardt and Helena Modjeska. She'd wanted to have the same stage presence that her own mother, Nellie Fields, had displayed. Faith had never envisioned anything for herself other than the life she'd known.

Had she?

A momentary loneliness squeezed her heart, but she drove it away with ruthless determination. She wasn't lonely, and she didn't want a life different from what she had. She was content. She had everything she'd ever wanted or needed—her children and her work. And when Becca was well, she would be happy to return to the stage.

Truly, she would.

Drake stood at the window of his second-floor bedroom and watched Rick Telford lift the little girl from the wagon bed. A few moments later, Faith Butler and the young boy whose hand she held accompanied the doctor and Parker McCall into the house. Drake heard the front door open, listened to their voices and footsteps as they made their way up the stairs to the third floor. It was the most noise and activity the house had heard or seen in seven years, and it left Drake feeling restless, unsettled.

He didn't want them there. He cursed himself for the hundredth time for not sending word to her that he'd changed his mind about allowing them to stay in his home. Raking his fingers through his hair, he turned from the window and strode across the room to the door. He opened it, then stepped into the hallway.

"Ma, can I go outside?" he heard a young voice ask from the floor above.

"Not yet, Alex. Come back into the room. We must get settled first."

"But, Ma—"

"Alex."

Silence followed, then the closing of a door.

Drake set his jaw. *Hellfire and damnation!* He never should have allowed her to come. He wouldn't have a moment's peace as long as she and her children were here. Not one solitary moment of peace!

With another string of silent curses, he descended the stairs and stalked into his library, closing himself in where he could be alone—and undisturbed.

"You just let me know if you need anything, Mrs. Butler," Parker McCall said from the doorway. "Take your time with settlin' in. We're used to mostly doin' for ourselves. You take care of the little lady there, and when you're ready, I'll show you around the place, give you the lay of the land, so to speak."

"Thank you, Mr. McCall."

He set a dusty hat back on his head. "I reckon you'd better call me Parker."

"Then you must call me Faith."

He grinned, his sun-bronzed face crinkling around his dark eyes and the corners of his mouth. "Be right pleased to do so, ma'am."

"Faith," she reminded him, returning his smile.

"Faith."

The warmth of his smile lingered with her as he closed the door. Perhaps it wasn't going to be so bad here. Parker McCall made her feel welcome. Just maybe the others . . .

"Look, Ma. There goes Dr. Telford on his way back to Dead Horse. Golly, look how high up we are!"

She turned to find her son hanging halfway out the window, barely visible beyond the heavy draperies. "Alexander Butler!" She grabbed hold of his shirttail before he could topple, headfirst, out the opening. "Lord, I could use a bit of help here," she muttered as she yanked her son back into the room.

Alex immediately tried to wriggle free.

"Hold still, young man." She placed her index finger beneath his chin and tipped up his head. "Alex, I already have my hands full with your sister. I won't have you breaking your fool neck. Is that understood?"

He looked as chagrined as a seven-year-old boy full of vinegar could manage. "Yes, ma'am."

"Do you know what folks think of us? They think performers are simply charlatans, people of low character. They think we don't know how to properly raise our children. They don't believe we know good manners. I won't have you confirming their suspi-

cions." She knelt on the floor. "I know this is exciting
and new, Alex, but you must be on your best behav-
ior, at least until I can prove myself as a housekeeper
to Mr. Rutledge."

This time his apology was in earnest. "I'm sorry,
Ma. I promise not to cause any more trouble."

Now it was Faith's turn to feel bad. "I know you
won't." She gave him a tight hug. "You've always
been a good boy. I'm proud of you, Alex. I've always
been proud of you. But I'm going to need your help
now more than ever." Releasing him, she rose and
glanced about the gloomy room. "Since Mr. McCall
told us these are our rooms, shall we have a look at
them?"

In a flash Alex forgot the scolding, curious to discover all he could about his temporary home.

Parker had given them two rooms with a connecting doorway between. The first room, where Becca
lay sleeping, had two narrow beds and a small fireplace. A window—the one Alex had nearly fallen out
of—was set into a steeply pitched roof. Once Faith
removed the draperies that covered the window, she
found its northern exposure gave them a clear view of
the valley and the town below.

"There," she said as she dropped the dark fabric to
the floor. "That's much better."

The second room, she discovered, was larger than
the first and had both a bed and a sitting area with a
sofa and two chairs. There were two windows in this
room, one on each side of the fireplace, which looked
out upon the bunkhouse, barn, and corrals.

The draperies were promptly removed from these
windows, too, allowing morning sunlight to spill into
the room, chasing gloom into the corners. The light
also revealed dust motes floating in the air, reminding

Faith she had a job to do. She'd been hired as a housekeeper, and she didn't suppose that meant just cleaning up her own living quarters.

"Alex, I want you to sit with your sister while I find the kitchen and see about fixing us all something to eat. Then you can go outside for a while, but only where Mr. McCall says you may. Understood?"

Her son nodded.

"Good." She opened her trunk and withdrew the new apron she'd purchased at Gold's General Store with funds she could ill afford to spend. Pushing away her constant concerns about money, she tied the blue-green apron around her waist. With a quick glance in the mirror, she checked her hair to make certain it was still tidy, then left their quarters and descended the stairs to the ground floor.

"Mr. McCall?" she called softly.

First, she looked into the parlor. It was dark, gloomy, and sparsely furnished, but she recognized the familiar shape of a piano in the far corner. She wondered if her mysterious employer ever played the instrument but found it difficult to imagine that the heart of a musician beat within such a man.

With a shake of her head, she crossed the hallway and looked into what was obviously the dining room. Despite the shrouded windows, she could see a long table in the center of the room, surrounded by numerous chairs with tall backs.

"Parker?"

Still no reply.

Well, she thought, undaunted, the kitchen can't be too far from the dining room.

Squinting in the darkness, she saw what appeared to be a door at the opposite end of the room. Certain it must lead to the kitchen, she headed toward it—

and smashed her toe into the leg of a chair, set askew at the table.

"Ooh." She doubled over, the pain making it hard to breathe. "Ooh," she groaned again, then, "Blast it all!" She glared at the black skeleton of the chair, then sent an even harsher glance toward the window coverings that blocked out the light. She straightened, muttering, "If this place weren't as dark as a mausoleum, a body wouldn't find herself running into things."

Limping slightly, she continued toward the back of the dining room, moving much more slowly this time to avoid any other unpleasant surprises. When she pushed on the swinging door, she discovered herself in a narrow passage containing a table and a service window to the pantry. Beyond the passage was the kitchen.

Here, for the first time, she found a room not bathed in darkness. The kitchen had windows facing the south and west and a doorway that opened onto a small veranda. There was a black cooking stove in one corner. In the center of the room was a long table with benches on both sides and a chair on each end. Along the outside wall was a large cupboard, an icebox, and a counter with a sink and a pump handle. The connecting pantry was enormous, but the shelves were almost empty. Another door led to the back hall, a second stairway, and a third entrance, this one opening onto a porch that faced the bunkhouse.

It was on this back porch that she found Parker McCall, leaning his hip against the rail while he talked to a tall, slender cowpoke with a dirt-smudged face and sweat-darkened shirt and trousers. Parker turned as Faith stepped onto the porch.

"Here she is now," he said, motioning for Faith to

come forward. "Faith, I'd like you to meet Gertie Duncan. Gertie, this is Faith Butler, our new house-keeper and cook."

Gertie removed her hat, revealing a riot of short chestnut curls, then she dropped her cigarette and ground it into the dust with the heel of her boot. "Howdy, Miz Butler. It'll be nice to have some decent grub for a change. Parker here's a lousy cook."

Faith tried not to reveal her surprise as she returned the greeting, but she doubted she was suc-cessful.

Gertie laughed. "If it makes you feel any better, Miz Butler, you're not the first t'be taken aback when they see I'm a woman. 'Course, most folks seem t'for-get it quick enough." She slapped her ragged hat back on her head. "I'd better get back t'work. Them horses ain't gonna break themselves."

Faith watched the tall woman stride away, know-ing she was staring but unable to keep from it.

"Gertie's one of the best wranglers I ever worked with," Parker told her.

She turned toward him. "I'm afraid I was rude. It's just I—"

Parker shook his head. "Gertie's used to it. She's got feelings as tough as rawhide. She doesn't hurt easy. Wouldn't't've lasted ten minutes around here if she did."

Faith looked back to watch the woman disappear around the corner of the barn, hoping the foreman was right but feeling sorry for her bad manners all the same.

Parker pushed off from the railing. "Well, let me show you around the kitchen for starters. Like Gertie said, I'm a lousy cook and everybody's already glad you came."

"I'm certainly going to do my best," Faith promised as she rubbed her palms on her crisp new apron, praying that she didn't appear as nervous and unsure of herself as she felt.

A trickle of sweat wound its way down the back of Faith's neck as she dipped the last strip of salt pork into the cornmeal and dropped it into the melted fat in the skillet. While the meat browned, she opened the oven to check on the potatoes, baking in their jackets. Just a few more minutes and they would be ready.

Straightening, she said a quick prayer of thanks for Wiley Pritchett, the crotchety old stage driver who'd hired on with Raymond Drew's company last year. Wiley had taught her how to fix this rather simple but tasty meal. Not to say she'd ever cooked it all by herself, but she'd helped Wiley often enough to feel a measure of confidence. Luckily the Jagged R smokehouse was full of meat, and by some miracle she'd found the remaining necessary ingredients for the meal in that woefully stocked pantry.

But what about tomorrow?

Pot roast. She could fix a pot roast. And fried chicken. She knew how to make good fried chicken. Well, edible, anyway. And her rice pudding was passable.

But then what?

She glanced quickly about the kitchen. What she needed most of all was a cookbook with recipes even *she* could follow. If there wasn't one to be found here, she would have to go into Dead Horse and buy one at the general store.

Caught woolgathering, Faith remembered the meat

in the frying pan just in time to keep it from burning. Quickly she removed the strips of pork, then drained off all but a couple of tablespoons of fat. To this she added flour, browned it while stirring well, then mixed in some canned milk and let it simmer into a thick gravy before returning the strips of meat to the pan.

Finally, heart pounding nervously, she leaned forward and tasted the concoction. Her eyes widened and she smiled. It was actually good! She'd done it. She'd prepared her first meal without burning a thing and without anyone's help. Grinning like a schoolgirl, she scooped the pork and gravy into a large blue bowl.

"Mmm, mmm. Somethin' shore smells good in here, and it's been callin' t'me t'come see what's cookin'."

She glanced toward the back door to find a grizzled cowboy standing in the doorway.

He whipped off his hat, spit on his hand, and smoothed his graying hair back on his head. "M'name's Dan Greer, and you must be Mrs. Butler."

Before she could answer, more cowpokes came pouring through the back door, forcing Dan Greer into the kitchen before them. She looked from one man to the next, growing increasingly nervous at the sight of them.

"All right. All right." Gertie Duncan pushed her way through the crowd of dusty cowpokes. "Give 'er a chance, boys. She ain't the first filly you ever laid eyes on." Her gaze met Faith's. "You ready for us t'be in here, Miz Butler? If not, say the word, and I'll run the lot of them out."

Faith nodded, then shook her head, and finally swirled about, gasping, as she remembered the baking potatoes. She grabbed a towel to protect her hand and yanked open the oven door. Fortunately, she wasn't too late.

"I'm ready for you," she said with a relieved sigh.

While she pulled the potatoes from the oven, she heard the ranch hands taking their seats among plenty of good-natured jostling and joking. She recognized Parker's voice and felt a flash of comfort, knowing she had at least one friend amid all the strangers.

She smoothed strands of hair that had pulled loose to straggle about her face, then brushed her hands over her apron. The newness of the fabric had already disappeared beneath splatters of grease and a dusting of flour.

I must look a sight.

But she wasn't on the stage, and those hungry men behind her hadn't come to look at the cook, she reminded herself. They'd come to eat.

Drawing in a deep breath for confidence, she picked up the serving platter stacked with potatoes and the bowl of salt pork and gravy, then turned to face the waiting ranch hands.

Except for Gertie, they all rose in unison from their chairs. The men grinned as Faith approached the table.

Dan Greer jumped forward to pull out a chair for her. "You sit here, ma'am, by me."

"Oh, I don't know, Mr. Greer." Her gaze flicked to Parker McCall. "Perhaps I—"

"Go on and sit down, Faith," the foreman said. "You gotta eat, too. Besides, everyone wants t'get to know you. Can't think of a better time than now."

"Well . . ."

The boy to her right—perhaps eight or nine years older than Alex, Faith thought—held his hat against his chest and nodded in her direction. "The name's Johnny Coltrain. Pleased t'meet you, Miz Butler."

"I'm Will Kidd," said the man beside Johnny.

Across the table, a giant blond fellow said, "They call me Svede." His thick, rolling accent told her why. "Svede Svenson."

"And I'm Roy Martin," said the man to Svede's left. "We're right glad you've come to work at the Jagged R, ma'am. Right glad."

The last remnants of nervousness vanished as she looked at them. "Thank you." She smiled, then added with a laugh, "I'm right glad, too."

With an impatient sound, Drake slammed the ledger closed after realizing he'd been staring at the same column of figures for over half an hour. He leaned back on his chair and gazed at the ceiling, trying to ignore the muffled voices beyond his closed door.

The cowpokes had come in for lunch an hour before, just as they did every day. But this day was different because they'd lingered instead of eating quickly and getting back to work. And he knew it was because of *her*.

His fingers tightened on the arms of his chair as he squeezed his eyes closed.

He'd heard her laughter, light and airy, drifting to him from the kitchen. The men's laughter had been louder, more boisterous, and it was easy for Drake to imagine them all preening and vying for her favors.

Damn!

He rose abruptly and began pacing the room, feeling caged, wishing it was night so he could saddle up his horse and outrun the rage. When he heard the rap on his door, he snapped, "What is it, Parker?"

The door opened. "It's not Mr. McCall. It's me. I've brought you something to eat."

He whirled on Faith Butler. "What are you doing in here? Didn't I tell you to stay out of my way?"

She didn't turn and flee as he'd expected. Probably because she couldn't see him clearly. Probably because she didn't know the man who'd hired her.

Lowering his voice, he growled, "Come in." Then he returned to his desk. "Put the tray on the table over there."

With his back still to her, he turned up the lamp, allowing light to spill into virgin corners of the library. He heard Faith's hesitant footsteps as she entered the room, taking the tray of food to the small table near the fireplace. Then he turned.

For an instant, before she looked at him, her face was serene, and he realized he'd failed to judge the extent of her beauty. But her serenity was shattered when her gaze lifted toward him. He recognized her surprise. He knew what she saw—the wretchedly scarred face, the black patch over a sightless eye— and he knew what she felt.

She felt what Larissa had felt. Revulsion. Loathing. Disgust.

But, surprisingly, her voice didn't reveal any of those things when she spoke. "Your food is getting cold, Mr. Rutledge. Why don't you sit down and eat? I'll return for the tray later." She walked toward the door, then paused and turned to face him. "I . . . I want to thank you again for hiring me, Mr. Rutledge. I'm going to do my very best to prove myself an excellent housekeeper." Her smile was soft, gentle, perhaps even courageous.

Unable to return the smile, Drake showed his back

to her, reaching out to the lamp, turning it down, plunging the room into familiar darkness. A moment later the door closed, leaving him alone—just as he wanted.

Faith's calm demeanor disappeared instantly. She leaned against the wall, pressed her hands against her chest, and consciously slowed her breathing.

She didn't know what she'd expected. She'd known her employer was an angry man. She'd known he wore a patch over his right eye. She'd known he was tall and strongly built. None of those things had surprised her when she'd looked up and seen him clearly for the first time.

But she hadn't expected to feel a sharp jab of sorrow pierce her heart. She hadn't expected to feel a stranger's pain as if it were her own.

She closed her eyes and saw him again in her memory. His hair was as black as a raven's wing, worn long, like Buffalo Bill Cody's. He had a neatly trimmed mustache above a grim, unsmiling mouth. His chin was squared, stubborn, strong. A narrow white scar cut his right eyebrow in two, then disappeared beneath his eye patch and appeared again on his right cheek.

She'd felt a strange urge to reach out and touch him, to offer some sort of comfort. But for what?

"Faith?"

She gasped as her eyes flew open.

"Sorry," Parker said. "Didn't mean to startle you. You all right?"

She nodded as she straightened away from the wall. She glanced quickly toward the library door, then headed toward the kitchen.

Parker followed. "Maybe I should tell you a bit more about Drake."

"That isn't necessary."

"I think maybe it is."

She felt again that sharp pain in her chest, pain that belonged to another. "Another time, perhaps," she whispered. "I need to check on Becca."

Like a coward, she fled up the back stairway. But she couldn't escape the memory of Drake Rutledge or the curious sense that her life would change because of him.

3

Gertie Duncan leaned against the top rail of the corral and watched the white stallion as he paced the width of the enclosure, tail held high, nostrils flaring. The wild horse was a beauty—or would be as soon as she was able to take brush and curry to him. If there was one thing Gertie knew, it was horseflesh, and this stallion was one of the best she'd ever seen.

"You might as well get used t'me, fella," she said softly. "We're gonna spend a lot of time together. We're gonna get to be good friends, you 'n' me."

The stallion snorted and tossed his head as he whirled and pranced in the opposite direction.

"Golly! Look at him."

Gertie glanced down to find a young boy standing beside her, staring wide-eyed through the fence rails. She grinned. "He's somethin', ain't he?"

"Is he yours?" the boy asked without taking his eyes off the horse.

"Nope. Shore wish he was, though. He belongs to Mr. Rutledge."

Finally the boy tore his gaze of admiration from the stallion and looked up at her. His eyes widened even more. "You're a *girl!*"

She laughed. "Yeah, but it ain't fatal. The name's Gertie. What's yours?"

"Alex."

"Miz Butler's your ma?"

He nodded.

Gertie tipped her head toward the corral and the pacing stallion. "I'm the Jagged R wrangler. That means I take care of the horses here. This one, we just brought in off the range. I've been tryin' to catch him for three years."

"He looks mean."

"He is for now." She watched the wild animal, studying his fine lines, well-shaped head, intelligent eyes. "He's smart, too. What he's gotta learn first is to trust me. The rest'll come easy after that."

Alex climbed up on the fence so he could peer over the top rail. "Could I be a wrangler when I get bigger?"

Gertie pushed her hat back on her head and glanced over at the boy a second time. "I don't know. You like horses?"

He nodded.

"How old're you?"

"Seven. But I'll be eight come September."

"You ever had a horse o' your own?"

Alex shook his head.

Grabbing the boy just beneath his arms, Gertie lifted him off the fence and set him on the ground. "Come on. I got somethin' t'show you." She didn't shorten her long strides or look behind her to see if he followed. If Alex really wanted to help, Gertie figured he'd keep up.

The doors at both ends of the barn were thrown open to the afternoon sunlight. The cavernous building smelled of straw and hay, leather and manure, dust and sweat—familiar scents that made Gertie feel at home. She'd always been more comfortable with horses and other animals than she'd been with people. Kids were different, though. She liked kids. Maybe because she knew they didn't think she was some sort of freak like most grown folks did.

Stopping at one of the stalls, she looked inside at the buckskin mare. "This here is Sugar," she told Alex when he stopped beside her. "She's got a bad cut on her left front fetlock, and I've got to doctor it twice a day. I've also got to keep her stall mucked out so it's nice and clean for her. And she needs to be walked a bit so she don't stiffen up. You think you could help me do all that?"

"Yes!"

She grinned at his enthusiastic response. "Well then, I guess it's up to your ma. If she says it's okay with her, then it's okay with me."

"I'll go ask her." With that, he darted off.

Gertie chuckled as she watched him disappear through the barn doors. Too bad Parker thought the Butlers would be at the Jagged R just a few months. Gertie figured it was going to be a pleasure having them around the place. The lunch Alex's ma had served today was a heck sight better than anything Parker had whipped up lately. And Faith Butler was nice and friendly to boot, even if she was prettier than a newborn heifer in a flower bed.

Turning her gaze toward the buckskin mare, Gertie remembered the way all the cowpokes had removed their hats and slicked their hair with the palms of their hands as soon as they'd laid eyes on Faith. Gertie couldn't think of a time in her entire life when a man had ever looked at her like they'd looked at the red-haired housekeeper. It hadn't surprised her at all when she'd learned Faith was actually an actress. Faith Butler was surefire too pretty to be hidden away on a Wyoming cattle ranch, cookin' grub for a bunch o' mangy cowpokes.

Gertie removed her hat and ran her fingers through her unruly mop of curls. She wondered what it would be like to have hair as shiny and pretty as Faith's. She wondered what it would be like to be small and shapely and have men staring at her like she was the first water hole after five days on the desert.

Slapping her hat against her thigh, she snorted in disgust. As if she needed a man of her own! She lived with a couple dozen of them, day in and day out, year in and year out, and she didn't see there was much call for having one all to herself. More trouble than they was worth, the lot o' them. And since the good Lord hadn't seen fit to make her any of the things men seemed to want in a woman, it must be that she wasn't meant to belong to anybody in particular. And that suited her just fine.

She turned on her heel, then headed back to the corral and the things she did best.

Faith stood on a chair beneath the parlor windows. Minutes before, she had removed the draperies, dropping them into a pile on the floor. Now she was washing off the accumulated grime from the windowpanes with a mixture of vinegar, water, and plenty of elbow grease. When a good portion of the glass was clean, she paused to admire the view.

In the valley below, Dead Horse appeared just a wide spot on the old stage road. A few houses, a few businesses, and a smattering of green-leafed poplars, planted when the town was born. Not far beyond Dead Horse was the river, running high on its banks this time of year—a ribbon of life-giving water in the high desert country, winding its way south. And in the distance, to the east and to the west, rose mighty mountain ranges, purple peaks and pine-covered slopes—a sight of great beauty that left her almost breathless.

Pushing loose strands of hair away from her face with the back of her wrist, she returned her attention to the task of cleaning the large windows, wondering as she did so why anyone would want to shut out the spectacular view with draperies and gloom.

But she suspected she already knew the answer. Her employer was hiding from the rest of the world. Was it because of his scar? Because of the blindness of one eye? Or was there another reason for his seclusion?

She recalled again the moment Drake Rutledge had turned up the lamp in the library. He'd wanted to frighten her. Why? Simply so she would leave? If that was what he'd wanted, he could merely let her go, turn her out. Would he have her believe he was a hard, cruel man? If so, he'd failed. He'd given her and her children a place to live when they'd needed one so desperately. Nothing he could do could eliminate that one act of kindness, no matter how gruff and unpleasant he might try to be.

Shaking her head, she thought, I can best thank him by getting this house in order and letting in the sunlight again. With renewed vigor she began scrubbing another pane of glass.

Suddenly her son barreled into the room. "Ma! Ma!"

Fear pierced her heart at the sound of his voice. Then she realized his cry was one of excitement, not pain or panic. She glanced down at him. "What is it, Alex?"

"Gertie says I can learn to be a wrangler, just like her, if it's okay with you."

"A wrangler?"

He nodded. "That's the cowboy who takes care of the horses. Can I, Ma? Can I?"

"Oh, Alex, I don't know. Mr. Rutledge might not like—"

"But Gertie said it's okay. Please, Ma."

Faith released a sigh as she stepped down from the chair. "I suppose it might be all right, but I need to talk to Miss Duncan first." She wagged a finger at him. "And you, young man, remember your manners. You're to call her Miss Duncan, not Gertie. Now I want you to go upstairs and check on your sister. I'll come for you there."

Alex opened his mouth to argue, then appeared to think better of it. With hands shoved into his pockets, he left the parlor.

"A wrangler," Faith whispered to herself as she removed the kerchief from around her hair. She could only imagine what sort of trouble her son might get himself into. "Oh, Lord, however shall I see Alex properly raised?" With another sigh, she headed toward the back of the house and out the rear door.

She found Gertie inside the corral, talking to a pacing white horse with crazed eyes and flaring nostrils. She watched as the other woman reached out a hand toward the wild animal.

"You might as well settle down, fella," Gertie crooned. "I ain't goin' nowheres. Come on now. Settle down. . . . That's right. Easy, boy. Easy."

The horse stopped suddenly. He bobbed his head up and down, then stomped his right hoof, stirring up a cloud of dust that drifted across the enclosure on the light breeze.

"Thatta boy. I ain't gonna hurt you."

The horse snorted and tossed his head, then burst into motion, resuming his restless pacing.

Gertie laughed as she watched the animal, never moving from where she stood.

"Miss Duncan," Faith called softly, uncertain if she should interrupt or not.

Gertie glanced over her shoulder, then turned and walked across the corral. "Alex didn't waste no time, did he?" she said as she stopped at the fence.

Faith shook her head.

"Didn't think he would." She grinned. "You got a nice boy there, Miz Butler."

"Thank you." Faith returned the smile, then asked, "Miss Duncan, are you sure you don't mind? About this wrangler business, I mean. I don't expect others to be watching after my son. And I know he can get underfoot at times."

"I don't mind. Really I don't. And nobody calls me Miss Duncan. I'm just Gertie."

"You'll be Miss Duncan to Alex. I'll not have him showing disrespect for his elders."

Gertie hooted with laughter. "Don't think I've been called anybody's elder before." She scratched her head. "Not sure I care for the thought much."

Faith didn't know how to respond. She was no

stranger to odd characters. She'd known more than a few during her lifetime in the theater.

But Gertie Duncan was quite different from anyone else. Everything about the wrangler's appearance was masculine, from her lean but muscular build to her shirt, trousers, boots, and hat. Her face had been browned and freckled by the sun, despite the wide brim of her Stetson. She wore her hair shorter than many men, and there was nothing feminine in the way she walked or talked.

Although her appearance was unusual, something about the woman appealed to Faith, something that made her want to be friends with Gertie Duncan. Maybe it was the ever-present twinkle she saw in Gertie's dark blue eyes or the oft-used smile that revealed the slight gap between her front teeth or the laughter that seemed to come to her so easily.

With a fluid motion, the wrangler stepped up onto the fence rail, then swung her legs over the top and dropped to the ground beside Faith. She removed her dusty hat and combed her fingers through her mop of hair. Her smile was gone as she met Faith's gaze. "Listen here, Miz Butler. Parker told me about your little girl bein' sick and all. You got yourself plenty on your platter t'handle. I guess I can keep an eye on one small boy now and agin."

Faith felt a sudden welling up of tears. She looked away, her vision blurred. "Everyone has been so very kind," she whispered around the lump in her throat.

"Shoot. Folks out here just take care of one another. Got to. This is hard country. Nobody can make it all on their own."

Faith nodded, still unable to look at Gertie.

Nobody can make it all on their own. What would it be like to have someone to lean on, to depend on?

It seemed to Faith she had been making it on her own all her life.

Her father, Jack Fields, hadn't really wanted the responsibility of raising a child, but he'd been so infuriated by his wife's request for a divorce, he'd refused to let Nellie ever see her daughter again. Faith had tried to be a good daughter; she'd tried to take care of Jack, to make him happy. She'd failed. He'd deserted her before her fifteenth birthday. If not for Raymond Drew keeping her on with his traveling troupe, she might have starved—or worse.

A few years later Faith had met George, and she'd believed everything would be perfect from then on. She'd tried to take care of her husband after they were married. She'd tried to make him happy. But just as with her father, she'd failed. George had deserted her, too.

Once upon a time, she'd entertained a lovely dream of what her life would be like. Once upon a time, she'd been in love and believed in her husband and . . .

Drawing a ragged breath, she drove off the memories, reminding herself she was better off as things were, that she didn't need anyone to lean on, to depend on. And she certainly didn't need to go around feeling sorry for herself.

Gertie's fingers alighted on Faith's shoulder. "I'd be obliged if you'd let the boy help me, Miz Butler."

A wry laugh escaped Faith. "I don't know if he'll be much help, but he does seem to want to learn about what you do."

"He'll help all right." Gertie slapped her hat back on her head, smiling broadly. "I'll see that he does."

Faith glanced toward the house. "Mr. Rutledge won't mind, will he?"

"No reason he should." Gertie stepped forward, her gaze following Faith's to the house. "Never have figured what Rutledge is doin' out here. He don't seem t'take much interest in the place. I've only talked to him a half dozen times in the years I been here. Always closed up in that back room o' his. 'Cept when he takes his horse out for one of their midnight rides."

Faith glanced at the woman beside her. "Midnight rides?"

"I seen him once. Like he was runnin' from the hounds of hell themselves, racin' that pinto across the plains. A wonder he didn't end up with his neck broke. And his horse, too." Gertie shook her head, her eyes downcast. "Powerful sadness in that man. Powerful sadness."

"I know," Faith whispered, remembering what she'd seen when Drake Rutledge had turned up the light on his desk. Remembering also the strange way it had made her feel. Earlier that day she'd run from those feelings, refusing to listen to Parker when he'd wanted to tell her about their employer. Now she wanted to know. "What happened to him?"

"That scar and his eye, you mean? Don't know. Parker does, I reckon, but he's never said an' I never asked."

Faith nodded again, even though she hadn't really been asking about the scar. It was something much more intangible that continued to tighten her heart whenever she thought of Drake Rutledge.

"Well . . ." Gertie cleared her throat. "I'd best be gettin' back t'my work. Rutledge don't pay me t'stand around jawin'." She stepped up on the bottom rail of the corral. "You send that boy out t'me when you can spare him, Miz Butler, and I'll see that he does what he's told."

"Thank you, Gertie. And please, call me Faith."

The cowgirl responded with another one of her broad smiles. "It's gonna be right nice havin' you around the place, Faith Butler." Then she swung over the fence as she had before and approached the white stallion, talking softly as she went.

The house had fallen into silence with the coming of night, and at last, Drake felt free to leave his library.

Anger and frustration had warred within him for the better part of the day, and he blamed it all on the new housekeeper. Faith Butler was the reason he'd felt trapped in his library with his books and ledgers and dark, restless thoughts. If not for her . . .

With a soft expletive, he strode down the hall. But he stopped abruptly outside the parlor, his good eye widening in surprise. Moonlight, spilling through the large window, silvered the room. The clean tang of vinegar lingered in the air.

He took a step into the parlor, gazing about him, surprised to find that the room had warmth and appeal. The chairs and sofa had been rearranged, grouped near the fireplace in an invitation to sit and converse. The piano had been polished to a high sheen, and a sheet of music had been set out, beckoning whoever entered the room to create a melody on the ivory and ebony keys of the instrument. Knickknacks and bric-a-brac that had belonged to the previous owner of the house, suddenly free of dust after so many years of neglect, glittered in the moonlight.

She had done this. In just her first day at the ranch, she had done all this.

Damn her!

He didn't want her meddling with his house. He didn't want her coming in here and rearranging things. He didn't want a cozy home. He merely wanted a refuge from women like her!

Cursing one more time, he strode out of the parlor. He yanked open the front door and stepped onto the porch, dragging in a quick gulp of crisp night air as if his life depended on it. Only when he heard a softer gasp did he realize he wasn't alone even here.

Damn her!

He turned and glared toward the porch seat as Faith rose to her feet, her hands smoothing the folds of her dress.

"I . . . I hope it's all right that I sit out here," she said when he didn't speak. "I just needed a moment of quiet before retiring for the night."

"You must be tired. You've made yourself busy today."

He'd meant it as an insult. He'd meant to call her a meddlesome busybody. But he saw her smile in the silvery glow of moonlight. It was a smile that could have lit up the night by itself. As if he'd just paid her a compliment.

She lifted her left hand and brushed away loose strands of hair from her face. "Yes, it's been an eventful day, but it feels good to have accomplished so much."

Drake wanted to tell her to leave his house alone. He wanted to tell her to let the draperies be, to let the dust accumulate, to keep things as they were, as they'd been for years. But just as he'd been unable to deny her a place to live, it seemed he was unable to deny her whatever had brought about her smile.

Obviously unaware of his inner turmoil, she stared down at the valley and the small lights of Dead

Horse. "When Dr. Telford brought me to your ranch the other day, I couldn't imagine why anyone would want to build a house up here on this ridge. But tonight, I understand. It's so peaceful here." Her voice changed slightly. "'Every man shall eat in safety / Under his own vine what he plants; and sing / The merry songs of peace to all his neighbours.'"

There was something about the way she recited the words that painted the image of them in his mind, in his heart. He could almost believe in such a place. He could almost believe in such a peace.

"Well, I'd best be to bed," she whispered as she turned and walked to the door.

Although he didn't glance behind him, he somehow knew she paused there and looked over her shoulder.

"Mr. Rutledge . . . thank you again." Another pause, then, "Good night."

"Good night, Mrs. Butler."

He heard the door open and close. He felt her going like a sudden chill upon his skin and heard her words repeat themselves in his mind.

. . . *and sing the merry songs of peace to all his neighbours.*

He didn't even know his neighbors. Hadn't wanted to know them. Had intentionally remained here on his ridge and watched as the town faltered, as family after family moved away. What was it to him whether Dead Horse was there or not? If it disappeared tomorrow, it wouldn't change his life one iota.

It hadn't always been so. Once he had enjoyed a vast array of friends. At least he'd thought they were his friends.

But that was long ago, and the young man he remembered had been someone else entirely.

4

The temperature had climbed into the nineties by early afternoon, rare for June. Rick Telford was more than a little tempted to use the heat as an excuse to visit the Dead Horse Saloon.

What could one drink hurt? asked a small voice in his head.

He knew the answer. One drink would lead to two. Two would lead to more. More would lead him back.

And Rick wasn't willing to go back.

He might not be much of a doctor these days and he might not have much of a medical practice in Dead Horse, Wyoming, but at least he was sober when someone needed him. That was something. Some days, that was everything.

"Father Telford, are you going to come in and eat or have I wasted my time cooking for you?"

"Be right there, Nancy," he answered his daughter-in-law, trying to ignore the intolerant tone of her voice.

He had no right to complain, he reminded himself. He'd come to Dead Horse with nothing. His son had made him welcome in his home even though no one would have blamed James if he'd turned his father away.

And Rick wouldn't have blamed him, either.

With another quick glance toward the saloon, he rose from the porch swing and entered the house. "Aren't we going to wait for James?" he asked as he watched Nancy set a plate of biscuits on the table.

She shook her head. "No. He said he would eat something at the hotel." She sat down on her usual chair. "Are you certain you'll remember everything that must be done while we're away, Father Telford?" She spread butter on a biscuit, then passed the plate to her father-in-law.

Rick swallowed a sigh. "I think I can manage. Claire has little need of my help. After all, she and her husband built that hotel. She knows all about running it. But I'll be there if she needs me."

"*Mrs.* O'Connell works for us now." Nancy glared at Rick, then jabbed her fork into the broiled ham on her plate. "Although heaven knows, I wish she didn't. We'd be gone from this godforsaken place if James hadn't bought that wretched building."

"The town won't be godforsaken if James is successful in Green River City. If he can get the railroad to see the profit in bringing—"

Nancy's fork clattered onto the table as she jumped up from her chair. "I hope he fails. I hope no one will even talk to him. I don't know why he wants to stay here. If it weren't for you, he wouldn't." Tearfully, she fled from the room.

Rick leaned back on his chair, staring at the uneaten food before him, knowing that what Nancy had said was true. If it weren't for him, James might have moved away from Dead Horse long ago. There weren't many places where a man like Rick Telford got a second chance. Because of its desperate need for a doctor—any doctor—Dead Horse was one of the few. James had stayed to lend support and make certain his father got his second chance.

His appetite gone, Rick left the table and headed for the back door. He walked swiftly to the small stable behind the house, hitched up his horse and buggy, and set out for the Jagged R, trying not to think about the past, trying not to think about a drink, trying not to think.

Faith waited anxiously beside the bed as the doctor examined Becca.

"Well, Mrs. Butler," he said as he removed the stethoscope from his ears, "your daughter is doing remarkably well, considering her condition just one week ago."

Faith let out a sigh of relief. "I was hoping that's what you would say." She smiled at Becca. "Would you allow me to take her outside to sit in the shade? It's so terribly hot up here this time of day."

"I don't think it would do her any harm to be moved, as long as she's carried up and down the stairs." Rick wiped a trickle of sweat from his brow. "I'm sure she would be more comfortable outside where she might feel the occasional breeze."

"Do you hear that, Becca?" Faith sat on the edge of the bed and took her daughter's hand. "The doctor says you may leave your bed for a short while. There are some lovely trees around the house with plenty of shade for you to sit beneath. Won't that be nice?"

Becca's answering smile lasted only a moment, but Faith knew she was truly delighted by the news.

Rick Telford snapped his bag shut and reached for his suit coat, which lay on the foot of the bed. "I'll ask Parker or one of the other men to come carry her down. I'd do it myself, but I strained my back a couple of days ago." He glanced once more at Becca. "You mind what your mother tells you, young lady, and you'll be fine before you know it."

Unshed tears burned the back of Faith's throat as she watched her daughter nod solemnly at the doctor. She was encouraged by Becca's improving health, but she knew there was still such a long way to go to full recovery. Becca was so frail. Just the effort of a smile seemed to drain her of any energy.

As Becca's eyelids drifted closed, the girl asked, "Will Alex come sit with me under the tree, Mama?"

"Of course he will, darling. Your brother loves to spend time with you."

More tears stung her eyes and throat. The statement wasn't entirely honest. Alex was good to his sister and truly fond of her, but he was understandably restless whenever Faith requested he stay with Becca. It was hard for him to be confined to this room. Gertie Duncan had taken Alex under her wing, and the boy was completely smitten with the female wrangler. There was so much to see and do on the ranch, especially for a seven-year-old boy, and he wanted to see and do it all.

"Mrs. Butler?"

At the sound of the unexpected voice, a shiver ran up Faith's spine. She lifted her gaze toward the doorway as Drake Rutledge stepped into the bedroom. It was the first time she had seem him since their brief encounter on the porch four nights before. It was also the first time she had seen him in the full light of day.

"I met the doctor on the stairs. He asked me to carry the little girl downstairs."

There was something equally frightening and appealing about her employer. She felt both drawn to and repelled by him. His face was handsome, despite the eye patch and scar.

His scar. So that's why it's called the Jagged R! she thought with sudden insight.

But his looks had nothing to do with her confused emotions. The effect he had on her went much deeper than mere appearances.

Faith rose from the bed. "I'd expected Parker." Her throat was tight, her words barely audible.

He scowled. "I guess I was the first person Telford found." He strode toward the bed.

It was on the tip of her tongue to refuse his help. Then he stopped and glanced down at Becca, and a flicker of compassion crossed his face. Others might not have recognized it. Faith did.

"It's like an oven up here," he said.

"I know."

Drake met her gaze. "Perhaps you should move to one of the lower bedchambers."

"These rooms are fine." She couldn't help the smile that crept into the corners of her mouth. "They cool off quickly when the sun goes down. And Alex loves the view from this window."

He didn't say anything in response, only continued to stare at her.

Discomfited by her reaction to him, Faith looked down at her daughter. "If you'd carry her outside so she can lie in the shade, I'd be most grateful, Mr. Rutledge."

Drake tried to summon a return of the anger he'd felt when he'd climbed the stairs to this room. He'd been furious with the doctor for waylaying him, for expecting him to do this. He'd been furious with Faith Butler for coming to his house, for moving in and changing things.

But the moment he'd looked down at the small child on the bed, his anger had vanished, and even her mother couldn't force its return.

He leaned over and lifted Becca Butler into his arms. She weighed next to nothing. She seemed delicate, breakable. As he straightened, she opened her enormous green eyes, met his gaze, and smiled.

"Are you going to carry me downstairs?" she whispered.

"Yes."

She leaned her head against his chest and released a trusting sigh. "Thank you."

An odd warmth spread through Drake. His heart constricted in his chest even as his arms tightened around the child. He didn't allow himself to remember how long it had been since he'd actually held another human being, how long it had been since he'd allowed himself to feel anything other than bitterness. He tried not to acknowledge the protective feelings that surged to life within him.

It was better to feel nothing. It was always better to feel nothing.

Avoiding Faith's gaze—knowing he would be sorry if he looked at her—he turned and carried the little girl down the back stairway, in a hurry to be rid of Becca and the unwanted feelings she and her mother caused within him.

Once off the rear porch, Drake stopped beneath the leafy canopy that stretched overhead.

The previous owner had planted numerous trees, as well as a narrow swath of lawn, around the circumference of the house. Now, in late June, trees and grass provided a cool green oasis, an inviting escape from the summer heat.

Faith stepped past him, blankets and pillows in her arms. "Just a moment while I lay these on the grass." She paused to look about her, then pointed. "Let's go over there, where Becca can see the horses."

Drake watched as Faith knelt near the trunk of a tall cottonwood, spreading the blankets on a thick carpet of grass beneath it. As she straightened, she glanced over her shoulder and met his gaze.

For a moment, he stood riveted by the tender look in her eyes. It didn't matter that he knew the look was for her daughter. It spilled over onto him, and he felt it touch some hidden place deep inside him. A place that hadn't been touched in many years.

Faith stretched out her arm in invitation. "You may put Becca down, Mr. Rutledge," she said in her soft, musical voice.

He gave his head a slight shake to break free of the spell she'd cast over him. Then he moved forward and gently laid Becca on the blanket.

Before he could draw away, the girl opened her eyes again, looking directly at him. "It's nice out here, isn't it?"

"Yes, Becca. It is."

She smiled, then turned her head on the pillow, staring off toward the barn. "There's Alex. What's he doing, Mama?"

Drake glanced up—and discovered that the three of them had become the focus of attention. Faith's boy, lead rope in hand, stood with a horse near the barn. Gertie Duncan and Rick Telford watched from beside the corral. Parker McCall, wearing an amused expression, leaned against an awning post outside the bunkhouse.

Drake stiffened and rose swiftly to his feet. Hating the stares of others, he felt his anger return with force. She'd done it to him again. Faith Butler had caused him to do something he didn't want to do.

"Alex is helping Miss Duncan with the horses," Faith answered her daughter, obviously unaware of Drake's building rage.

"Can I help, too?"

"Maybe when you're stronger, darling." She looked up. "Mr. Rutledge, you are always so kind to us. I cannot thank you enough."

He ignored her words of gratitude. "Next time, get someone else to carry her down," he replied gruffly, then spun about and strode back to the house.

But he found no solace inside. Except for his library, daylight streamed into every room of the house. Gone were the draperies that had shrouded the windows. Woodwork had been polished. Floors had been scrubbed. Rugs had been beaten. Intrusive brightness was everywhere. Nothing was as it had been. Nothing was as he'd wanted it.

Damn the woman!

He stepped into his library and slammed the door behind him.

Faith stared at the back door long after her employer had stormed through it.

"Why was he angry?" Becca queried.

"I don't know, darling." She turned toward the bunkhouse. *I don't know, but Parker McCall does.*

Parker knew, and now Faith wanted to know. She

wanted to understand more about Drake Rutledge. Suddenly she felt a sharp need to know whatever Parker could tell her.

"I'll be back in a little while." Faith rose from the ground and set off across the yard.

Squinting his eyes against the sunlight, Parker pushed his hat back on his head as Faith drew near. "I reckon I've just witnessed some sort of miracle." He grinned. "Can't say the last time I saw Drake outside in the middle of the day. Must be years by now."

"Tell me about Mr. Rutledge. I'd like to understand."

"He doesn't frighten you, does he?"

"A little." She gave a slight shrug. "At least, he did at first. But now . . . " She shrugged again.

He motioned toward a bench beneath the awning. "Sit there where you can keep an eye on the girl, and we'll talk."

Faith moved into the shade and settled onto the wooden bench. Parker followed her but didn't sit down. Instead he leaned his back against the wall of the bunkhouse. Faith watched as he removed his hat and began sliding his fingers around the brim, turning the Stetson in a steady circle.

"I first met Drake up in Montana, oh, 'bout ten, eleven years ago, I reckon. Rich man's son from Philadelphia, playin' at bein' a cowboy. Closest he'd ever been to a cow was a T-bone steak. Green as peas. All his fancy schoolin' didn't mean nothin' out here on the range, and he knew it, too." He shook his head, as if remembering more than he was saying.

Faith waited patiently for him to continue.

His face crinkled with amusement. "Lord, he was a handsome dude, and if there was a female within fifty miles, she'd find him. But Drake didn't have no mind t'get himself harnessed t'any one gal in particular. He was bound and determined t'make himself a cowboy." He chuckled, then sobered instantly. "He did it, too. Earned my respect right quick. If there was any man you could count on, it was Drake Rutledge."

Faith wasn't surprised. Somehow she'd sensed that about her employer.

"His pa was some important lawyer back in Philadelphia. He was all set on havin' Drake join him in his firm. But that wasn't what Drake wanted. He wanted to stay out west. I think he would've done it, too, if his pa's heart hadn't gone bad. There wasn't much Drake could do when his ma sent for him but go help his family, like they needed."

Parker pushed away from the bunkhouse wall and set his Stetson back on his head. Then he stepped toward the edge of the shade, staring off toward the house. "Can't say exactly what went on those couple years he was back in Philadelphia. He wrote once t'tell me he was engaged to a society gal named Larissa something-or-other and that he was practicin' law in his pa's firm. Looked like he'd given up on his dream of comin' back west. But I reckon he was happy enough, judgin' by his letter. Next thing I knew, he wrote me agin, sayin' his parents were dead. Told me he'd bought this place in Wyomin', sight unseen, and asked if I'd be interested in bein' the ranch foreman." Parker rubbed his fingers along his jaw as he turned to look at Faith. "But he wasn't the same when he came back."

Her chest felt tight as she read the compassion in the cowboy's eyes.

"I tried to ask him about it once," Parker continued. "He told me he'd killed his parents."

She gasped.

"Ain't true. I saw the piece that was wrote up in the newspaper back east. Seems there was a carriage accident. Drake was drivin'. His ma died in it, and that's how he lost his eye. Don't know for sure what happened to his pa. Paper didn't mention him as bein' in the carriage."

"And his fiancée?" Faith asked softly.

Parker shook his head. "Don't know what happened to her, either. Drake never mentioned her again."

She left him, Faith thought with certainty. The girl named Larissa hadn't wanted Drake Rutledge any longer. Because of his scarred face? Because he'd lost an eye? Because she'd blamed him, as he'd blamed himself, for his mother's tragic death? Faith couldn't know for certain. But she knew without question it was because of Larissa that Drake had come to this ranch and cloaked himself in bitterness.

"He must have loved her very much," she whispered.

"I reckon he did, at that."

Turning her gaze upon the house, she thought of the dark and angry man inside. She thought of the way he'd shut himself in, closing out the world and everything and everyone in it. She thought of Drake and the girl he had loved, the girl who had left him— and she felt her heart nearly break in two.

If thou wilt leave me, do not leave me last,
When other petty griefs have done their spite,
But in the onset come; so shall I taste
At first the very worst of fortune's might,
And other strains of woe, which now seem woe,
Compared with loss of thee will not seem so.

Faith understood about loss and rejection, more than Parker McCall might ever dream. She knew what betrayed love did to a person, down deep in a secret part of the soul.

She rose from the bench and stood beside Parker, placing a hand on his arm. "Thank you for telling me what you know. I shall keep your confidence."

Then she headed back across the yard to sit beside her daughter in the shade of the tall cottonwood.

5

Lying on the bed, Alex stared at the ceiling and listened to the rain battering the roof. He frowned as his frustration grew. Why did it have to go and rain today of all days? Gertie—or rather, Miss Duncan—had been going to start giving him riding lessons, and now the weather had ruined everything.

He glanced over at his sister and glowered. She was sleeping, as usual. It was bad enough that he wouldn't get to ride that horse today, but now he was stuck looking out for Becca, too. Their mother had gone into town for supplies with Miss Duncan this morning, before the downpour had begun. Now Alex didn't know when they would get back.

He silently repeated a few curse words he'd learned from Mr. Drew's stage hands, wanting to say them aloud but not able to do it. He knew Ma would wash his mouth out with soap if she ever heard him talking like that. She was awfully strict about such things.

Making as little noise as possible, he got up and opened the window. He leaned forward, turning his face upward and closing his eyes against the cold splatter of rain. In a matter of moments his head and shoulders were drenched.

Ma would be really mad if she was to see me doing this, he thought with a grin.

Opening his eyes, he pulled back inside and turned once again toward his sister. Becca slept on. All she *ever* did was sleep. He figured she wouldn't wake up for hours. He'd bet his favorite marble she wouldn't.

Quietly he moved toward his sister's bed. "Becca," he whispered.

No response.

Even more softly, "I'm goin' down for something to eat. You hungry?"

Again no response.

"I won't be long," he mumbled as he headed for the bedroom door.

The Rutledge house was big, much nicer than any place he could remember staying in before. But Alex hadn't paid much attention to the house once Miss Duncan had said he could help with the horses. However, with nothing else to do today, this seemed like a real good time to do some exploring.

He liked being on the third floor. It felt like he was on top of the world whenever he looked out the window in his room. He liked racing down the stairs, just to see how quickly he could reach the bottom. If he got up enough speed, he could take three steps at a time without falling.

His mother had told him to always use the back staircase, which had suited him just fine for running races 'cause it was pitched so steep and all. But today, with no one to see him, he decided it was the best opportunity he would ever have to test his theory about the perfect curve and pitch of the banister on the front staircase.

The oak railing was wide and winding, an unhindered slope all the way to the entry hall. It seemed to have been designed to tempt a seven-year-old boy, bored by a rainy day. It seemed to have been designed for sliding down.

Oh boy! Ma would tan his hide if she ever found out.

But, of course, that thought didn't dissuade him from the adventure. Besides, his mother wouldn't find out. There'd been no sign of her on the road from Dead Horse. She and Miss Duncan were probably holed up at the store, waiting out the storm.

With a quick glance at the floor far below, Alex scrambled onto the polished railing, backside first. Then he took a deep breath, leaned forward, and pushed with his hands as hard as he could. Within seconds he was sliding down the steep decline.

"Whee!" he shouted with glee.

He gained more speed as he went—faster and faster and faster, until, all of a sudden, he was afraid. Maybe this hadn't been such a brilliant idea after all.

He squeezed his eyes shut as he prepared to hurtle off the end of the banister and crash against the opposite wall. But instead he felt himself yanked away by strong hands. For a moment he was suspended in midair, then he met with a broad chest. He opened his eyes, glancing up at his unexpected savior.

The man who held Alex firmly in his grasp scowled at him with his one good eye, the other covered by a patch. "What the hell do you think you're doing?"

Alex shivered, knowing he was facing Mr. Rutledge. "I was . . . I was . . . I . . . " His mother was going to tan his hide for this. He hung his head in shame. "I . . . I'm sorry, sir."

"Sorry? Did you even think that you could have killed yourself?" He set Alex on the floor, then stepped back from him. "What's your name?"

"Alex, sir. Alexander Butler. I . . . I . . ." His words died abruptly as he looked up. He swallowed the hard lump in his throat and croaked, "I'm real sorry, sir. I won't do it again. I promise."

"See that you don't," came the man's gruff reply.

With a nod, Alex scurried toward the kitchen; then, with a safe distance between them, he paused and looked back.

Drake's anger slowly drained from him, an anger born of fear when he'd seen what had surely been a disaster about to happen. He'd done something quite similarly stupid when he'd been about the same age as this boy. Except Drake's wild flight down the banister of his parents' Philadelphia home had resulted in a broken arm and fifteen stitches in the back of his head.

"What happened to your eye?" Alex asked from the other end of the hall.

Drake had thought the boy gone and was unprepared for the question.

"Is it missing?" Alex stepped forward. "Your eye, I mean. Do you just got a hole under that patch?"

"No. My eye is still there."

Alex looked disappointed. "How'd it happen?"

"Don't you have something you're supposed to be doing? Where's your mother?"

"She's in town with Miss Duncan, getting supplies. How'd it happen?"

The boy was tenacious, he'd give him that. "I don't believe that's any concern of yours." Drake wanted the silence of his library and a stiff brandy.

"I never knew anybody who wore a patch over his eye before. I was just wondering what it was like."

"Why don't you wear one yourself and find out," Drake replied tersely, then strode into his private sanctuary and closed the door securely behind him.

Bothersome little brat.

He moved swiftly toward the sideboard and the decanter of brandy.

What was it like? It had been hell at first. With only one eye, he'd lost his depth perception. He'd fallen down stairs, run into walls and doors. He'd felt constantly startled by little, everyday things. He'd been afraid and unsure of himself.

He was more used to his blindness now. He'd had over seven years to get used to it, to learn to judge things by shadows, to learn to listen more closely to what went on around him.

Drake took a quick swallow of brandy, feeling the warmth as the liquid slid down his throat.

Is it missing? Your eye, I mean. Do you just got a hole under that patch? Surprisingly, he grinned as he remembered the boy's words. No one in all these years had ever had the courage to ask such a question.

Leave it to Faith Butler's son to be the one.

Faith stared anxiously out the window of the general store at the continuing downpour.

Nearby, Gertie whispered an expletive. "We'll be up to our hubs in mud 'fore we get home. Shoulda known this wasn't a good day t'come into town.

Shoulda took one look at the sky and known we were in for a drencher."

"Maybe we should leave now," Faith suggested. "What if it doesn't let up all day?"

"Won't do us no good t'get stuck out in the middle of this storm. We're better off waitin' here. It's gotta let up sometime."

Faith glanced over at the woman beside her. "I'm worried about the children. Alex will be so restless. We've been gone a long time already. And they'll need to eat and—"

"Needn't be worried." Gertie offered an encouraging smile. "Parker'll look in on 'em, see that your little girl's okay."

"He shouldn't have to do that."

Gertie pulled a pouch of tobacco from her shirt pocket and began rolling a cigarette. "Ah, he likes doin' it. From what I've seen, he's right partial to kids. Shame he doesn't have a passel of his own." She moistened the cigarette paper with the tip of her tongue. "Cowboyin's a lonely business. A man ain't likely to run across a marryin' kind of woman very often. For most of 'em, that don't matter much. Who'd want 'em, anyhow? But for a man like Parker . . ." She shook her head, then said, "Well, I'm gonna slip outside and have me a smoke." With those words, she opened the door and stepped onto the boardwalk, sheltered from the rain beneath the wide awning.

"Mrs. Butler?"

Faith turned toward the proprietress of the general store. "Yes?"

"Is there anything else you'll be wanting?" Sadie Gold asked as she laid a hand on top of a large tin of Arbuckle's coffee. A heavyset woman with streaks of gray in her brown hair, Mrs. Gold watched Faith with an inquisitive gaze.

"No." Faith shook her head. "I believe that's everything for today."

"Well then, why don't you join me in the back for a cup of coffee? I don't imagine there's going to be many customers on a day like this, and we might as well get better acquainted. I've been mighty curious ever since I heard you'd taken up housekeeping for Mr. Rutledge." She motioned for Faith to follow her. "I hear tell you're an actress."

Gertie leaned against the wall of the general store, one knee bent, her foot braced against the wall for balance. She drew deeply on the cigarette, then exhaled a stream of smoke, watching as it dissipated in the whistling wind that accompanied the falling rain.

The storm was the only thing breaking the silence of Dead Horse. If it weren't for the horses and wagon from the Jagged R standing in front of the store, the entire town would look deserted. Like a ghost town.

Gertie shook her head. It could come to that, too, if James Telford didn't have any luck down in Green River City. The railroad would save this town and the folks who lived here. And, if it was to happen, it had better happen soon.

Across the street, she saw the front door of the hotel open and Rick Telford emerge. She felt a funny little skip in her heart at the sight of him.

Odd. It was just Doc.

Rick spied her and waved. Then, with his arm over his head in a useless attempt to shield himself from the rain, he dashed across the muddy street and up onto the boardwalk. "What brings you to town, Gertie?" he asked breathlessly, shaking the water from his hair.

"Faith needed supplies."

He glanced through the window into the general store. "How's she working out?"

"Real good. Ain't seen so many just washed cow-pokes at meals in all my life."

He laughed at her good-humored sarcasm. "No, I don't reckon you have." He removed his glasses and wiped them dry with his handkerchief.

Well, I'll be damned!

As if seeing him for the first time, Gertie realized the doctor wasn't a bad-looking man. At least, not for his age, which she figured to be several years past forty. His abundant hair was the same stone gray as his eyes, but his face wasn't wrinkled much, except for around the corners of his eyes and mouth. He carried himself straight, like a man half his age, and his arms were strong. Rick Telford was no weakling, city-dude sort. Gertie figured he could hold his own against plenty of the much younger cowpokes she'd known in her day.

Sometimes, when they'd been talking, she'd felt that Rick was a lonely man. She understood loneliness. She understood what it was like to be different from those around her. She'd always been different, a bit of an outcast, just 'cause she'd been born female.

But the cause of Rick's loneliness was of a different nature.

Gertie knew all about what had happened to his wife, about how he'd been drunk and hadn't cared for her proper and how she'd died. About how he'd pretty much been run out of the town he'd been living in, nobody wanting a drunk for a doctor. It wasn't like any of it was a secret. There wasn't a soul in Dead Horse who *didn't* know the story, not with the way Nancy Telford had of flapping her jaws like a sheet in a strong wind.

But Gertie had always admired Rick. Dead Horse had been just eager enough for a doctor of its own that it had given him the chance he'd needed. And Gertie had to give him credit for what he'd done with that chance. He'd proved himself a good and caring doctor to one and all. As for the liquor, Gertie had never so much as smelled it on his breath since the day he'd arrived. Not once. Never so much as even seen him go near the saloon.

Yes, she'd admired him. But had she ever really taken notice of him?

"How's that arm of yours?" he asked, drawing her out of her reverie.

"My arm? Oh, it's fine, Doc. You fixed it up real good."

"Mind if I have a look?"

She flicked the cigarette into the street. "Naw, I don't mind." She rolled up her sleeve and held out her arm toward him.

Her pulse did a funny little dance through her veins as he cradled her forearm in his hands and leaned forward for closer inspection.

Well, I will be damned!

It was unbelievable. It was too incredible for words. But the truth was, she'd give that very same right arm he was looking at for him to kiss her just once.

Doc Telford?

That was crazy!

Ridiculous!

Downright plumb loco!

Doc Telford?

"I guess you won't be needing my services any further," Rick said as he straightened.

Their gazes met, and a warm tingling sensation spread through her. Her knees weakened suddenly. She felt herself blush, and her eyes widened in disbelief.

Blushing? Good Lord all Friday, she hadn't never blushed before in all her born days.

Her glance fell away as she pulled her arm free of his gentle grasp. She quickly rolled down her shirtsleeve. "Well, I sure hope I won't be needin' 'em," she mumbled. "Can't say I take much pleasure spendin' my hard-earned wages on doctorin'."

When he didn't say anything, she dared to look up again. He was watching her with a peculiar expression, as if he were seeing her for the first time.

He has just about the finest mouth I ever laid eyes on.

How many times in the past few weeks had he held her arm while he'd doctored her wound? Plenty. And not once had she ever given thought to anything other than making sure her arm healed up and wouldn't interfere with her work. What on earth was wrong with her now?

She felt her blush grow hotter.

If she didn't do something to stop herself right quick, she was going to give in to that irresistible urge, throw her arms around his neck, and plant one right on his lips. Right here on Main Street.

She sidled away. "Looks like the rain's lettin' up. Think I'll see about loadin' those supplies into the wagon so me and Faith can get on back to the ranch." She reached for the door and yanked it open.

"It was good seeing you, Gertie."

"Yeah. You too, Doc," she answered without looking behind her.

Like a scared jackrabbit, she hurried into the general store and away from the source of her consternation.

"You know, Mrs. Butler," Sadie said as she refilled Faith's coffee cup, "this town hasn't had a proper Fourth of July celebration in three years. Maybe you'd think of doing a Shakespearean reading or something for us." After pouring more of the dark liquid into her own cup, she set the speckled coffeepot back on the stove, then settled onto her chair again. "Treat us to a bit of real culture. It sure would be good for my young'ns."

"I don't know, Mrs. Gold. Independence Day is less than two weeks away."

"Are you telling me you don't have plenty of scenes just swimming about in that head of yours?" Sadie waved her hand in dismissal. "I don't believe it for a moment. Besides, the folks of Dead Horse need a bit of cheering up, and I think you're just the ticket. My guess is you're a right fine actress."

Faith felt warmed by the woman's praise. Not once had Sadie Gold made Faith feel ashamed of how she'd made her livelihood. Not once had she so much as hinted that there was any unworthiness in such a profession. Faith appreciated it more than she could say. "That's very kind of you, Mrs. Gold. I suppose I *could* find something appropriate to perform, even on such short notice."

"Of course you can. We'll have us a regular festival. See if we don't." Sadie grinned. "Maybe you can even get Mr. Rutledge to come. I swear, sometimes I haven't even believed the man is real."

Picturing Drake in her mind—tall, masculine, *disturbing*—Faith whispered, "Oh, he's quite real."

Changing the subject abruptly, as she had often done throughout their brief visit, Sadie said, "We'd have us the railroad by now if Mr. Rutledge had just given his support to our efforts. From what I've heard, he's rich as Croesus. Money like as always gets attention. And with all those cattle he's runnin' on his range, he'd benefit from the railroad coming through here as much as anybody."

"Has anyone talked to him about it?"

"They've tried, but he's always sent folks away without seeing them." The older woman shook her head. "I sure will hate to leave Dead Horse if things don't turn out. We've been happy here." She sighed heavily. "Starting over isn't easy, especially when you're my age. Me and the mister have done more than our share of starting over."

Before Faith could answer, Gertie appeared in the doorway between the living quarters and the store. "Faith, the rain's let up. I think we'd best git while the gittin's good. No tellin' how long it'll take us t'get back as it is. I'm gonna start loadin' the wagon."

"I'll be right there." Faith rose from her chair and offered a smile to her hostess. "It's been such a pleasure to visit with you, Mrs. Gold. I appreciate your kind hospitality."

"The pleasure's all mine. You don't be a stranger now. There's few enough of us womenfolk in these parts. You just drop by for a visit any time. Don't wait until you need supplies."

"I won't."

"And I'll be up to see you as soon as we put

together something for the Fourth of July. Good heavens! I'm as excited as my children will be when they hear about it."

Still buoyed by the woman's friendliness, Faith walked through the general store, feeling lighter than she had in years.

Perhaps—just perhaps—coming to Dead Horse, Wyoming, hadn't been such a bad thing after all.

6

Laughter, soft and bright, drifted through the open window of Drake's sanctuary. It wasn't the first time he'd heard the pleasant sounds in the past half hour. This time, however, he rose from the chair behind his desk and followed it.

Two days of rain were only a memory now. Lingering was the fresh scent of an earth washed clean. The blue sky held not so much as a hint of clouds. The mountains seemed nearer and even more purple than usual.

And here, much closer to him, golden sunshine filtered through a web of leaves and branches to cast an aura of light around the mother and daughter resting on a blanket spread on the lawn.

Sitting up, her back braced against her mother's side, Becca wove a long strand of grass between her fingers. There was more color in her face than there had been on the day Drake had carried her down from her room, and he found himself gladdened by the subtle change.

Faith tenderly brushed aside Becca's strawberry
blond hair before kissing the child's forehead. "You
should be napping." Her words were full of motherly
concern.

"Tell me another story first."

"I have work to do, Becca." She checked the watch
pinned to her bodice. "The men will be expecting
their supper when they return. I've food on the stove
to tend to."

"*Please*, Mama. I promise I'll take a nap as soon as
you're finished."

Faith laughed again.

Odd, how such a simple sound could bring about a
more complex reaction. Drake felt something hard
and secret inside his chest yield, soften.

"All right," Faith answered Becca. "You may listen as I practice my soliloquy for the Independence
Day celebration. And then you must keep your
promise, close your eyes, and sleep. Agreed, young
lady?"

The child nodded.

Faith rose from the blanket. She took two steps
away, her back toward the house. For a long time
she didn't move, and when she did turn, it seemed
she had become someone else right before Drake's
eyes.

"'Thou knowest the mask of night is on my face, /
Else would a maiden blush bepaint my cheek / For
that which thou has heard me speak tonight. / Fain
would I dwell on form, fain, fain deny / What I have
spoke; but farewell, compliment.'"

The brilliance of the midday sun faded to nothing.
With only a few words, by the mere magic of her
countenance and the lilting sound of her voice, Faith
drew Drake into another time and place. With just a

few lines from an ancient play, she turned day into night, light into darkness.

Drake leaned forward, resting his forearms against the windowsill, straining to better hear her words, straining to see her more clearly, to watch each subtle expression on her face as she spoke.

"'Dost thou love me? I know thou wilt say "Ay," / And I will take thy word. Yet if thou swear'st / Thou mayst prove false. At lovers' perjuries, / They say, Jove laughs. O gentle Romeo, / If thou dost love, pronounce it faithfully; / Or if thou think'st I am too quickly won, / I'll frown, and be perverse, and say thee nay, / So thou wilt woo; but else, not for the world. / In truth, fair Montague, I am too fond, / And therefore thou mayst think my 'haviour light.'"

She was beautiful. Everything a fair Juliet should be. The radiance of her flame red hair. The pale white of her smooth complexion. The earnest, innocent look of love in eyes of blue green. The perfect swell of her breasts and the narrowness of her waist beneath a dress of buttercup yellow.

"'But trust me, gentleman, I'll prove more true / Than those that have more cunning to be strange. / I should have been more strange, I must confess, / But that thou overheard'st, ere I was ware, / My true-love passion. Therefore pardon me, / And not impute this yielding to light love, / Which the dark night hath so discovered.'"

The world held its breath for a heartbeat, and Drake held his with it, caught in the wonder of watching Faith as she stood beneath the spreading arms of the tall trees, her own arms outstretched toward her invisible Romeo.

And then her spell was broken as Juliet's line

repeated in his head. *But trust me, gentleman, I'll prove more true . . .*

He straightened and drew sharply back from the window, angered at allowing himself to be drawn into her expertly cast web once again.

Trust a beautiful woman to be true? Not in his lifetime. Not in any lifetime.

Out of the corner of her eye, Faith caught a movement at the library window. She looked yet saw nothing but the dark draperies, shutting out the daylight.

Closing in the man.

Had he been watching her? she wondered, and felt an odd mixture of emotions at realizing he might have been.

"Do something else, Mama."

She glanced down at her daughter. "No. You promised you would rest, and I must get back to my cooking or I'll have my hands full with a bunch of hungry cowboys and nothing to feed them."

"I wish Alex was here."

"Alex and Miss Duncan will be back later." Faith frowned slightly as she placed her knuckles against her hips. "Close those eyes, little girl, or I'll have to see you back to your room."

Becca let out a long and pitiful sigh of the oppressed, and Faith nearly laughed aloud at the dramatic display. It would seem Becca had inherited at least some of her mother's talent for theatrics.

Smiling and shaking her head, Faith walked toward the back door of the house.

Thanks to the two days of rain, the kitchen was much cooler than it had been when Faith had first started cooking for the Jagged R crew. She knew the respite from heat wouldn't last but was glad for it nonetheless. At least she had more confidence in her ability to feed everyone without poisoning them. The cookbook she'd purchased at the general store in Dead Horse was responsible for most of that confidence.

She glanced once again at her watch, then hurried over to the stove, where the navy beans were cooking. Fortunately the water hadn't all boiled off while she was spending time with Becca.

She paused long enough to read over the recipe in the cookbook, left open on the counter, then she removed the kettle of beans and drained the water into the sink. Afterward she poured the beans into a pot and began adding the other prepared ingredients—tomatoes rubbed through a colander, brown sugar, ginger, mustard, black pepper, salt, and dark molasses. The molasses, according to the instructions, was to give a good brown color to the beans. Faith wasn't sure how important that was to those who would be eating them.

She envisioned young Johnny Coltrain or crusty Dan Greer refusing to eat her beans because they weren't the proper shade of brown, and she chuckled. Not very likely, she thought with an amused shake of her head. The cowpokes who worked at the ranch had praised everything she'd set before them and eaten every last crumb. They didn't seem particularly choosy, but that didn't lessen Faith's desire to do a good job.

With one final glance at the recipe, she added strips of bacon over the top of the mixture. Then she placed the pot into the oven, where the beans would bake for three hours, and closed the oven door with a sense of great satisfaction. This would be the best meal she'd prepared since arriving at the Jagged R. Three apple pies were already cooling on the windowsill. Beefsteaks were waiting to be fried, and she'd mastered the art of making biscuits several days before.

She wondered if Drake Rutledge had noticed the difference in her cooking during this past week. Then she wondered if Drake Rutledge noticed anything about her at all.

She frowned as she washed her hands and dried them with a towel, recalling what Parker had told her about their employer. Then she considered Sadie Gold's comments about the need for the railroad to come to Dead Horse and the help Drake Rutledge could have been to the town.

Her eyes widened in sudden realization. *The townsfolk need his help, and he needs theirs, too.*

She turned toward the hallway.

Drake Rutledge might manage to fool others, but he didn't fool her. She knew he hid a kind heart beneath that gruff, unfriendly facade. He had shown it by giving Faith and her children a place to live. Now it was time for her to return the favor. Before she left the Jagged R, she was going to find some way to help him begin living again.

But how?

She stepped into the kitchen doorway and glanced down the hall toward the library door. Closed off from the world. She wondered if she might have chosen the same path of escape after George left her if it had been available, if she hadn't been forced to provide for her children.

That was it! A jolt of excitement shot through her. That was how she could help him.

She squared her shoulders and smoothed her hair with her fingertips, then grabbed her dustcloth and walked swiftly toward the library.

The three quick raps on the door didn't surprise Drake. For some reason he'd been expecting them—and her.

"Come in, Mrs. Butler."

He watched as she entered and walked briskly across the room, stopping before his desk. Grudgingly he had to admit she'd earned his respect and admiration. Despite his attempts to intimidate and frighten her, she'd always held her ground.

"I'm sorry to disturb you, Mr. Rutledge," she said as she peered at him in the dim light, "but I really must clean the library sometime, and there never seems to be an hour of the day when you're not closeted in here. Why don't you take a break from your work and allow me to dust and sweep?"

Drake leaned back on his chair, away from the low-burning lamp. "I like things as they are. Leave this room alone."

"Oh, pish! No one wants to spend his day shut up with dust and grime." Her smile brought more of a glow into the room than the lamp on his desk. She turned on her heel and walked straight to the window, drawing open the draperies and allowing in the daylight. "I'm glad to see you aren't averse to letting in a bit of fresh air. I'm sure it hasn't done you any harm."

"Mrs. Butler!" He rose from his chair as the unwelcome brightness spilled into the room.

"Yes?" She turned, her eyebrows raised in innocent question.

Blast the woman! As sure as she was standing there, she was daring him to throw her out.

And he found he couldn't do it!

"Nothing," he grumbled.

Once again she smiled. "Did you happen to hear me practicing my Shakespeare a while ago?" Without waiting for a reply, she turned to the nearest bookshelf, pulled a cloth from the pocket of her apron, and began dusting. "Mrs. Gold asked me to do a reading for the town's Independence Day gathering. She said they hadn't observed the holiday in several years. I've chosen a selection from *Romeo and Juliet*."

And a very beautiful Juliet you make.

He sank onto his chair and scowled at her back. How did she manage to do this to him? How did she manage to make him a prisoner in his own house, in his own library? Why didn't he just order her out and be done with her?

"Dr. Telford says he doesn't care for Shakespeare's works, but I see from your books that you must enjoy them." She ran her fingers lightly over the spines of the books on one shelf as she let out a sigh. "It must be wonderful to have so many choices of what to read."

"It *would* be wonderful if I had some peace and quiet in which *to* read."

She looked over her shoulder, her mouth curving gently. "It seems to me you have far too much peace and quiet, Mr. Rutledge."

The truth of her words struck him dumb.

"Not that a mother with young children doesn't understand the need for a moment to escape," she added with a soft laugh as she returned to her dusting.

Drake searched his mind for something to say, for some rejoinder or even an insult, but nothing came to mind. He seemed to be helpless to do anything other than watch her as she moved about the room.

How did she do it? he asked himself again. How did she manage to destroy with such ease the order and rhythm of his life?

As for Faith, her mind was filled with things to say next, but none of them seemed right. She wanted to ask him to come to the town's celebration the following week. The folks of Dead Horse needed Drake Rutledge, and whether he knew it or not, he needed them, too. The last thing a man like Drake should do was shut himself away like a monk.

For some reason, that thought brought a blush to her cheeks. The man sitting behind her wasn't the sort she would ever envision as a monk. He fairly exuded masculine power.

What would it be like, she wondered unexpectedly, to be held by his strong arms? To be pulled close against his broad chest? To feel his mouth upon hers? Would his mustache be soft or prickly against her skin?

Her hand stilled as her pulse raced.

What on earth was the matter with her? Not once in the two years since George had gone away with his mistress, leaving Faith to fend for herself and their children, had she ever considered what it would be like to be with a man again. In truth, long before George had left her, she had ceased wanting to share the intimacy of her body. There had been no pleasure, merely an invasion.

Why now was she thinking of sharing such things

with this stranger? For that's what he was to her. A stranger. All she knew of Drake Rutledge was what others had told her. Why then was she imagining what it would be like for him to hold her, kiss her, caress her?

"What happened to your husband, Mrs. Butler?"

She sucked in a breath of air, startled by his question, and felt her cheeks grow even more heated. Had he read her thoughts as she'd stood there, imagining the two of them embracing?

"Are you a widow?"

She began rubbing with her dust rag again, trying desperately to compose herself before she might be forced to meet his gaze. "No, Mr. Rutledge," she answered in a near whisper, "I'm not a widow."

Again she envisioned herself in Drake's arms, imagined his chest bare against her own naked bosom.

"George . . . my husband . . . he's not an actor." It wasn't an answer to his question, but at least it was the truth. And for now it seemed important that Drake not know her husband had deserted her.

"Why isn't he with you?"

"He went to California on business." There was a shred of truth in her reply, but only a shred.

"I see."

But, of course, he didn't see. Faith didn't want him to see. Instinct told her it would be dangerous if he saw too much.

She heard his chair squeak as he rose, listened to his footsteps as he crossed the room to the window. She knew without looking that he braced the heel of one hand on the sill as he gazed outside. In her mind's eye she saw him, tall and strong and dark, the patch making his handsome face look dangerous and yet . . .

"Your daughter is much improved."

Her heart skittered. "Yes."

"I'm glad."

"Thank you." Her voice sounded breathless.

"Well . . ." He cleared his throat. "I'll leave you to your cleaning."

She turned toward him. He looked much as she'd imagined, sunlight adding a hint of midnight blue to his black hair. She thought again what it might be like to feel his arms around her, to kiss those unsmiling lips.

Fighting another blush, she spoke quickly before he could leave. "Mr. Rutledge, I was wondering if you might take me and the children into town for the celebration next week."

"I don't go into town."

"But why not?"

The moment the question was out of her mouth, she wished it back. That wasn't what she'd meant to say. She didn't have to know the man better to understand what a poor choice of words she'd made.

She saw him stiffen, saw the chiseled lines of his face harden.

"I don't believe that's any concern of yours," he replied in a voice as cold as a Wyoming winter.

"No, you're right. It isn't any of my concern." She stepped toward him. "I apologize, Mr. Rutledge. I hope you'll forgive me."

He offered an abrupt nod, then headed toward the door.

Faith whirled about. "Wait!"

Drake stopped but didn't look behind him. "What is it, Mrs. Butler?"

"Please think about my invitation."

Without a word, he opened the door and left.

Faith's disappointment was entirely out of proportion to the circumstances. She hadn't really expected him to join them, had she? And what possible difference would it have made? Drake Rutledge had lived in this house for many years, and no one in town knew him. Nancy Telford imagined him a murderer. Sadie Gold had even wondered if he existed at all. Why should Faith's invitation make any difference to him?

It didn't, of course. It couldn't.

Only she'd wanted it to. She'd very much wanted her invitation to make a difference to Drake.

The curtain of night dropped over the earth, bringing with it a cool breeze to rustle the leaves of the tall trees surrounding the house. A quarter-moon hung suspended over the mountains, casting a soft light upon the valley below.

One foot on the lower rail of the corral, his forearms resting on the top rail, Drake stared at the horses without seeing them, his thoughts troubled. Troubled because of Faith Butler and her irritating interference.

I don't go into town.

But why not?

It had been hours since she'd walked into his library, opened his curtains to let in the daylight, disturbed the careful order of his life, then asked him to accompany her into Dead Horse. Hours, and the words still lingered in his head.

I don't go into town.

But why not?

Why not? Was she more blind than Drake himself? Couldn't she *see* him with those blue-green eyes of hers?

Blast the woman!

He heard footsteps and turned his head, not surprised to find Parker approaching but glad for it. Anything to keep his mind off Faith.

"Evenin'," the foreman said as he stopped beside Drake. He glanced up at the star-studded sky. "Nice night. Rains've kept it cool."

Drake grunted a response.

Parker patted his belly. "Sure has been a pleasure havin' a woman to cook for us." Like Drake, he placed one foot and both arms on the corral rails, then stared off toward the mountains, dark shadows in the distance. "Be great if we could keep her on after the little girl's well. Sure would. The boys'd all give money to keep her here."

Drake felt like grinding his teeth. He'd wanted to forget Faith, and here was Parker bringing her up within moments. "I imagine she'll want to rejoin her husband as soon as she's able," he replied curtly.

"Husband?" Parker turned to stare at Drake.

He nodded, feeling a grim satisfaction from catching his friend unaware. "He's out in California, according to Mrs. Butler."

"You sure about that, Drake? I got me the feelin' she's alone exceptin' for those kids of hers."

"I'm sure. She told me herself."

"Well, I'll be." Parker scratched the top of his head. "She don't wear a weddin' band. Guess I figured—"

Drake's mood darkened. "You figured wrong."

"Well, I'll be," he repeated. "It just don't—"

"Do you think we'll get more rain?" Drake asked in a weak attempt to change the subject.

Parker didn't answer.

"We could use more. The grass is drying out early this year."

"Hmm." The foreman turned and glanced toward the house, muttering, "Just don't figure."

No, it didn't figure, Drake thought. There wasn't much about Mrs. Butler that *did* figure. She shouldn't be any of the things she seemed to be.

He remembered that afternoon, envisioned her as she'd spoken the lines Shakespeare had written so long ago. Her expressions, her movements, seemed to have been engraved upon his mind. Her melodious voice whispered in his memory, entrancing him again.

"Well"—Parker pushed away from the rail—"guess I'll turn in. Swede and I are headin' up to the north range tomorrow." He started away. "'Night."

"'Night," Drake returned absentmindedly.

I don't go into town.

But why not?

Why not? Why not go into Dead Horse? He didn't care what the people there thought. What others thought had ceased to matter to him long ago.

As Parker had done moments before, Drake turned and stared up at the third-story window through the shadow of tree limbs.

Hadn't it?

Haloed by soft moonlight, he stood alone near the corral.

Faith knew Drake couldn't see her, yet she drew

instinctively to one side of the window, one hand touching the hollow place between her breasts, as if to stop the frantic beating of her heart. Her skin felt suddenly warm, and she was grateful for the cool night air.

What is the matter with me? she wondered. Why does he make me feel so strange?

Was it merely his dark and dangerous looks, or was it something more? Was it only because she wanted to help him in repayment for what he'd done for her and her family? Or was it something else?

A need stirred deep inside. A need to be held and caressed, to be loved as a woman. A need long since silenced.

She closed her eyes and leaned against the window encasement, her knees almost too weak to hold her upright. Once before she had felt desire. Once before she had longed for a man's touch. She'd been eager for George to teach her all that she had not known. He had taught her about broken hearts. She had loved George with the true simplicity of guileless youth, but George had not known how to love in return.

Wonderful, laughing, handsome George Butler.

Was ever book containing such vile matter
So fairly bound? O, that deceit should dwell
In such a gorgeous palace!

With her back to the wall, she slid down until she sat on the floor. She drew her legs up to her chest and rested her forehead on her knees, wrapping her arms around her shins. Hot tears seared her eyelids before slipping free to moisten her cotton nightgown.

She didn't cry for love lost. Those tears had long

since been spent. She cried instead for the loss of innocence, for the shattering of dreams.

And, although she didn't realize it yet, she cried for the dark and tortured man who stood in the moonlight beneath her window.

7

July arrived in Wyoming on hot, dry winds. The sun beat mercilessly upon the small town of Dead Horse, bleaching the last remnants of paint from the board siding of the saloon and turning the street to a sea of dust. Horses stood with drooping heads, and dogs crawled under bushes and boardwalks, seeking the smallest bit of shade.

Seated on the porch of the Telford house, Rick wiped the sweat from his forehead with his handkerchief while reading the telegram from his son. It was a short message but a hopeful one. James was making some headway with the railroad officials. He and Nancy were leaving for Cheyenne today, but they hoped to be home by the end of next week. James closed by asking Rick to keep an eye on things at the hotel.

Rick shook his head as he folded the telegram and stuck it in his pocket. Keep an eye on the hotel. That wouldn't take much, he thought grimly. If it weren't for the hotel restaurant and Claire O'Connell's cooking, they could just lock the doors and forget it. There hadn't been a guest registered since Faith Butler and her children had moved up to the Jagged R nigh on two weeks ago.

Remembering the Butler family, he turned his gaze toward the ridge to the south of town, squinting against the bright sunlight. It had been nearly a week since he'd been to see his youngest patient. He supposed he should ride up there today, although he was quite certain his services were no longer needed. Becca Butler was out of the woods. As long as she got plenty of rest, she should continue to improve from this bout of illness. Only God knew when she might take sick again. Only God knew if she would grow to adulthood.

A cloud of dust rose above the road leading into Dead Horse, drawing the doctor's attention. He stared, too hot to look away, waiting to see which Jagged R cowpoke had decided to come into town for a drink at the saloon.

He licked his lips, his mouth suddenly drier than just moments before. Again he wiped his forehead with his handkerchief.

God, help me.

The thought of a drink made his belly twist. His hands began to shake, and he glanced down at them, his eyes narrowing.

When would it stop? he wondered. When would he stop thinking about holding a glass of whiskey in his hand, about staring into the amber liquid, about drinking until oblivion overtook him?

He squeezed his eyes shut as he drew his forearm across his forehead. He practiced taking one deep breath, then another, silently rehearsing an old litany that had kept him sober for close to four years now.

If he could make it through one minute without a drink, he could make it through two. If he could make it through two minutes, he could make it through ten. If he could make it through ten minutes, he could make it through an hour and then a day. If he could make it through a day, he could make it through another week and then another month and then another year. He swallowed hard, took another deep breath, then opened his eyes again, relieved that the dreaded moment was passing.

He focused his gaze once more on the horse and rider drawing close to town. He recognized Gertie Duncan even before he saw her face. The young woman didn't sit a horse like any man Rick knew. She slowed her horse to a walk at the outskirts. A billow of dust and dirt rolled on ahead of her, obscuring her momentarily from view. When the air cleared, she had nearly reached his house.

"Hey, Doc," she called when she saw him on the porch.

"Afternoon, Gertie."

"Hot 'nough for you?"

"It is."

"Same for me." She grinned as she reined in her lanky dun mare. "You all ready for the Fourth? Mrs. Gold's been workin' so hard, it's a wonder she ain't drowned in her own sweat."

"I know. Sadie has decided I'm to carry the flag in the parade."

Gertie cocked an eyebrow. "A parade?"

"Right down Main Street."

She laughed, a riotous sound coming straight up from her belly. "Well, don't that beat all. I heard tell there was gonna be fireworks, but this is the first I knew of a parade."

"It's for the children," Rick explained, looking down the empty street through town. "Lord knows there's little enough to celebrate around here."

"Say, Doc . . ."

He drew his gaze back to her, watched as she dismounted.

Holding on to the end of the reins, she stepped toward him, placing one foot on the lower step of the porch. Then she touched the brim of her Stetson with two gloved fingers and pushed the hat back on her head. "Mind if I ask you somethin'?" Her smile had disappeared.

"Of course not, Gertie. What is it?"

"Well, I was thinkin'. . . I was thinkin' you might like some company at the picnic. I can't cook a lick, mind you, but Miz Butler'll pack me somethin' t'feed the two of us."

Rick's eyes widened in surprise.

"Now don't go thinkin' I'd ask just anybody to join me," she added quickly, a rush of color infusing her cheeks. "I just figured, you bein' here alone, without your son an' all, that you might like somebody t'see that you're fed right."

"Your invitation is most kind and very much appreciated. I'd be glad to join you."

She removed her hat and raked fingers through her tousled hair, then slapped the Stetson against her thigh, raising a small flurry of dust. "Well, good. Glad that's settled. I just didn't want t'see you alone." She turned and quickly remounted her horse. "See ya on the Fourth." She tapped her heels against the mare's sides and, without a backward glance, rode off in the direction of the general store.

Rick stared after her, thinking that Gertie Duncan was an odd but thoughtful young woman. She would have made someone a nice daughter-in-law. Him, for instance.

Immediately he was ashamed. James loved his wife. It wasn't up to Rick to be wishing his son had married someone else. It was Rick's own fault that Nancy didn't like him. He was the guilty one, after all.

Drake sat beneath the tall cottonwood, staring at the river as it rolled by, his thoughts drifting with it.

Unable to sleep, he'd left the house at dawn and walked to this quiet refuge. There certainly wasn't any peace and quiet to be found in his own home. Not with Faith Butler there. His entire routine had been blithely destroyed by the woman.

And he wasn't the only one affected. His men weren't inclined to get much work done anymore. They loitered around the kitchen and the back porch all hours of the day, talking to Faith, grinning and making fools of themselves.

Idiots!

That thought had no sooner formed than he heard the crunching of dried twigs. He swore beneath his breath. Couldn't he even be alone *here*?

He glared in the direction of the sound just as Alex Butler pushed his way through the dense underbrush. The boy carried a bucket in one hand, and over his right eye he wore a patch. Just as he reached the river's edge, he stumbled over a rock and nearly pitched headfirst into the water. By sheer luck he toppled sideways instead, but he remained precariously close to danger.

Drake was instantly up and rushing forward. He

grabbed the boy by the arm and pulled him away from the river.

Alex looked up. Alarm lingered in his expression for only a matter of seconds, then disappeared, replaced by a grin as he scrambled to his feet. He pushed the patch up onto his forehead. "You were sure right about the patch, Mr. Rutledge. It makes it really hard to see, don't it? I walked into a door yesterday. Almost blacked my eyes. Didn't even know it was there."

"Is that so?" Drake responded darkly.

Alex nodded. "Yeah. Makes me feel real funny, too. Like I've been spinnin' around a lot. All dizzy like. Is that what it's like for you, too?"

Drake turned away.

"Are you used to it now?" the boy persisted as he tagged after him.

"Yes." *Go away.*

"Hey, thanks for grabbin' me just then. I'm not a very good swimmer."

"You're welcome." He glanced down at the boy and scowled, hoping it would make Alex leave.

The boy was oblivious of the subtle hint.

"Does your mother know you're down here?"

Alex's gaze dropped guiltily to the ground.

"You might have drowned, boy."

Drake remembered how quickly an accident could snuff out a life, how it could change everything for those left behind. Then he thought of Faith Butler, imagined her beautiful eyes full of tears for her lost son. He didn't know her well, but he knew she loved her children. He knew she would suffer if one of them was lost.

Drake took hold of Alex's arm a second time, causing the boy to look up. "You don't come down to the river again unless an adult is with you. Do you understand me?"

"Yes, sir," he whispered, dutifully chagrined.

"See that you mind."

Alex shuffled one foot, kicking up pebbles. "You're not going to tell Ma, are you?"

Drake subdued a groan as he released his hold on the boy and sat down again, his back against the cottonwood's trunk.

"Please don't tell her. She's been real happy since comin' here, and I don't want her worryin' about me. Ma's always worried too much."

Despite himself, Drake was intrigued. "What about your father? Where is he?"

"I haven't seen my pa in a long time. Don't hardly remember when it was. Pa isn't ever coming back." He held himself a little straighter, and his tone was belligerent. "But I don't care. We can take care of ourselves. We're doin' all right without him." His voice lowered. "He just made Ma cry anyway."

Drake had the urge to hit the absent Mr. Butler.

"Hey, you oughta see what I've learned to do. I can saddle a horse all by myself. Gertie taught me. I'm going to be a wrangler, just like her." Alex motioned toward the house and barn. "You want to see?" He reached out, as if to help Drake up from the ground.

Drake stared at the small hand for a moment, then looked up into a pair of hopeful, excited eyes.

The last thing in the world he wanted was to get mixed up in the problems of his housekeeper and her children. The last thing in the world he wanted was to watch this boy saddle a horse in the middle of a hot July day. The last thing in the world he wanted was to leave this cool, serene place by the river.

But for some unknown reason, he took hold of that small hand and allowed himself to be led away.

"Go on, Mrs. Butler," Johnny Coltrain urged. "Do some more."

"Cain't say I like anythin' so much as listenin' to you recite them lines," Will Kidd added.

Seated on a bench near the back porch, Faith lowered the mending into her lap. She glanced from one man to the other and found herself unable to deny her new friends what they'd asked.

She knew it wouldn't matter what play or scene she chose. She'd found that the cowboys at the Jagged R were easily pleased, whether it was her cooking or her acting. Would that all of her audiences through the years had been so, she thought as she gave her head a slow shake.

Then, drawing a deep breath, she began with a line from *Romeo and Juliet*. "'Come, civil night, / Thou sober-suited matron all in black, / And learn me how to lose a winning match / Played for a pair of stainless maidenhoods. / Hood my unmanned blood, bating in my cheeks, / With thy black mantle till strange love grown bold / Think true love acted simple modesty.'"

She closed her eyes as her cheeks grew warm. Why was it *this* scene that had come so quickly to mind? Why the soliloquy where Juliet longs for her new husband to join her for their wedding night? The words produced unwelcome images. Images of a man with a pirate's patch and an angry soul. Images of him holding her, kissing and caressing and loving her.

But it was more than just repeating Juliet's lines that caused those images and her accompanying distress. For days she had been tortured by them, especially at night when she was alone in her room. She would imagine him then, Drake Rutledge, lying there beside her in bed, touching her in the most intimate of fashions, in ways she had long tried to avoid.

Her voice lowered, and her breathing quickened as she continued. "'Come, night; come, Romeo; come, thou day in night;/ For thou wilt lie upon the wings of night / Whiter than new snow on a raven's back.'" Her heart raced. "'Come, gentle night; come, loving, black-browed night; / Give me my Romeo, and when I shall die / Take him and cut him out in little stars, / And he will make the face of heaven so fine / That all the world will be in love with night / And pay no worship to the garish sun.'"

It was wrong to be thinking these things, feeling this way. It was wrong and perilous.

"'O, I have bought the mansion of a love / But not possessed it, and though I am sold, / Not yet enjoyed. So tedious is this day / As is this night before some festival / To an impatient child that hath new robes / And may not wear them.'"

Silence fell, and then her small audience applauded, drawing Faith abruptly back to reality.

"Well, I swear," Will said almost reverently, "if that ain't the prettiest thing I ever heard. I could just stand here and listen t'you all day."

She opened her eyes, feeling the flush in her cheeks growing hotter as she looked up.

"Me too," Johnny declared.

Will set his hat back on his head. "Now"—he cleared his throat—"if I could just figure out what you was sayin'."

Faith laughed along with the two cowboys, the unwelcome images fading from her memory. Of course, it was just a performance. She was an actress who threw herself into her part. She'd been imagining Romeo and Juliet, that was all. She'd been feeling Juliet's emotions, not her own. She'd been imagining Romeo, not Drake Rutledge.

"Come on, Johnny." Will slapped the young cowboy on the back. "There's work t'be done."

Johnny touched his hat brim. "Thanks, Mrs. Butler. I sure did enjoy that."

"You're very welcome."

She shook her head as she returned her attention to the mending. She would do well to practice some comedies, she decided. She had fallen victim to her own performances. She had only been feeling what Shakespeare had wanted the audience to feel. Nothing more.

"Pure silliness," she muttered to herself. "Pure and utter foolishness."

Then, as if to mock her, Drake walked into the yard, holding the hand of her son. Her heart tightened in her chest at the sight.

She could hear Alex chattering, although she couldn't make out his words. His face was alight with pleasure as he gazed up at the man beside him. A moment later they disappeared through the open door of the barn.

Curious, Faith laid aside her mending, rose from the bench, and crossed the yard.

The interior was stifling, even with the doors at both ends thrown open to catch any breeze. Earthy scents, singular to barns, filled her nostrils as she stepped inside. She paused just beyond the square of sunlight, giving her eyes a moment to adjust.

"See?" she heard Alex say. "You gotta be real careful to make sure this strap is laid flat or you could cause a sore right here behind her leg."

Across the barn, Drake leaned his forearms on the top railing of a stall, watching as Faith's son tightened the cinch of a saddle on a buckskin-colored horse.

"Gertie says I'm a quick learner and that I'll make a good wrangler when I grow up." Alex glanced over his shoulder. "You think so, Mr. Rutledge?"

"I suppose so," the man answered.

"Maybe I can work here at the Jagged R. I like it here a lot." Alex caught sight of Faith just then. "Ma, come see what I can do."

She sent her son a smile, responding to his youthful enthusiasm. Then Drake turned, and she felt her heart skip a beat, unwanted images returning. She ignored them as she stepped forward, crossing the barn toward the stall. She moved to the opposite side of the stall door, standing as far away from Drake as good manners allowed, and forced herself to concentrate on her son.

"This is Sugar," Alex told her as he stroked the horse's neck. "I've been helpin' Gertie doctor her leg. See?" He reached down and lifted the buckskin's left front hoof. "She was hurt real bad, but she's almost better now."

"Miss *Duncan*"—she emphasized the name—"says you've been a big help to her."

Alex beamed.

"Your son wants to be the next Jagged R wrangler."

Her pulse skipped as she turned to look at him. *Be careful!* her mind warned, but her heart didn't listen. "I know," she replied softly.

Drake had never seen eyes quite like Faith Butler's. Not blue, yet not truly green. Large eyes, framed by long mahogany brown lashes. Expressive eyes that seemed to change with her mood.

What was it he read in those unusual blue-green eyes now?

She looked away, as if to keep him from finding the answer to his unspoken question. "Unsaddle the horse, Alex, and come inside. It's time for me to start preparations for supper, and I could use your help."

"Ah, Ma. I don't—"

"Alexander," she warned softly.

"But—" Alex tried again.

"You'd better do as she says," Drake interrupted.

She turned to meet his gaze a second time, and he was struck afresh by her loveliness. But there was more, he realized. It went deeper than handsome ancestors and patrician bone structure. She had a beauty of the spirit, too.

Color infused her high cheekbones as Drake continued to stare without speaking.

In that moment he forgot all about his anger, all about the many reasons Faith Butler irritated him, all the reasons he had for avoiding a beautiful woman like her. He forgot that she had turned his routine existence upside down. He forgot that he wanted to be left alone in his once dark library. He forgot all about bitterness and loneliness, bad memories and unwelcome tomorrows. He forgot everything except the lovely woman standing before him.

He saw Faith swallow, saw the tip of her tongue moisten slightly parted lips. There was a provocative innocence in the action that caused a jolt of awareness to shoot through him.

As if she'd seen something that frightened her, Faith took a step backward. "I'd best see to supper," she said, barely above a whisper. And then she hurried away.

"Don't see why I have to help with supper," Alex

muttered from behind him. "I got horses to tend to. Gertie needs me to—"

"Do as your mother says," Drake responded absently. Then he, too, left the barn, silently pondering what had just happened and what it might mean in the days to come.

8

The pewter sky of twilight was broken by pink-stained clouds on the western horizon. Mountain ranges had turned the color of ripe grapes, and tall trees—lodgepole pines and ponderosa, tamaracks and quaking aspen, chokecherry and box elder—stood as ebony sentinels over a cooling earth.

With the children in bed and the last of her chores finished, Faith stepped out the back door and watched the colorful spectacle at the close of day. She was thankful for a moment to herself, yet her thoughts brought her anything but peace.

"I should leave Dead Horse," she whispered. "I should at least go to Cheyenne. I should find a way back to New York."

But she knew she wouldn't go. Not yet.

Becca was better, but she wasn't strong enough to travel. Chances were slim—no, nonexistent—that Faith could find another job that would provide a home and decent food for her children. And Alex was so incredibly happy here. And . . .

She pressed her hands against her stomach, trying to drive away the knot that had formed there earlier in the day and had lingered ever since.

What's wrong with me?

She knew the answer to her own question.

Drake.

"But why?" she asked aloud, as if challenging the sky to explain it to her.

She received no reply. Not from the sky or from within.

She settled onto the stoop, her arms wrapped around her shins, her feet on the next step down. She rested her chin on her knees and watched as the first stars began to wink in the darkening heavens.

She tried to summon her husband's image to her mind, tried to remember when she had dreamed of George's touches, of his kisses. She knew she had done so once, but she couldn't remember the feelings themselves. She should, but she couldn't.

It had all been so very long ago.

Faith tingled with triumph. Applause still thundered in her ears as she walked along the darkened streets of New York toward the small apartment she and George had rented for the run of the show. Exhilaration quickened her steps.

Opening night had been everything she had hoped it would be. In truth, it had been even more than she'd hoped. Only one thing had marred this night: George's absence. He hadn't come to the theater to watch her.

But Faith refused to think about that now. When she told him about the enormous success of the play, his mood would change. Things would be better between them. Things would be as she'd dreamed they would be when they were first married.

Perhaps they'd be able to buy a little house of their own. George would find a job that he liked, one he would keep, perhaps start his own business. Yes, this play would change their luck. George was forever complaining about their luck. From now on it was going to be better. They wouldn't be without money. Faith would become a famouse actress, and George would be proud of her. The children would have warm clothes and plenty to eat. George would remember to be kind to her. He would learn to be tender. He wouldn't . . . he wouldn't be so . . . so . . .

A light snow began to fall, and Faith pulled her threadbare coat more tightly about her, fighting a sudden urge to cry.

Why should she cry? Things were going to be wonderful now. There was no more reason to cry.

A few minutes later, Faith climbed the stairs to their fourth-floor apartment and let herself in. The parlor was dark, but she didn't need a light to find her way to the bed tucked in the back corner of the room.

She leaned down and kissed her sleeping children. Alex, not yet five, slept with both arms thrown above his head, taking the lion's share of the thin mattress. Little Becca, barely three, was curled into a ball, her thumb in her mouth. Smoothing their hair away from their foreheads, Faith whispered that she loved them.

A house with a yard and a white picket fence for them to play in. No more cramped apartments that smelled of cooking grease and garbage. If this play made her famous, the Butlers could have all of those things. They could be a happy family.

She straightened and turned toward the bedroom, where a soft light glowed beneath the closed door. George was still awake. He'd waited up for her. When she told him the news, things would get better. She knew they would.

"George," she said softly as she pushed the door open.

She heard him swear, saw him roll over and sit up in bed. She watched as the girl with the flowing golden hair slowly pulled the sheet up to cover her bare breasts. A blessed numbness spread through Faith, a numbness that seemed to separate her from what was happening, as if she were watching it happen to someone else.

George swore again. Tossing aside the covers with one hand, he reached for his trousers with the other. The naked girl, lying where Faith always slept, laughed softly as she blew him a kiss on the air.

The numbness didn't last.

"What are you doing?" Faith asked, knowing the answer but unable to say anything else. "What are you doing? The children." She glanced over her shoulder. "The children."

"Listen, Faith." George started toward her.

She pressed her back against the doorjamb. "Who is she? Why is she here?"

But, of course, she knew the answer to that question, too. She'd seen the answer with her own eyes.

He'd been making love to her, here . . . in their bedroom . . . in their bed.

In Faith's bed.

She thought she might be sick.

The blonde rose, her lithe body confidently displayed as she reached for Faith's wrapper. "George and I are lovers," she stated simply.

"Lovers?" Faith echoed.

"Tell her, George. Tell her she doesn't know how to please you." She ran her tongue over her kiss-swollen lips. "In bed or out. Tell her I know what you want." She gave Faith a wink. "Tell her you're going away with me."

Faith looked at her husband.

He took another step toward her. "It's true, Faith. I'm leaving with Jane. I can't stay here. I wasn't meant to live like this. I was meant for better things."

"But I'm your wife. And the children. What about the children?"

George shrugged. "You're their mother. You'll see that they don't starve. Besides, you're the one who wanted them."

Jane came to stand beside him, wrapping her arm possessively around his back. "George is going to do great things, and I can help him." She splayed the fingers of her left hand across his bare abdomen, just above the waistline of his trousers. "Can't I help you, George?" she whispered huskily.

Faith swirled about and bolted for the kitchen, where she emptied her stomach into the sink. By the time the retching stopped, George had joined her in the tiny room off the parlor.

"I've got an opportunity to make a name for

*myself out in California. Jane has some money her
father left her, and we're going to start our own business."*

His own business . . . Hadn't she thought that very
thing on her walk home? She wanted to laugh. She
wanted to scream.

"And what of our marriage?" she asked instead,
her voice hoarse.

"I'll seek a divorce."

"I see." She turned slowly, leaning her hip against
the sink to steady her shaky legs. "She isn't the first,
is she?"

He shrugged again, not even trying to lie.

The pain in her chest was almost unbearable. "I
loved you, George."

"I know, but it just didn't work out the way it was
supposed to. You can't expect me to be tied down this
way. I'm meant for better things, Faith."

Jane, dressed in her own clothes now, appeared in
the parlor. "It's time to go, George."

"I'm coming." He reached out and touched Faith's
cheek. "No hard feelings, honey."

Faith closed her eyes as those words from the past
echoed in her head.

No hard feelings?

No. At least not anymore. Over the past couple
of years, she had sorted through the confusion
and the pain and come to terms with the truth.
There was nothing she could have done to keep
George with her. She hadn't been the wife he'd wanted.

Perhaps she'd suspected, even on her wedding
day, that he would never stay. But she'd been only

eighteen and in love with a dazzling man, a charmer. And she'd trusted him as only a girl of eighteen could trust. Later, she'd pretended not to know about his affairs. She'd pretended to desire him long after desire had been destroyed. She'd even pretended not to know that she'd stopped loving him. She'd tried so hard to, at the very least, keep the illusion of love alive.

Faith had decided the night George walked out the door with Jane that she would never risk her heart again. She had no need of a man to survive. She'd proven it many times already. As for foregoing the more intimate rituals of marriage, she'd never missed them.

Until now.

She took a deep breath, driving away the persistent, unwelcome images of Drake Rutledge. She hadn't missed a man's touch, a man's kisses. She didn't want them or need them.

Faith caught a whiff of cigarette smoke, a momentary warning that she wasn't alone. She straightened and turned, watching as Gertie stepped up to the back porch.

"Nice night, ain't it?" the wrangler asked, then drew again on her smoke. The end of the cigarette glowed brightly in the night air.

"Yes."

"I'm not disturbin' you, am I? If I am, you just say so an' I'll make myself scarce."

"No, you're not disturbing me." In fact, Faith was glad for the company, hoping it would turn her thoughts in a different direction.

Gertie leaned her back against the porch railing, looking up at the canopy of stars now twinkling overhead. She inhaled once more on her cigarette, then blew out the smoke, a pale cloud against the dark backdrop of night. "You ever wonder what them stars look like on the other side of the world?"

"Much the same as they do to us, I imagine."

"You ever been to another country, Faith?"

"No."

Gertie dropped the butt of her cigarette, then ground it into the earth with the heel of her boot. "Me neither. Doc has. I heard him tell once about goin' t'England and Paris and Rome." She grunted. "Hell, I ain't been further east than Kansas. Don't have no notion how the rest of the world lives. All I've ever known is mountains and plains and horses."

Faith nodded but remained silent.

"I don't have no education. Don't even speak proper, and I know that for a fact. There ain't nothin' I like better than listenin' t'you."

"Why, thank you, Gertie."

"I can't read, neither. Leastwise, not much more'n my name." She removed her hat, then turned toward Faith. "You reckon I could learn?"

"I'm sure you could."

"You reckon you could teach me?"

"Me?" Faith shook her head. "I'm not a teacher."

"You're teachin' Alex, ain't you?"

"Yes, but—"

"I won't be no bother."

Faith smiled gently. "I suppose I could try."

"Thanks." Gertie slapped her hat against her thigh a couple of times, then sat on the bottom step.

Faith had the distinct impression that her new friend had more on her mind than just learning to read. She didn't have long to wait to find out what it was.

"You reckon a fella could ever take notice of a gal like me?" Gertie's voice was hesitant.

So *that* was the problem. A man.

Perhaps a man was always the problem.

Gertie twisted on the step and looked up at her. "I guess what I'm really askin' is, do you think you could help make me look more . . . more like a woman? I know it'd be like turnin' a sow's ear into a silk purse, but I . . . I . . . Well, you see, I invited Doc t'eat with me at the picnic on the Fourth and . . . well, I just thought . . . " Her voice drifted into silence.

Hearing the earnest desperation in Gertie's voice, Faith couldn't help smiling again. She leaned forward. "You're no sow's ear, Gertie Duncan, and I'd be delighted to help."

"I don't expect no miracles, mind you."

"I don't think it will take a miracle," she replied gently. "Why don't you come up to my room tomorrow morning after breakfast?"

"All right." Gertie cleared her throat. "There's one more thing. I know I already asked enough favors. But, you see, I promised Doc you'd fix the lunch. I can't cook a lick, and I'd sure as heck hate t'poison him."

Faith laughed as she placed a hand on Gertie's shoulder. "No, I don't think that would help matters any. Of course I'll fix the picnic lunch for you. It's no bother. I'll be making up a basket for the children and me anyway."

"Well then . . ." Gertie rose and set her hat on her head. "Guess I'll be turnin' in for the night."

"Good night, Gertie."

"'Night, Faith. And thanks again." She set off with long, yard-eating strides, quickly disappearing around the corner of the house.

Dr. Telford and Gertie.

They were an unlikely pair, Faith thought as silence settled around her once again.

As unlikely as Drake Rutledge and me?

She groaned as the images she'd sought to forget came rushing back. With her elbows on her knees, Faith rested her forehead against the heels of her hands.

"Go away," she whispered. "Go away and leave me alone."

Drake rode again that night.

He began by following the familiar pattern of galloping madly across the plains. But for some reason, midway in his flight, he reined in, drawing his pinto to a halt alongside the riverbank.

As he stared into the ribbon of water, glittering with reflected starlight, Drake realized with surprise that the bitterness, the loneliness, the private fury, hadn't returned as he'd expected it would. The peace that had settled over him as he'd stood in the barn with Faith remained with him still.

Purposefully he thought about his parents and Larissa and waited for the familiar rage to fill him. But it didn't come. It wasn't there. All he felt was a gentle sorrow at what had been lost so very long ago.

Then he thought of Faith Butler. He thought of how his house had changed since the day she'd arrived, how darkness had become light, how his routine had altered, even how his ranch hands were different. But he felt no anger as he had before, as he'd felt just that morning, in fact.

Instead he experienced a measure of hope, as if life

had begun anew for him. The fury was gone, dead. Faith had wrought this change without even knowing what she'd done.

He envisioned the look on her face that afternoon, a mixture of surprise, dread, and something more . . . *Desire?* Could it have been desire? Desire for *him?*

She was a married woman with two children. She was an actress who only needed a temporary home until her daughter was well. She was beautiful and talented, and there was no reason in the world to believe she might remain at the Jagged R longer than a matter of weeks.

But he hoped she would. He hoped he would be granted a little more time to know her. Not long. He knew that wasn't to be. But he could hope for the remainder of summer. Or perhaps until the leaves had turned to gold. Or maybe until the first snows had fallen.

Alex's words echoed through his memory. *Pa isn't ever coming back. . . .*

Drake wasn't a whole man. He was half blind and his face was scarred, disfigured. There was no reason to believe any woman would ever choose to be with him.

But maybe . . . just maybe . . .

Drake nudged the pinto's ribs with his heels, turning his horse in the direction of the ranch house. After a short while, he kicked the gelding into a gallop.

But this time he wasn't racing from the past. Instead he was riding toward his future.

9

Gertie looked into the mirror with a mixture of curiosity and horror. Surely that creature wasn't her!

"It's too short, of course," Faith said, kneeling on the floor as she checked the hem of the dress, "but there's plenty of fabric here. We can let it down. And we'll have to take it in here and there because you're so slender. But you'll look lovely when it's done."

"Who're you tryin' to fool, Miz Butler? I ain't never looked this ridiculous since my ma tried t'put my hair in ringlets when I was just knee high." She turned away from the mirror. "Tryin' t'be what I ain't. If this ain't the stupidest idea I ever come up with, then I don't know what is."

"You're wrong, Gertie." Faith stood. "You're just not used to wearing a dress. When we alter it to fit you properly, Dr. Telford won't be able to take his eyes off you."

Gertie wanted to believe everything could be fixed with a bit of sewing, but she couldn't. Not when she only had to look at her reflection to know otherwise. She'd never been cut out to look like a woman, and she knew it. Especially when she stood next to Faith Butler.

"Hell," she muttered, "who said I cared what Doc thought, anyways?"

Faith's laughter was soft and airy. "You're not going to lie to me now, are you, Gertie?"

Gertie let out a deep sigh as she sank onto the edge of the bed, her knees apart, her hands clasped between them in the folds of the skirt. "It ain't no use nohow."

"Why not?" Faith sat down beside her.

"You think an educated man like Doc would ever take notice of the likes o' me? Hell, I'm just another cowpoke from the Jagged R Ranch, far as he's concerned. He don't know I'm female underneath my trousers." She snorted in derision. "Shoot, I didn't hardly know it myself 'til I thought about kissin' him." At the admission, heat rushed to her cheeks.

Lord Almighty, she was *blushing* again!

Faith put her arm around Gertie's shoulders and gave her a squeeze. "Looks aren't the only thing that attracts a man to a woman, and if they are, you don't want him anyway."

Gertie cast a sideways glance at Faith, noting the firm set of her mouth and the look of sadness in her blue green eyes. Briefly she wondered who'd put that hurt there. Then Faith smiled and the sadness was gone, leaving Gertie to wonder if it had been there at all.

"Tell me about Rick Telford," Faith encouraged.

"What attracted you to him? Was it merely *his* appearance?"

"'Course not."

"Then tell me what."

Gertie thought about it a moment, then answered honestly. "He's smart, for one thing. You don't become as good a doctor as he is without bein' smart. And he's a gentleman, too. Real refined and distinguished like. I never seen anybody with better manners. And I admire him a lot for what he's done, quittin' drinkin' and all." She shook her head. "He sure as all git out has got plenty of patience. Just look at who he's gotta live with. You're too new here t'know, but if you ask me, that there daughter-in-law of his would drive a saint to commit murder. But he's always been kind as can be with her. I don't know how he does it. There's plenty of times I'd like to've punched her square between the eyes."

Faith laughed again. "It's probably just as well that you didn't."

"Yeah. It's not somethin' a lady would do, I reckon. But then, I ain't never been mistaken for a lady." Gertie shrugged. "Or a woman either, for that matter."

Faith rose, then turned and took hold of Gertie's hands, drawing her to her feet. "Come over here," she said, pulling Gertie back to the mirror. "Now, I want you to quit seeing yourself as a wrangler or cowpoke or whatever. You *are* a woman, and Rick Telford would be blind not to notice. See how pretty that curl in your hair is, and look at the way it shines in the sunlight after it's been washed. You're lucky to be able to wear it short like that. You don't have to spend lots of time in the morning with a hairbrush and hairpins. And see how slender you are. Why, you'll never go to fat, Gertie. Not in a hundred years. And your eyes are the prettiest shade of blue I think I've ever seen."

Gertie met the other woman's gaze in the glass. "You're a right fine actress, Faith Butler. You almost got me believin' what you're sayin'."

"I'm just telling the truth, Gertie. Rick will know that I'm right."

Drake leaned back on his chair, his fingers steepled against his chin as he stared across the desk at his ranch foreman. "In your opinion, what are the chances of getting the railroad through Dead Horse?"

"Without the promised shipment of Jagged R cattle, probably none," Parker answered. "They'll most likely choose another route. But with your support, I'd say the chances are good. The railroad cares about one thing. Making money. If we can show it's more profitable for them to come up our way, they'll do it."

Drake glanced toward the window. "What sort of man is James Telford?"

"Young. Bright. He's a good representative for the town."

"And he owns the hotel?"

"Yeah."

Drake rose and crossed the library. He leaned his right shoulder against the window casing as he gazed out into the yard. Two cowpokes stood talking outside the bunkhouse. Another—Johnny Coltrain, he thought—worked a young horse inside a corral. Alex Butler sat on the top rail, observing the training session. Swede Swenson stood in the shade of the barn, shoeing a big white gelding, an ugly animal with pink-rimmed eyes and a deep scoop in his nose.

"It won't matter one way or the other to the Jagged R if Dead Horse survives," he observed. "We'll be here no matter what. What's kept the rest of them from leaving before now?"

Parker remained silent.

Drake glanced over his shoulder. He understood Parker's surprise. He realized today was the first time he'd shown any interest in Dead Horse and its inhabitants. "I'd really like to know."

Parker came to join him by the window. "Well, let's see now. The Golds, Sadie and Joseph, run the general store. They're Jewish and haven't always been welcome where they've lived. They've moved around and know how hard it is to start over. They've got six kids. They'd like to stay. Folks in Dead Horse have always made them welcome. Their religion's never caused them any problems here. They know they might not be so lucky next time if they're forced to go."

Drake nodded.

"James and Nancy Telford own the hotel. A young couple, just starting out. No children yet. James used to work for the bank, when the town still had one. He bought the hotel after Seamus O'Connell died."

Drake narrowed his eyes thoughtfully. "If James is so bright, like you said, why invest in a dying town? Why not move someplace where he'd get a better return on his money?"

"Because of his father."

"His father?" Drake was intrigued. "What about the good doctor?"

"Rick needed a place to start over. Dead Horse gave him the chance he needed."

Parker hadn't really answered the question, so Drake waited for him to continue.

"Rick was a drunk, plain and simple. Didn't have much of a practice, from what I hear tell. Then his wife died. He blamed himself—and I guess so did the folks in the town where he was livin'. So he came to Dead Horse to stay with his son, and he sobered up. After a while, he started practicin' medicine again. When things started goin' bad for the town, James didn't want to move away, maybe pull the rug out from under Rick, so he and Nancy stayed and took over the hotel."

Drake thought of his own father, remembered what it had been like, watching Clyde Rutledge grow old before his time, watching Clyde grieve himself into an early grave, all the while blaming his son.

What would Drake have given, what would he have done, to be able to help his father? Or to have had Clyde's forgiveness?

Just about anything.

He understood what James had done for Rick. Perhaps better than most would. "Go on," he told Parker, wanting to blot out the memories. "Who are the others?"

"Well, there's Jed Smith, the postmaster. He lost a leg back during the war. Only place I've ever seen him is on the boardwalk in front of the post office. Sits there, smokin' his pipe and talkin' to anyone who stops by. Stretch Barns owns the saloon. Beatrice . . . Hmm, don't rightly know if she even has a last name. Anyways, Beatrice works for Stretch, serving drinks and such. Claire O'Connell, Seamus's widow, she runs the hotel restaurant for the Telfords." He scratched his head thoughtfully. "Oh, yeah. There's the widow Ashley. She calls herself a dressmaker, but

I doubt she's had much work the last few years. She's gettin' up in years. Don't suppose she's got anywhere else to go."

While Parker talked, Drake tried to imagine the town and the people who lived there, but he couldn't. Seven years he'd been in this house, and he didn't know any of those places of business, didn't know any of the people Parker named.

What did that say about him? he wondered.

He focused his attention on the activities outside his window, realizing he didn't even know the men who worked for him. Oh, he knew their names and what they looked like. But what else did he know?

"Parker," he said without turning his head, "it's been a long time."

After a moment Parker responded, "Yeah, boss, it has."

"You've been a good friend."

The foreman's hand touched lightly on Drake's shoulder, then was gone. "I've tried to be."

Another silence filled the room.

Finally Drake said, "Someday I'll tell you about it."

Parker didn't ask what Drake meant. He must have known. "When you're ready." Without another word, he crossed the library and let himself out, closing the door behind him.

"Blast it all, son." Clyde Rutledge dropped a sheaf of papers onto Drake's desk. *"You're not applying yourself. How will you ever be ready to take over the firm if you don't take your work more seriously? I'm not paying you to gallivant about town in that fancy carriage of yours. You've got clients to attend to. They need your attention."*

Drake stared at the legal documents fanning out before him. The last thing in the world he wanted to do was go over them with his father. Most of the work the firm did was boring, uninteresting, as far as Drake was concerned. How his father had tolerated it all these years he'd never know.

"Can we talk about this later, Father?" he asked as he rose from his chair. "I'm supposed to pick up Mother at her dressmaker's in a few minutes, and then I promised to take Larissa to the Cavanaugh house party."

"I'm counting on you, Drake. You've got to buckle down. This firm needs you."

But it didn't need him. This stuffy old firm would get along just fine without him, and everyone knew it. For a moment, Drake remembered what it had been like to gallop alongside a stampeding herd of cattle—the dust, the noise, the smell, the danger. How alive he'd felt!

Clyde Rutledge sank onto a chair, his hand pressed against his heart. "I won't always be around, son. When I'm gone . . . well, you know I won't be with you for long. Your mother will need you."

Wasn't it enough that he'd been forced to give up his own dreams? Drake wondered as he stared at his father. Wasn't it enough that he'd returned to Philadelphia when his mother had sent for him?

Anger flared to life, but Drake managed to hide it, even while his thoughts kept churning.

It wasn't as if the Rutledges needed their son to earn his way or to support them in their old age. They were wealthy enough to live out the rest of their lives in comfort, even if Drake never handled another case for the firm.

And he sure didn't have to sit there and watch his father play out his weak-heart routine.

Drake picked up his gloves, then reached for his fur-lined coat. "I'd better be going. We don't want Mother standing out in the cold." He motioned toward his desk. "I'll go over those papers later." Then he escaped before his father could say another word.

He left the law firm of Rutledge and Seever, but he couldn't leave behind the memories Clyde Rutledge's comments had started whirring around in his head. As Drake drove his fine pair of matched bays down the street to Madame Celesta's Dress Shop, he couldn't help remembering those brief but adventuresome years he'd spent out west.

His friends in Texas and Montana, and all points in between, wouldn't have been accepted in the upper echelons of Philadelphia society, but Drake hadn't cared. They'd been honest, hardworking men. They'd done their share of good-natured ribbing of the greenhorn among them, but in the end they'd accepted Drake and done their best to teach him all he needed to know.

Cowboying had been tough work, but even its worst chores were better than being stuck in an office with a stack of dry, boring briefs. The men he'd worked with on ranches and cattle drives had had little education. Even so, he'd preferred their down-to-earth, commonsense views of life to the stuffy narrow-mindedness of the men in his father's firm.

It had always been in the back of his mind to return to the West one day, but then he'd met Larissa Dearborne. Beautiful, exquisite Larissa, who could twist him so easily to her will. After he'd asked her to marry him, he'd known he would never leave Philadelphia. Larissa would never be able to survive in the rough and rugged West he'd known. So he'd given up that dream.

And wasn't being Larissa's husband worth giving it up?

That question lingered as he greeted his mother inside the doorway of Madame Celesta's, as he helped Constance Rutledge into his shiny black carriage with its bright green upholstery, as he guided the horses along the quiet streets toward the Rutledge estate.

Perhaps that was why, when they met Teddy Westover at the entrance to the park, he so quickly took up Teddy's challenge for a race. Perhaps he missed the wild and reckless days of his youth. Perhaps it was because he felt everything slipping through his fingers. Because he saw his dull, staid future, and it frightened him.

And so, with his mother in the carriage, crying for him to slow down, he raced his team against Teddy Westover's.

He would never know what caused his coach to slide out of control, what caused it to tip and roll. He would never remember the following seconds that would change his life. But he would live with the aftermath forever.

"Show me how to make a *B* again, Mama."

Faith looked across the kitchen table at Becca. The girl's face was wrinkled in concentration as she stared at the paper and chewed on the end of her pencil.

"I don't remember how," Becca added, glancing up. "Show me again."

Faith subdued a sigh. At this rate she would never finish the alterations on Gertie's dress. But how could she complain about her daughter's curiosity? Or her improving health? If Becca weren't feeling so much better, she wouldn't be bored and restless. It was getting more and more difficult to find ways to occupy Becca's time and still make certain she got the rest she needed.

Faith put down her sewing and went around to the other side of the table. She took the pencil from her daughter's hand, then leaned forward and drew the letter slowly. "Now you show me."

Becca drew a whole line of *B*'s, her tongue sticking out between her lips as she frowned in concentration. When she was done, she glanced up at her mother with an air of triumph. The smile disappeared a moment later.

Faith followed her daughter's gaze across the room, straightening abruptly when she saw her employer standing in the doorway.

"Look who's up," Drake said. "She must be feeling better."

Faith placed a hand on Becca's shoulder. "Yes."

His gaze dropped to the girl, and then he did something totally unexpected.

He smiled.

Faith knew that he said something to Becca, but she wasn't sure what. She was completely captivated by the curve of his mouth beneath his dark, closely trimmed mustache. His smile had the strangest effect on her.

He moved into the kitchen, stopping on the opposite side of the table. He placed his hands on the back of the chair where Faith had been seated only moments before. "Learning your letters already?"

"I can write my name." Becca looked up at her mother, then admitted, "Well, sometimes I forget."

Faith pressed her free hand against her abdomen, trying to stop the fluttering sensation inside. "Was there something you needed, Mr. Rutledge?"

He looked up, their eyes met, and her heart skipped another beat.

"Not really," he replied.

"Oh." The word came out as a whisper of air with little substance.

"Mama's helpin' make a dress for Miss Duncan to wear into town for the celebration."

"Miss Duncan? *Our* Miss Duncan?" His left eyebrow arched, and the corners of his mouth lifted another notch. "In a *dress?*"

Faith nodded.

"I'd like to see that."

"You can." Why did it seem she had so little air in her lungs? "My invitation is still open."

"Invitation?"

"To join the children and me in Dead Horse for the Fourth of July." She had a sudden vision of the four of them, sitting on a blanket, watching fireworks against a black sky. Her heart began to race, and her knees felt ridiculously weak.

Drake stared at her for what seemed an eternity, his dark gaze never wavering, his expression unreadable. Finally he shook his head. "Another time, perhaps," he said in a low voice as he stepped back from the chair. "But thank you for asking me, Mrs. Butler. I do appreciate it." Then he turned and strode out of the kitchen.

A dozen heartbeats later Faith whispered, "You're quite welcome, Mr. Rutledge."

"Mama, are you all right? You look sort of funny."

She glanced down at her daughter, then drew a deep breath. "I'm all right, sweetheart. I was just thinking."

Forcing herself to move, Faith returned to her chair and picked up her sewing. As she slipped the needle and thread through the fabric of Gertie's dress, she wondered if she'd told her daughter the truth.

Perhaps she wasn't all right.

Perhaps there was something wrong.

Terribly, dangerously wrong.

With her heart.

She looks a little like Jane, but I don't care. I want her anyway.

The bitch. If Jane was here now, I'd gladly squeeze the life from her. I hope she choked on one of those jewels that bastard bought her with. Money. That's all she ever cared about. Just her precious money. Wasn't my fault when it was gone.

Money. Ha! I'm nearly out myself. Too little to pay a whore for a quick tumble. But I want her, damn it. I need her. Look at me. I'm hard already. Besides, who said I have to pay her anything? She might find she likes me so much she'll give it to me free.

I never used to pay a woman for her favors. Hell, they used to pay me. They used to keep me real nice. I never had to work in the old days. Even Faith always made sure I had plenty to spend. Yeah, Faith didn't do too bad by me. A shame she was a cold fish in bed. Wonder what became of her after I left?

Jane was different. Lord, she was hot. Wonder if the whore is as hot? Guess I'm going to find out.

Cheap hotel. Hope the bed's clean. Be my luck to get chiggers off the sheets and the clap from her. She's not much to look at up close. Not pretty at all. Maybe this is what Jane looks like now. Ha! Old and worn out, like she deserves to be. Slut. She wasn't any better than this one. Just a whore. Got lucky, that's all. But still just a cheap, no good, lying whore.

I'd kill her if I ever got me the chance. Yeah, I'd kill her. Nice and slow like, so she knew she was dying before it happened. So she'd beg me not to do it. So she'd tell me she was wrong for what she did to me and say she was sorry.

Nice and slow. That's how I'd do it.

I'd pinch her breasts. Like this.

What's the matter, baby? You don't like it like that? Sure you do.

And when she complained, I'd slap her. Like this.

Shut up. Don't make so much noise.

Got to get this dress off of her. Got to get inside her. Got to . . . got to . . .

Shut up. Shut up, you stupid whore. You like it this way, baby, and you know it. Shut up.

What do you think of that, Jane? How do you like it that way? Hurt you, did I? But you always liked it rough, didn't you? Do you get it rough from your rich husband? Do you? Does he know how to make you scream? Does he ever put his hands around your throat like this and squeeze, real slow and tight?

Go on, baby. That's the way. Try to get away. Yeah. That's right.

Get up. Get up and get out of here. You weren't worth paying for. Get up, I said. Get up, damn you.

What's the matter with you?

I'll be damned. I killed her.

It should have been Jane.

10

Reverend Harold Arnold, the circuit rider who came to Dead Horse once every four to five weeks, was in town for the Fourth of July. His sermon that morning, preached beneath a Rocky Mountain maple that grew behind the hotel, was on the true freedom that came from knowing God.

When the reverend led the small body of worshipers in song, Faith joined in, her voice full of joy. She had much to praise God for, she thought as she glanced down at Becca.

When the hymn was finished and the service complete, Faith introduced herself and her children to the minister. "It's been far too long since I've heard a sermon preached by an ordained minister, Reverend Arnold. You were very inspiring."

"Thank you, Mrs. Butler. It was a pleasure to see some new faces amongst my flock this morning. I suspect several of those men from the Jagged R were here because of you more than me." He grinned. "I hope you plan to remain in Dead Horse."

"I'd like to stay." Realizing what she'd said, she felt a jolt of surprise.

Would I like to stay in Dead Horse? she asked silently, testing her earlier response.

Yes.

"That would be wonderful," Reverend Arnold continued. "Perhaps next time I'll get to meet Mr. Rutledge himself." He leaned down and shook Alex's hand. "How about you, young man? Would you like to stay in Dead Horse?"

"Would I ever!"

What had she done? She'd given the minister and Alex the impression they might remain here, but she hadn't the slightest idea how long Drake Rutledge meant to keep her on as his housekeeper. When he'd hired her, he'd told her only that she could stay until Becca was well.

Listening now as Alex regaled Reverend Arnold with his aspirations of being a wrangler when he was older, Faith comforted herself by remembering the changes she'd observed in her employer. He no longer seemed so angry at having Faith and her children in his home. Perhaps he would decide he needed a housekeeper for more than just a few weeks or months.

Becca tugged at her skirt. "Mama?"

"What is it, dear?"

"I'm hungry."

The reverend chuckled. "Your daughter has the right idea. I'm rather hungry myself. I'm sure the good women of Dead Horse have prepared a fine feast for this day. Mind if I walk with you, Mrs. Butler?"

She shook her head. "Of course not."

Alex ran on ahead as Faith, Reverend Arnold, and Becca moved at a more sedate speed toward the picnic area near the river where long planks had been set up on sawhorses and covered with sheets. Men stood in small groups beneath the shade of the trees, talking and laughing, while the women loaded the makeshift tables with food, their voices rising in a friendly hum.

Faith excused herself and, with Becca close beside her, went to claim the picnic basket from the back of the Rutledge buggy. Then they approached the tables.

Sadie Gold greeted Faith with enthusiasm, giving her a hug and treating her as if they were lifelong friends. Hooking her arm through Faith's, Sadie drew her into the midst of the other women. "I'm sure you saw most everyone at your church service, but let me introduce you again."

Faith felt uncertain and shy. And hopeful. She wanted so much to fit in, to belong. She didn't want to be judged and found wanting, as had happened so often in her past. It had never mattered to her before. It mattered now.

Unmindful of Faith's trepidation, Sadie began, "This is Claire O'Connell. Claire runs the restaurant over at the hotel. But, of course, the two of you must have met when you were staying there. And this is Mary O'Rourke. Mary and her husband have a farm south of town. These are my daughters. Ruth here is my oldest, then Naomi, Esther, and Tamar. My two sons are off somewhere. Getting into mischief, no doubt." She grinned and gave a small shrug. "But then, when aren't young boys into mischief, I'd like to know?"

Names swirled in Faith's head, but she didn't have a chance to respond or even draw a breath before Sadie continued with the whirlwind introductions.

"This is Madge Ashley. Madge here makes the prettiest dresses and hats. Prettiest you've ever seen." Sadie swept the picnic area with her gaze. "Where's Agnes? She was just here a minute ago. Hmm. I guess she went to nurse her new baby. I don't see her anywhere now. You'll have to meet her later."

The other women quickly made Faith welcome. No one seemed to give a second thought to having an actress in their midst. She felt none of the condemnation she'd felt from others in the past. It just didn't seem to matter to the women of Dead Horse, Wyoming, how Faith had made her living before coming here.

I'd like to stay in this place, she thought again as she began emptying her picnic basket. I would very much like to stay.

The day was a complete delight. Faith knew it would become a treasured memory.

Alex found a couple of soul mates in Samuel and David Gold. When they weren't busy stuffing themselves with the vast array of food the women of Dead Horse had prepared, they were capturing grasshoppers or climbing trees or tossing a ball.

Becca made friends with three-year-old Alice Horne. The two of them sat quietly on a blanket and played with their rag dolls. It did Faith's heart good to see the rosy color in her daughter's cheeks and hear her laughter. Today it was even possible to believe the doctor was wrong about Becca's fragile health. Today it was possible to believe only the best of everything.

Faith was delighted by the stir caused when Gertie arrived. She stifled the laughter rising in her throat as the female wrangler, riding astride her horse in her dress, swung down from the saddle, giving one and all a generous glimpse of her knees and calves.

But Rick Telford saved Gertie from complete embarrassment by hurrying to welcome her and offering her his arm. Faith hoped Rick would look beyond the awkward exterior and see the warmhearted woman that was Gertie beneath.

There were moments when Faith thought about Drake, all alone in his house on the ridge, and felt his aloneness as if it were her own. Moments when she wished he were there with her, sitting on the same blanket, eating the picnic lunch she'd prepared. Moments when she admitted her growing attraction for her darkly handsome employer and knew she was dancing too close to a dangerous flame. Moments when she knew she must move away or get burned.

After everyone had eaten their fill, the town's celebration continued with a parade, followed by three-legged races. Parker joined with Alex, and the two of them won the first race, much to Faith's delight. There were also pie-eating contests, horse races, and ring tosses.

As the day waned, Matt Horne brought out his harmonica and Lon O'Rourke his banjo, and everyone sang along to familiar tunes such as "Darling Nellie Gray" and "I'll Take You Home Again,

Kathleen." Even though some folks sang a trifle off key, the warm camaraderie more than made up for a few sour notes.

With the approach of twilight came the time for Faith's performance. A makeshift stage had been constructed near the general store, and torches had been lit, bathing the stage in a flickering light. The townsfolk stood in the street in a wide semi-circle.

Faith was surprised to discover she was more nervous before this small audience than she had been in years. She drew a deep breath to calm herself, then began.

"'Thou knowest the mask of night is on my face, / Else would a maiden blush bepaint my cheek . . . '"

Again she thought of Drake, thought of the feelings he'd stirred to life within her. She imagined herself saying these same words to him, and she felt Juliet's blush rise in her cheeks.

"'Dost thou love me?'"

She imagined him there, in the midst of the audience. He would stand a head again above the crowd. She imagined the breadth of his shoulders, his long, raven black hair, his scarred but handsome face.

"'O gentle Romeo, / If thou dost love, pronounce it faithfully . . . '"

Her voice faltered slightly, and it was that which drove Drake's image from her mind. She forced herself to concentrate on her lines, reminding herself silently not to confuse the play with reality.

When she was finished with Juliet's monologue, there was a long hush. Then the silence was broken by riotous applause, shouts, and cheers.

"Faith Butler, that was the most beautiful thing I've seen in all my born days!" Sadie exclaimed as she came forward, taking Faith by the hand. "I was spellbound, pure and simple. Simply spellbound."

"Thank you, Mrs. Gold," she responded, even as her thoughts betrayed her with the wish that Drake could have seen her, too.

Gertie let out a long sigh and cast a sideways glance at the man beside her. Rick was grinning from ear to ear, still staring at the stage, still captivated by Faith Butler's presentation. It was plain as the nose on Gertie's face that he didn't even remember she was there.

She couldn't blame him. She'd been enthralled herself. She'd listened to Faith a time or two out at the ranch, but she'd never expected to feel like she'd been transported somewhere else, as if by magic. Faith had almost had Gertie understanding what that Shakespeare fellow was saying with his *knowests* and *dosts* and *thous* and whatnots.

And there sure wasn't nobody nowhere as pretty as Faith Butler. No wonder every jack-man present was acting like he'd been kicked in the head by a wild mustang.

Gertie looked down at the skirt of her dress and knew she'd been acting just as loco as any of the men. What had ever made her think Rick Telford would notice her? Oh, he'd been a right nice gentleman all afternoon long. He'd never so much as snickered at her like she knew some of the Jagged R cowpokes had been doing. She'd have the devil to pay for her foolishness. The boys would be ribbing her for weeks to come. It would have been worth it if Rick had just once acted like he might take a cotton to her. But, of course, he hadn't.

"Faith was wonderful." Rick turned to look at Gertie as he spoke.

"Yeah, she was."

"We won't any of us forget this Fourth of July any time soon."

"No, I don't reckon we will," she answered softly. She sure as heck knew she wasn't going to forget it. Not when she'd made such an idiot out of herself.

He took hold of her arm. "I'll escort you back to the blanket. Then I've promised to help with the fireworks."

"I can see for myself just fine. You go on and do what you gotta do."

"I wouldn't think of it, Miss Duncan." He began walking, drawing her along with him.

Lord o' mercy, how her heart did hammer!

A fool. That's what I am. A dad-burned crazy fool.

"I'd like to thank you, Gertie."

"Thank me?"

"For inviting me to join you today, for seeing that I wasn't alone while James and Nancy are away." He patted her hand where it rested in the crook of his arm. "And for putting on that dress. I know how you must hate it."

It was the first time he'd mentioned what she was wearing. She'd begun to wonder if he'd even noticed.

"It was very kind of you to do that for an old man like me."

I wasn't bein' kind, Doc, she wanted to say, *and you're not old.* But the words just wouldn't come out.

"I imagine you've turned a few heads today," Rick continued.

But not yours, she replied silently, feeling her heart sink.

"James and Nancy will be sorry they didn't return in time when they hear all about today."

"Yeah," she whispered, "I reckon they will."

They reached the blanket where, earlier in the day, the two of them had sat together, eating fried chicken and biscuits with honey and cake with frosting and more.

As Rick let go of her arm, he placed a fatherly kiss on her cheek. "It's been a great Fourth. Thanks again for spending it with me. I know you would rather have been racing your horse with the other cowboys."

"I . . . I wanted t'spend it with you, Doc."

He patted her shoulder. "You're a thoughtful young woman, Gertie Duncan."

"Oh, hell," she muttered.

Then, thinking she couldn't very well make things much worse than they already were, she grabbed him by the upper arms and yanked him toward her, kissing him square on the mouth.

When she let him go, she said, "You ain't old and I ain't your daughter, and if you can't figure out what's goin' on, then you're . . . you're . . ."

With a strangled sound of frustration, she left the sentence unfinished, whirling around and striding toward the horses, holding the skirt of her dress up to her knees to keep the blasted thing out of her way.

Drake watched Faith's performance from a distance, staying far back from the rest of the crowd, hidden from view by the night. He was mesmerized by her voice, her movements, her expressions. She became Juliet, an innocent young girl in the first flush of love.

He heard the lines she recited and wanted to make his own reply.

"'But trust me, gentleman, I'll prove more true / Than those that have more cunning to be strange . . .'"

His heart missed a beat. Once before he had heard her speak that line, and he'd been angered by the words. But not this time. This time he believed they could be true. He believed *she* could be true.

Given half a chance, I could learn to care for her.

The soliloquy ended. The good folks of Dead Horse pressed forward, congratulating and praising Faith. Drake fell back farther into the darkness and observed the adulation while mulling over his unsettling thoughts.

He didn't want to care. It would be a great mistake to feel more for Faith Butler than benign friendship. He'd fallen victim to the wrong woman once before. He could admit it now. Larissa had been beautiful and charming, but she had also been selfish and spoiled. He shouldn't have been surprised by her reaction to the scars on his face. She had reacted as Larissa had always reacted to anything less than perfection. She had rejected it—and him.

His bitterness was gone, but the lesson learned shouldn't be forgotten. He needed to remember that Faith was in Dead Horse only because she'd had no other choice. She'd stayed for Becca's sake. And if the way the child had looked lately was any indication, the Butler family would be leaving Wyoming soon.

Faith had her profession as an actress. She had her children. Somewhere, she even had a husband. She didn't belong in Drake's life, and he didn't belong in hers. Better that he face the truth now. Better that he save himself the trouble.

And the pain.

The crowd began to disperse, moving back toward the river for the fireworks display. Drake turned to slip away, to return to the Jagged R before he was seen. He was too late.

"Mr. Rutledge? Is that you?"

He glanced over his shoulder and saw Faith walking toward him, that exquisite smile lighting her face.

How had she seen him? he wondered. How had she known it was he in the shadows?

"You came. You saw the performance." Her voice was as sweet as nectar, lulling him, holding him there, staying his departure.

"I saw it."

"I didn't think you were coming."

"How could I not come to see you, Mrs. Butler?" He asked the question softly, knowing he shouldn't ask it at all.

Her smile vanished. Her eyes widened.

Drake took a step forward, drawn toward her by some invisible cord.

"Ma, hurry up!" Alex called from Drake's blind side. "The fireworks are gonna start."

Drake whirled toward the sound even as Faith jumped backward. Not more than half a dozen yards away stood Alex and Becca, waiting for their mother.

"Come on, Mama," Becca added.

"I think you'd better go with your children, Mrs. Butler," Drake said gruffly.

She hesitated a moment, and he wondered if she might ask him to stay with her.

"Yes." The word was barely more than a whisper. "I must go."

He didn't move as she hurried away from him, took hold of her children's hands, then walked into the darkness of night, leaving Drake alone once again.

11

Faith spent a restless night, tossing and turning in her bed, unable to sleep. Every time she closed her eyes, she envisioned Drake at the precise moment he'd stepped toward her, light from the flickering torches dancing across his mysteriously handsome face.

He'd been going to embrace her, kiss her. She'd known it. Worse still, she'd wanted it. If Alex and Becca hadn't called for her, she would have allowed it to happen.

With a groan, she sat up and shoved her tangled mass of hair from her face.

Hadn't she trouble enough? she wondered. It was only by the grace of God that she was here. She could be serving drinks in a saloon right now instead of having a decent job and a home for her children. What would happen to them if she forgot her proper place?

She rose and walked to the window to watch the coming of dawn.

She was a fool to allow these feelings to continue. Like it or not, absent or not, she had a husband. George Butler might have deserted her and the children, but to the best of her knowledge, he'd never gotten his divorce. She was still legally his wife. She had no right to these feelings for another man, no right to have these desires.

And she had no future in Dead Horse.

She heard voices, and a moment later Drake and Parker strode into view. They walked to the corral, then led out their horses and began saddling them. Within moments the rest of the cowpokes joined them.

Faith felt a flicker of joy seeing Drake with the men of the Jagged R. He belonged there. She could feel it. She could see it in the way he moved. Confident. Strong. At peace. She knew she'd been witness to a small miracle over the past few days. She didn't know what had caused the rage within him to cool; she only knew it had been there and now it was gone.

Suddenly Drake twisted in the saddle, his head turning toward her third-story window. His gaze was shadowed by the brim of his hat, but she knew he'd seen her. Her pulse quickened as she raised her hand in a wave, unable to stop herself.

Then common sense forced her to step back from the window, where she remained until she heard the men riding away.

Guard your heart, Faith, she warned herself. *Don't let it happen again.*

For years, the Jagged R had been nothing more to Drake than a place to hide from the world. He had left the operation of the ranch to Parker, trusting his friend to manage it well, and the foreman had done just that. The ranch had become ever more prosperous over the years. Rutledge cattle grazed over thousands of acres of grasslands, a land still free of fences where feed and water were plentiful.

As he and the men rode across the range, Drake thought how good it was to be with them. And it was good to be out riding in the daylight. No one spoke, but it was a companionable silence. A shared silence among men who understood each other, men who were comfortable with themselves and their work.

The years fell away, taking Drake back to the carefree time of his youth when he'd been like these cowboys, when he'd been a whole man, able to see and to ride and to rope. He wouldn't ever be that young cowboy again, but he could be something different.

Perhaps he could *make a difference*, for himself and the people who lived in Dead Horse.

With sudden clarity, Drake realized that if it hadn't been for his accident, he would still be trapped in an office in Philadelphia instead of sitting astride a horse, surrounded by majestic mountains and the range land he loved. If he'd married Larissa, he would still be handling dull, boring cases for Rutledge and Seever during the day and escorting his beautiful, spoiled wife to staid suppers and musicales in the evenings. He would have been imprisoned by that life as surely as he had been imprisoned by his partial blindness.

He knew the guilt over his mother's death would never leave him, but he couldn't change the past. The accident had happened. His mother had died. His fault or not, he couldn't undo it. Nor could he ever earn his father's forgiveness. It was much too late for that.

Strange how such thoughts had lost their sting in a matter of days.

Drake was pulled from his private musings by Dan Greer's voice.

"We'll be back by the end of next week," the cowboy told Parker. His gaze shifted to Drake. Then he tugged on his hat brim in a friendly salute, turned his horse, and cantered south, accompanied by Swede Swenson on his ugly white gelding. Moments later, Will Kidd and Johnny Coltrain rode east.

"Come on." Parker turned his mount in the opposite direction. "I want to check on the line shack up on Cougar Creek."

They moved out at a walk, giving their horses a brief rest.

"You should have come into town with us yesterday," the foreman said, glancing over at Drake. "We had quite the holiday."

"Another time."

"It's not so bad, you know. Your face, I mean."

Drake shrugged, not wanting to remember the way he'd felt when women or children had turned away from him, as if he were some sort of freak or monster.

Faith didn't turn away.

No, Faith hadn't turned away, not when she'd first met him, not last night. But Faith was different from other women. He'd recognized that difference almost from the first moment they'd met.

He gave his head a slight shake, as if to dislodge the image forming in his mind. Then he asked, "Did you hear any more news about the railroad?"

"Nope."

"Is Telford expected back soon?"

"Rick seemed to think James and his wife would be back by the end of the week."

Drake nodded thoughtfully. "When he gets back, ask him to come see me."

Parker didn't grin, but there was something in the look he shot toward Drake that suggested one. "I'll do it," he replied simply.

Then the two men simultaneously nudged their horses into a canter and rode toward the mountains in the west.

Gertie glared at the wild-eyed mare. "We can do this the easy way," she warned the animal, "or we can do this the hard way. But we *are* going to do this."

To be honest, she halfway hoped the mare would give her a rough ride. It would match the turmoil going on inside her.

This woman nonsense was likely to drive her plumb loco. She'd been far better off before she'd started feeling all soft and fluttery inside whenever she looked at Doc. Just what did she think it was going to get her, anyway? Did she think she was suddenly going to be as pretty as Faith or something?

She swore beneath her breath, then slowly placed her foot in the stirrup and stepped up onto the saddle.

The mare stood docilely for several heartbeats before exploding into motion. Back arched, the horse rose above the ground, landing with a harsh thump as she twisted and jerked, trying to dislodge Gertie and the hated saddle.

Gertie grinned. "Go on!" she shouted. "Give me hell!"

Time and again the mare bucked and hopped, spun and whirled. Dust flew into the air, pelting Gertie's cheeks. The only sounds she heard were grunts, both her own and those of the horse. Sweat soaked her hatband. More streamed down her spine. She felt the jarring in her back with every landing, but she kept her seat.

She knew the moment the fight went out of the horse, even though the bucking didn't stop at once. Seconds later, the mare quieted.

Gertie felt both satisfied and saddened. She reached out and stroked the animal's sweat-coated neck. "It won't be so bad next time, girl."

"That was mighty impressive, Miss Duncan."

She looked up suddenly, startling the mare. The horse shied and dislodged Gertie from the saddle. Gertie fell with a thump to the ground. Her hat landed near her feet.

Before she could get up, Rick Telford was inside the corral, kneeling beside her. "Are you hurt?"

Disgusted and embarrassed, she didn't look at him. "No."

"Here." He placed a hand against her back and took hold of her arm with the other one. "Let me help you up."

Several choice swear words shot through her head. What'd he have to come out here today for?

Gently he drew her to her feet. "Are you certain you're not hurt?"

"I'm all right."

"Gertie."

She felt her face growing hot. "Look, Doc—"

"Gertie, look at me."

She knew her face must be covered with dirt and streaked with sweat. Her hair would be sticking flat against her scalp. Her shirt was damp under her arms and along her spine.

Why'd he have to come when she was looking like this?

She pulled her arm away. "What're you doin' here, Doc?" Screwing up her courage, she looked him straight in the eye and waited for his answer.

"I came to see you."

"Listen, Doc, I'm sorry about last night. I don't know what came over me." She looked away again. "Must've been that blasted dress I was wearin'." She went after the mare, now standing quietly in a far corner, reins dragging the ground, head hung low. Gertie figured she knew just how the poor critter felt.

"Gertie, we *need* to discuss what happened." He followed her across the corral.

"What for?"

"Well, for one thing, I'm old enough to be your father."

"But you *ain't* my father."

"Gertie." He touched her shoulder, urging her to turn to face him. "Take a good look at me."

She did. And she liked what she saw. She knew if she didn't do something plenty quick, she'd wind up throwing herself at him, like she'd done the night before. She'd just about die if that happened again. Especially since she knew he had no hankering for her kisses.

Before she could make a complete and utter fool of herself, she stepped around to the other side of the mare and began to loosen the cinch. "Let's just try and pretend it never happened. Okay, Doc?"

There was a long silence, then he said, "I think that would be wise."

Hellfire! She didn't want to be wise. She wanted him to hold her and kiss her and . . . and . . . and do all the things she knew a man ought to do to a woman. Shoot, she hadn't lived with a bunch of randy cowpokes for the better part of her twenty-five years without learning a thing or two about the private dealings between the sexes. She might still be as green as grass when it came to actual experience, but she knew what was supposed to happen.

And she wanted it to happen with Rick Telford!

She wished she could tell him just how she felt, but pride kept her silent. After all, Doc didn't want a sweaty, smelly, bronc-busting wrangler. And she couldn't very well blame him for it, any more than she could change the way she looked or what she was.

"I'd better tend to my business, Doc. I got other horses t'see to."

He said her name softly, as if in regret.

She didn't dare look at him. She felt a suspicious lump in her throat, and she feared she just might burst into tears, something she'd rather die than do. "You go on now. I can't be standin' around all day, jawin' with you."

She yanked the saddle from the mare's back, then turned and slung it over the top rail of the corral. She didn't turn back until she knew he was gone.

Laundry basket in hand, Faith stepped out the back door just in time to see the doctor get in his buggy and drive away. Quickly she glanced toward the corral, where she saw Gertie, leaning her head against a saddle on the fence.

"Wait here," she told Becca as she set the basket on the porch.

She hurried around the circumference of the corral, stopping when she reached Gertie. Then she whispered the wrangler's name. "Are you all right?" she added gently.

Gertie didn't even lift her head. "Hell, no."

Faith covered the other woman's hand with her own. "I'm sorry, Gertie."

"I busted my first bronc when I was fourteen. Got my first job on a ranch down in Texas when I was sixteen. They didn't even know I was a girl." She straightened, drawing her hand out from under Faith's, then turned and retrieved her hat from the dirt. She slapped it against her thigh a few times, raising a cloud of dust, before putting it on her head.

Faith remained silent.

Gertie's gaze swung around to meet Faith's. "Don't know why I ever thought Doc'd know I was a woman when every other cowpoke I ever worked with didn't notice."

"Oh, Gertie, I think you're wrong. I think Dr. Telford noticed."

"Lotta good it does me if he did." Her blue eyes were filled with sadness.

Faith offered a slight smile of encouragement. "Sometimes these things take time."

"I better stick with broncs. Even with the wild ones, you've got a good idea what they're gonna do next." She shrugged. "Never know what a man's gonna do." Gertie jerked the saddle off the corral rail, bracing it against her back with her hand on her shoulder. "Reckon I'd best get back to work."

Faith wished she could give the other woman a hug, but she knew such a gesture wouldn't be welcomed. She stood watching as Gertie led the mare out of the corral, thinking privately that the wrangler was right about men.

One never knew what they would do next.

She thought of last night, of Drake Rutledge, of the moment when she'd known he wanted to kiss her. She hadn't expected him to come into town. She hadn't expected him to watch her performance. Yet there he'd been.

What was this strange attraction between them? she wondered. Why did she yearn for a man she knew so little about? Why did she yearn for a man at all?

With a slight shake of her head, she returned to the house, picked up the laundry basket, and walked to the clothesline, Becca following in her wake.

"If I had any sense," she muttered to herself as she pinned a sheet to the line, "we'd pack up and leave."

"But I like it here, Mama."

She glanced over her shoulder, surprised that her daughter had heard her. The girl was seated in the shade, rocking her rag doll in her arms. Despite herself, she smiled. "I know. I like it here, too."

"I think we oughta stay forever."

Faith didn't reply to that. What could she say? That this wasn't their home, that they didn't belong here.

She sighed as she grabbed another sheet from the basket, allowing herself to daydream, if only for a moment. Imagining what it would be like if this were their home, if they did belong here.

As if to complicate matters, Drake and Parker chose that precise moment to return. She glanced up at the sound of horses trotting into the yard. Over the top of the clothesline, her gaze met with Drake's. Without breaking the fragile contact between them, he slowed his pinto to a walk, then stopped.

She felt the familiar flutter of her heart and bent down behind the cover of the sheet, ostensibly to pull another item from the basket. She tried to ignore the way her hands shook as she dropped more pins into her apron pocket.

Had George ever affected her like this?

Shocked by her own thoughts, she closed her eyes and tried to still her racing heart, telling herself the feelings would pass if she only waited them out.

"Would you like some help, Mrs. Butler?"

She gasped softly at the sound of his voice so near. She straightened so quickly that she made her head swim. She swayed unsteadily. In an instant he reached between the two sheets on the line and grabbed hold of her elbow to steady her.

"Faith?"

She drew in a deep breath. "Goodness. I don't know what came over me."

She felt the warmth of his hand on her arm. It made her skin tingle. The dizziness threatened to worsen.

"Why don't you sit down with Becca for a moment?" Drake suggested.

She pulled free of his touch. "I need to hang the laundry to dry."

"I can do it."

Her pulse hammered in her ears as she looked

at him. "I wouldn't think of it, Mr. Rutledge." She thought she sounded breathless, but she couldn't be certain because of the loud beating of her heart.

"I've managed to hang out laundry in the past. I think I remember how to do it."

His teasing words appealed to her. So did his smile. She smiled in return. "I'm quite all right now. I just stood up too fast."

"Then let me help you."

Drake knew she was struggling for the proper response to his offer. He could see her wavering between refusal and acceptance. Before she could decide it would be better to send him away, he reached down and picked up another bedsheet from the basket. "Pins?" he asked simply.

Her expressive eyes widened slightly. "Here." She dropped several into his outstretched hand.

"Thanks."

He'd thought about Faith Butler often while he and Parker had been out on the range. Even when Drake had been asking questions and gleaning information about the ranch from his foreman, a small part of him had been still aware of her, still thinking about her. When he'd ridden into the yard and seen her standing beside the clothesline, he'd known he had to talk to her, had to spend a little time with her. He had to find out if Faith was anything like the woman he'd been imagining.

He looked at her now and saw nothing but perfection on the exterior. She was wearing a gown of spring leaf green. Her hands and throat were unadorned by jewelry. Her abundant red hair was captured in a bun at the nape, and he thought how beautiful it must look fanned across a pillow.

She turned and found him watching her. She stilled, her wariness reminding him of a doe caught grazing in a meadow.

He expected her to bolt, just as a doe would, so he stopped her by saying the first words that popped into his head. "I've never been more impressed by Shakespeare than I was last night."

She remained silent, still.

He remembered her standing on the stage, the light from the torches flickering in her fiery hair. He remembered the wistfulness of her expression and the graceful gestures of her hands. "You make a beautiful Juliet," he told her, his chest tight with unnamed emotions.

"Thank you."

"Did you always want to be an actress?"

She shook her head, then nodded, then shrugged. Finally she laughed softly. "I don't know. I suppose so. My parents were actors. It's the only life I've ever known."

Her laughter was like music, touching him deep in his soul. He wished he could touch her in return. He wished . . .

"The theater is where I met my husband," she added.

The words were like the dropping of a heavy stage curtain between them. He felt the invisible barrier, knew that she had placed it there on purpose.

"Your husband," he repeated. The word left an unsavory taste in his mouth. He should turn away. He should go back to the house. He didn't do either. "You said he wasn't an actor."

"He's not." Her reply was scarcely audible.

Where is your husband, Faith?

She dropped her gaze to the clothesline, as if she'd heard the unspoken question. "George is . . . he's an investor." Her cheeks grew pale. "He travels a great deal."

Her sadness was like another presence. He hated George Butler in that moment. He didn't know what her husband had done to her, but he knew she'd been hurt by him. That was all Drake needed to know to hate the absent Mr. Butler.

Perhaps he hated him merely for being Faith's husband. He knew he shouldn't feel that way, but he did. The very thought of another man—any man—holding her, kissing her, loving her, was enough to drive him mad.

"Becca's looking well." He hoped the comment would drive away the sadness in her eyes. He hoped it would help him forget the unwelcome images in his head.

The ploy was successful. At least with Faith. A gentle smile curved the corners of her mouth as she turned to look at her daughter. "Yes, she does, doesn't she?"

He envisioned himself kissing that smiling mouth, an image even more disturbing than the ones that had gone before. He tried to erase it with another question. "Where's Alex today?"

"He's visiting at the Golds'. And I have no doubt Sadie's sorry she invited him to stay."

Secretly Drake agreed with her, but now was not the time to mention the boy's escapades on the banister or by the river.

"Alex has never had any friends his own age before," she added, her smile already fading.

He couldn't bear to see it go. "Faith . . . "

She lifted her eyes.

"You're welcome to stay on at the Jagged R for as long as you want. You needn't leave just because Becca is well."

She didn't respond for some time, only continued to look at him, a kaleidoscope of emotions shimmering in her eyes, emotions he couldn't quite name, wasn't sure he wanted to name.

Finally she said, "Thank you, Mr. Rutledge."

He waited a moment, uncertain what for, then turned and walked away.

It wasn't fair. She'd looked like any whore on the wharf. How was I to know she was some man's wife? Some important man's wife?

I didn't mean to kill her. But that doesn't mean anything to you goons, does it? Let go of my arm, damn you. I'm not going anywhere.

I should have checked one more time for my watch. The one decent thing I still own, and that's what gives me away. It's Jane's fault for having it engraved with my name. I should have looked for it harder. But who'd have thought the whore had a husband who was looking for her?

Nothing ever goes right for me. Nothing. Not since the day I came to California.

Jane and her damned inheritance. I thought it was a lot of money. I didn't know there was so little left. If she hadn't spent it all on herself . . .

The bitch. This is all her fault.

Let go of me, you dumb oaf.

Think, Butler, think. You've got to get away from these two before you wind up in jail—or at the end of a rope.

Stop your shoving. I can climb up into a wagon on my own.

I'm not hanging for no whore, married or not. I've got to get away.

12

It was dang sure hot, Alex thought as he sat on the corral fence, staring at the rangy mustang within. It was too sweltering for a breeze. Not a blade of grass, not a leaf on a tree moved. Hotter'n Hades, was what Gertie had said. Alex wasn't sure what Hades was, but he figured it must be plenty hot, too.

Alex let out a long sigh. It was too blamed quiet. There wasn't even the sound of flies buzzing to break the stillness. All the cowboys were out on the range, and he didn't know where Gertie had disappeared to. His mother had lain down with Becca to rest during the heat of the day. Mr. Rutledge was shut up in his library again, going over his ledgers, and Mr. McCall had ridden into town earlier in the morning.

Too blamed quiet.

Too blamed hot.

Nothing to do.

He swung his feet over the top rail of the corral and dropped to the ground, sending up a cloud of dust. Looking toward the river, he could see the tops of the cottonwoods just above the ridge. He thought how nice it would be to take off his shoes and plunge his feet into the water, but he knew he'd catch the dickens if he went down to the river without his mother or another adult. Mr. Rutledge had made that plenty clear.

Alex thought about saddling the little mare Gertie let him ride, but he knew he'd get in trouble for that, too. Gertie had told him he wasn't ready to ride alone just yet. He thought she was wrong, but he didn't want to make her mad at him.

He'd had a lot of fun with Samuel and David yesterday. He wondered how long it would take him to walk into town and see them again. But it was quite a piece to Dead Horse. Not much of a ride, but a long walk.

He shook his head, already eliminating the idea. He'd have to ask his mother, and she'd already told him he must help with the chores once it started to cool off. She wouldn't let him go into town. And if he bothered her now, she'd probably tell him to lie down and rest with her and Becca. He didn't want to spend the afternoon sleeping, that was for sure.

He bent down and picked up a small stone, turning it over and over with his fingers. Then he hurled it at the side of the bunkhouse. It hit the sun-bleached wall with a *thwunk*. He picked up several more stones and gave each a toss, one at a time.

Well, this isn't much fun either, he thought as he turned away.

Squinting against the glare reflecting off the hard-packed dirt of the yard, Alex headed toward the barn, thinking that he'd look in on Sugar. He'd cleaned the buckskin's stall that morning and led her around the yard a bit, just the way Gertie had instructed him to do. Gertie had said Sugar's leg was almost healed and the mare could be turned out with the other horses before too long.

The barn was cooler than it was outside, but not by much. Alex paused a moment just inside the doorway, giving his vision a second to adjust to the dim light. Then, as he walked toward the stall, he heard a sound overhead. Looking up, he saw a mangy-looking gray tabby hurrying across a thick beam. The cat disappeared into the hayloft, but not before a clamor of high-pitched meows arose.

Diverted from his former objective, Alex veered toward the ladder, climbing up the rungs as quickly as possible. The meowing of kittens had diminished by the time he reached the loft, but there was still enough noise to guide him to the cat's bed of hay in the corner. The tabby had already stretched out, and several kittens were attached to her teats. Three others were still seeking a place to nurse.

Alex squatted for a better look. The cat eyed him warily but didn't move.

"It's okay," he reassured the mother. "I'm not gonna hurt 'em." He leaned forward slightly. "Look at that. Their eyes aren't even open yet."

He reached to stroke one. The tabby hissed fiercely and swiped at him with a front paw. Alex jerked back, sending up a flurry of hayseed and dust as he landed on his behind. He sent the cat an angry glare, and the tabby growled in response.

"Okay, I'm going," he grumbled as he got to his feet. "Too hot up here anyway." More softly he added, "Stupid cat."

Turning, he noticed light filtering around the edges

of the hay doors. He walked over to them and lifted
the latch, letting the doors swing open.

"Wow!"

He had a great view of the house from here. He
could see his mother's bedroom window with its
gabled roof. If he leaned farther out, he'd bet he
could see clear to Dead Horse.

He bent at the waist and looked.

Almost. He could almost see the town.

He slid a little to the right and leaned out a bit
more.

Suddenly he heard an angry hiss from behind him,
then felt claws sink into his leg through his trousers.
He yelped and tried to kick free of the cat. As quickly
as that, he lost his balance, pitching forward. Wildly
he grabbed for anything to hold on to, but all he
found was air.

In a flash of thought, he wondered how bad it was
going to hurt when he hit the ground. Then he felt the
wind go out of him as something stopped his downward plunge by the band of his trousers. Before he
could wonder what had happened, he swung sideways in a wild arc.

In the past, Drake had preferred days like this. Days
when all the Jagged R Ranch hands were out on the
range. Days when silence settled over the house like
the curtain of night. There'd been comfort in the solitude. That was, after all, why he had come to this
place.

But today all it felt was lonely.

He walked out of his library and toward the
back door, his footsteps booming in the absolute
stillness of the house. He wondered where Faith

was. Would he find her outside, sitting in the shade of the trees?

He hoped so.

He paused just beyond the door, his gaze sweeping the lawn but finding no one there. Then he heard the boy's cry.

"Ma!" The single word was laced with fear.

Drake bolted off the porch, running in the direction of the voice. What he saw when he cleared the shade trees caused his heart to trip.

Alex hung from a rope outside the hay doors of the barn, a large hook caught in the back of his trousers. He was swinging from side to side, and it was easy to see that his security was tenuous at best. Even as Drake watched, the rope slipped on the pulley, causing the boy to drop a few inches before halting abruptly.

Alex yelped in fright.

"Try not to move!" Drake shouted at him.

"M-Mr. R-Rutledge, I'm s-scared."

He stepped forward, trying to sound calm and convincing. "I know you are, Alex, but it's going to be all right. Just try not to move."

Drake didn't know how long either the waistband or the loop in the rope would hold. If either gave, Alex was going to drop like a rock to the hard-packed earth below. With a critical gaze, he judged the distance from the rope to the hay doors. If luck was with him, he might be able to reach it and pull the boy toward him. But if luck wasn't with him . . .

"H-hurry, M-Mr. R-Rutledge. I . . . I th-think it's sl-slippin'."

Drake sprang into action, running into the barn. "I'm coming, Alex," he shouted as he climbed the ladder into the loft. "Try not to move. Hang on. I'm coming."

A thick beam protruded from above the hay doors about eight or ten feet. The pulley itself was attached to the beam close to three-quarters of the way out. Just inside the doors, the end of the rope was looped and secured around a metal bracket in the wall.

It took only one quick glance for Drake to know he couldn't risk trying to catch hold of the rope to draw Alex inside. The hook, normally used for lifting bales of hay into the loft, had only a precarious grip on the boy's trousers. There seemed to be only one option, and Drake decided to take it.

"Alex, I'm going to lower you to the ground. I'm going to go slowly. All right? I want you to hold real still. Don't try to help. You stay just like you are. Understand?"

"Uh-huh."

"Good. Here goes."

Praying for strength and a steady hand, Drake loosened the rope from the bracket, gripping it tightly and bracing himself against the boy's weight.

"All right. I'm going to start lowering you now."

"O-okay."

Drake's gaze didn't waver from the end of the large hook where it disappeared beneath Alex's waistband. It was almost as if he believed he could keep the hook from tearing free by sheer willpower alone. Slowly he allowed the hemp rope to ease through his hands, all the while holding his breath. Every inch seemed to take an eternity.

Since his depth perception was less than perfect without the use of his right eye, it was difficult for him to know how close to the ground Alex was when the cloth of his trousers ripped and the boy fell free. Drake heard Alex's cry of alarm as Drake fell backward into the hay, the rope and hook whipping upward until the hook clanged against the pulley. He was back on his feet in an instant, rushing toward the hay doors and looking downward. Alex lay, unmoving, on the ground.

"Alex!"

A heartbeat passed. Then another. And then the boy sat up, turning a dazed look toward Drake.

"Alex, are you hurt?"

"I . . . I don't think so."

Drake spun away from the opening and returned to the ladder. By the time he'd climbed down and reached the barn entrance, Alex was standing.

It was on the tip of Drake's tongue to give the boy a scolding he wouldn't soon forget. He had every intention of offering a lecture about safety and precautions and keeping out of places where a boy didn't belong. But before he could begin to harangue, he caught a glimpse of Alex's expression, remnants of fear lingering in suspiciously misty eyes and quivering lips.

Drawing a deep breath, Drake started forward again. "You sure you're not hurt?"

Alex drew a forearm beneath his nose, then answered, "I'm okay."

"You're lucky." He glanced up at the pulley. "You might have broken your neck." Looking once more at the boy, he asked, "What happened?"

The last vestiges of misgiving vanished, replaced by youthful indignation. "Your cat scratched and bit me. That's why I fell."

"*My* cat?"

"Well, she lives in your barn. That makes her yours, don't it?"

Drake hadn't had much to do with children, not since he'd been one himself, but it seemed to him that Alex was a bit too precocious—not to mention adventurous—for his own good. He supposed a firmer hand was what the boy needed. Yet he didn't offer one. Instead he said, "Yes, I suppose it does."

Alex glanced up at the hay doors. "Sir?"

"Yes?"

"Am I going to have to tell Ma about this?"

"Don't you think she should know?"

The boy shook his head and frowned. "It'd only make her worry."

"True." Drake fought the urge to smile, remembering how often he'd hidden his own childhood high jinks from his mother. More than once, he'd coerced the cooperation of one of the house maids or the butler to keep Constance Rutledge from discovering how close Drake had come to breaking his fool neck. Sometimes a boy needed an ally. "Where is your mother now?" he asked, trying to sound appropriately stern.

"Upstairs. She said it was too hot and she and Becca were going to rest awhile."

"She's right about it being hot." He glanced up into the glare of the sun, then suggested, "What do you say the two of us go fishing?"

Alex brightened. "Fishing? Really? I've never been fishing before."

Drake felt his own spirits brighten. He hadn't dropped a line in the water in years, not since he was a lad of about Alex's age. "Every boy needs to know how to fish. Maybe, if we're lucky, we can have trout for supper." He placed his hand on Alex's shoulder. "Come on. We'll see if we can find some poles."

*   *   *

Faith awakened slowly from her nap, feeling drugged by the still heat in her third-story room. She bathed her face in tepid water from the pitcher on her wash-stand, but it did little to lift her lethargy. The idea of firing up the kitchen stove and preparing supper was repulsive. Doing so was also unavoidable.

She checked her watch and was surprised to see she'd slept away the better part of three hours. She hadn't realized she was so tired.

Becca continued to sleep soundly, and Faith decided not to awaken her. Quietly she slipped from the bedroom and descended the back staircase. The ground floor of the house was cooler than the third story, but not by much. After propping open the kitchen door, she stepped onto the porch, hoping to find a cool breeze there.

She didn't.

Faith shaded her eyes with one hand as she swept the area for a glimpse of Alex. Her son knew he wasn't supposed to leave the yard without asking. He had always been obedient in the past, but there was so much going on around the ranch to tempt him. Today, however, things were quiet.

Too quiet.

She stepped off the porch. "Alex?"

No response.

She walked toward the barn. "Alex?"

Still no response.

The barn was as silent as everything else. An old dog, lying beneath a wagon near the doorway, lifted its head when Faith walked by but made no sound. The buckskin mare Alex was helping Gertie tend stood with drooping head in her stall.

"Alex?"

She felt a quiver of concern.

Where could he be? He wasn't with Gertie. The wrangler had told Faith she would be gone all day. All of the cowboys were out with the cattle except Parker, and he'd gone to town that morning. Since Parker's horse wasn't tethered to the hitching post or standing in the corral, she knew he hadn't returned yet.

As she left the barn, she glanced toward the house. He couldn't be bothering Drake. Could he?

"Alex!"

She lifted her skirts a few inches above the ground and quickened her steps. A few moments later, she arrived at the library. The door stood open. The room was empty. Drake was gone.

Alex wasn't in the house. He wasn't in the yard or in the barn. Where could he be?

Fear began to churn in her stomach, countless possibilities of what might have happened to her son racing through her head.

Why hadn't she made him lie down with them? What kind of mother allowed her seven-year-old son to run about unsupervised? Alex was a changed boy since coming to the Jagged R. He'd never enjoyed so much wide-open space before. It had always been easy to keep an eye on him in the theater or in the wagons or in the cramped quarters of a hotel or rooming house. Faith had grown lax, allowing Gertie or Parker or one of the other cowpokes—who all seemed so willing—to take the boy under their wing.

If something had happened to him . . .

Laughter reached her ears. Alex's laughter.

She ran to the door and looked out.

There they came, the two of them, fishing poles slung over their shoulders. Alex's feet were bare. His shoelaces were tied together, his shoes riding on the opposite shoulder from the fishing pole. Her son looked up at the man beside him with what was clearly adoration.

Something in Faith's chest gave, then broke. Wistful tears sprang to her eyes, but she wiped them away, not wanting the image of her son to blur, not wanting to miss memorizing the expression on his face.

In that moment she loved Drake Rutledge. Loved him for what he'd given her son. But that was the only kind of love she was free to give him, and this time she let the teardrops fall.

That night, as once again Faith tossed and turned in her bed, she had reason to regret taking a nap in the middle of the day. At least that was the reason she gave herself for her inability to fall asleep.

With a groan of frustration, she rose and padded on bare feet across the room to the window. A sliver of moon rocked in the sky just above the treetops. The night was still and untroubled. She rather liked the silence. For too many years she had endured either the bustle of the big cities or the rowdy saloon noises of frontier towns. This peacefulness was refreshing to her soul.

Now, if only her thoughts were equally serene.

But the image of Drake Rutledge with Alex wouldn't be shaken. It had stayed with her throughout their supper of fried trout. It had stayed with her as she'd tucked her children in for the night. It had stayed with her as she'd tossed restlessly in her bed.

What was it that drew her to him?

'Tis one thing to be tempted, Escalus,
Another thing to fall.

Truer words had not been written, yet she couldn't seem to stop herself from falling.

"'This love will undo us all,'" she whispered, and felt a chill, as if a cold breeze had entered through the window.

But was it love? she asked herself. Could it be nothing more than simple gratitude? Could it be mere loneliness? Must it be love?

That was when she heard the music, floating up from the lower level of the house. Plaintive notes that clutched at her heart. She knew without question that she would find Drake in the parlor. She knew she should not go.

But go she did. She put a robe over her nightgown and followed the music.

He played in the dark. No lamps brightened the room. He didn't seem to need them. His fingers flowed over the keys with a sureness that proved he needed no light.

Faith paused in the doorway to the parlor. She closed her eyes and listened, seeing Drake more clearly with her heart than she had when her eyes were open. As time passed, the melody changed from mournful to wistful and then suddenly to a song of joy. At last the music rose to a final crescendo, then stopped abruptly.

"Did I awaken you, Faith?" he asked in the sudden silence.

She opened her eyes, not surprised that he'd known she was there. "No. I couldn't sleep."

"Neither could I."

She heard the piano bench slide across the floor and sensed that he'd risen. "You play beautifully."

"Shocked?"

"Yes. A little."

"It was my mother's fondest wish that I learn to play. I think she hoped I would become a virtuoso. My father demanded I be an attorney." Footsteps brought him toward her. "I haven't played in a very long time. I'm a bit surprised I still remember how." He was silent a moment, unmoving. When he continued, his voice was low and thoughtful. "I guess most people wouldn't think of me as the musical sort. My father certainly didn't."

It seemed she could feel her own heartbeat pulsing throughout the room. "I doubt most people know the real you." *I think I know you, Drake,* she continued silently. *I think I know you in my heart. Why is that?*

A match scratched. A flame burst to life. Light flickered across Drake's face as he lifted the glass and lit the lamp's wick. When he was done, he turned toward her.

Shakespeare's words echoed once again in her mind. *This love will undo us all. . . .*

He inclined his head toward the piano. "Do you play?"

"No."

"But you sing." He moved a step closer.

"Yes," she answered breathlessly. "Sometimes, I sing."

"I've heard you when you're in the kitchen. Your voice is clear." He paused, then added, "And lovely."

She feared her heart might stop beating.

"Faith." He whispered her name as he lifted his hand to stroke her cheek lightly with his fingertips.

For a moment, she closed her eyes and leaned into his touch. For a moment, she pretended she belonged there with him. When he pulled his hand away, she looked at him and knew, before he could speak, what he was about to ask of her.

"Why isn't your husband with you? Where is he, Faith?"

She felt ashamed. "I don't know."

"Tell me." He spoke gently, yet with an authority that was difficult to resist.

Faith turned away, not wanting to meet his gaze. She hugged herself, feeling strangely cold despite the warmth of the night. "He left me for another woman. He said he was going to California. I haven't heard from him in over two years."

"But you're still married?"

She nodded. "As far as I know."

"You haven't sought a divorce?"

She shook her head.

"Do you still love him?"

"Still love him?" she echoed with a note of surprise. A bitter laugh rose in her throat. "No. No, I don't still love George."

Drake's hand alighted on her shoulder. "Are you certain of that?"

She could turn and step into his embrace. She knew it. Wanted it. But she held still, answering, "I'm quite certain. My love for George died a long, long time ago. Long before he left me, I suppose."

"Faith?"

With only a slight pressure, he turned her toward him. He lifted her chin with his index finger, forcing her to look up. He stared into her eyes with an unwavering gaze, looking down deep inside her. It felt as if he could see into the deepest secrets of her soul.

"You're safe here," he said at last.

Safe? She felt anything but safe when she was standing so close to him.

"Mrs. Butler . . . I'm going to kiss you."

He pulled her close and lowered his head with an

agonizing slowness. The chill she'd felt only a short time before was forgotten, replaced by a languid heat that radiated through her the moment their lips touched. The kiss was infinitely sweet, immeasurably tender, and far too brief.

With his mouth still hovering close to her own, he whispered, "George Butler is a fool."

Yes, she thought, but was unable to speak it aloud.

She wanted Drake. Wanted him with a fierceness she'd never experienced before. Wanted him in a way that made common sense flee. Wanted his kisses, his caresses, his all. It was wrong to want him so. It was terribly wrong. She wasn't free to feel these things. But she did.

He kissed her again, then drew back, his hands releasing their gentle grasp on her arms. "Good night, Faith."

"Good night," she whispered without moving.

Without another word, he turned her around and gently pushed her toward the stairs.

Drake watched as Faith ascended to her third-story room, then turned back into the parlor. He extinguished the lamp and sat once again on the piano bench. But he didn't resume playing. Not while Faith's faint cologne lingered in the air. Not while he remembered the way she'd felt against him. Not while he could still taste her sweetness on his lips.

It had been years since he'd felt like a whole man. Years since he'd believed a woman could look at him without horror and revulsion.

But Faith Butler made him feel whole again. When she looked at him, he'd seen the desire she tried so hard to deny. He'd seen that and more. He'd seen hope for a future he'd thought he would never have.

That was why he'd sent her away, even though his

own desire burned hot in his veins, even though he'd known he could have bent her to his will. Because he wanted that future, and the only way to have it was to see that Faith wasn't hurt in the process.

He allowed his fingers to run lightly over the ivory keys, then he rose and walked to his library. After lighting the lamp, he went in search of a particular volume from among his collection of legal tomes. He needed to learn all he could about the law pertaining to divorce.

Because if he was going to marry Faith, she had to be free, once and for all, of the husband who'd deserted her.

And Drake *was* going to marry Faith Butler.

13

Rick guided his horse through Dead Horse. The heat and the silence were both thick enough to cut with a knife. It was hard to believe the town's Fourth of July celebration, attended by every living soul within a half day's ride, had been only three days ago. Today Dead Horse looked as dead as its name.

He was returning from Matt and Agnes Horne's farm, where six-month-old Emma was suffering from the colic. Rick knew the baby's condition wasn't serious. He was more concerned about Agnes. He'd spent the better portion of his visit telling her she needed to get adequate rest. He'd also hinted that she should avoid getting pregnant again any time soon. The young mother, with four children under the age of five, had dark circles under her eyes and was far too thin. Rick was afraid Matt would find himself a widower if Agnes didn't take better care of herself.

He shook his head as he drew his horse to a halt beside the barn. Too many babies too soon. He'd seen it time and again during his years as a doctor. Women having babies, one right after the other, with scarcely time to draw a breath between them. Knowing his advice to Agnes had fallen on deaf ears, he'd suggested, as carefully as he knew how, that Matt do what he could to prevent another pregnancy, but he doubted it had done any good. Perhaps he should have been more blunt. Perhaps he should have just told Matt to keep his hands off his wife for the next year.

Problem was, young men like Matt had little restraint when it came to their husbandly rights, even when they were told the possible consequences.

Rick thought of Gertie Duncan, and he wondered if he would have any more restraint than Matt Horne. It amazed him the way the young woman had maneuvered herself into his thoughts. He kept remembering the way she'd kissed him a few nights ago. He kept seeing the way she'd looked the next day when he'd tried to talk to her. She'd told him they'd just forget the kiss ever happened. He'd agreed. Trouble was, he hadn't forgotten it.

Maybe he was getting senile. Gertie was not only young enough to be his own daughter, she was nothing like Esther Telford. His beloved wife had been a quiet, genteel woman, always a lady, no matter what the circumstances. Gertie, on the other hand, was as rough as any cowboy off the range. They had absolutely nothing in common.

Still mulling over his thoughts, he unhooked the mare from her traces and led her into her stall. He made certain there was plenty of water and hay, then walked toward the house. He was looking forward to sitting in the shade on the porch and remaining idle until nightfall. It was too hot to do anything else.

He heard the knock at the front door just as he entered through the back one. Dreading the idea of hitching the horse to the buggy again, he went to answer the summons.

He was surprised to find Jed Smith, the town's postmaster, standing on the porch. Jed rarely left the bench in front of the post office because he refused to wear the pegleg that had been issued to him by the army. As for crutches, he grumbled that they made his arms sore. He much preferred to let folks come to him, he always said.

Jed nodded abruptly. "Saw you ride into town. Thought maybe you should have this right away. Looked important." He held out an envelope.

Rick had the strange feeling the postmaster already knew what was inside the envelope with a return address marked Union Pacific Railroad.

Jed made no move to leave.

"Maybe it's news from James and Nancy," Rick said as he tore open the top of the envelope and withdrew the folded letter within.

. . . train derailment . . . regret to inform you Mr. and Mrs. James Telford died instantly . . .

The words jumped off the page and seared into his brain. James dead? He read the brief missive again, trying to make it say something else, anything else, but it was always the same.

He shook his head. It couldn't be true.

But it was. James and Nancy were dead. His son wasn't coming home. He was dead.

The paper slipped from his hands as he staggered backward, then sank onto a cane-back chair.

James was dead. He wasn't coming home.

"Rick?"

He tried to focus his gaze but failed.

"You all right?" Jed stepped into the house.

"James and Nancy are dead."

The other man cleared his throat. "I feared as much. Heard about the train wreck. Lotta folks died."

A lot of folks died, but only one was his son, only one was his daughter-in-law. "They never had children. They were still so young. So much ahead of them."

"I'm real sorry," Jed murmured. "Real sorry."

Rick stared at his hands, palms turned up. A physician's hands, meant to heal. For years those same hands had often trembled, shaken by the effects of whiskey. Today they'd been steady and sure, but what good had it done him? They hadn't been able to help his son. They hadn't been able to help Nancy.

"Well . . . " Jed sounded uncomfortable. "Guess I'll be gettin' back to the post office. You be all right?"

Rick nodded.

"Okay then. You need anythin', you let me know."

"Thanks," he replied, still staring at his hands.

A moment later the door closed and Rick was alone with the silence of the house. Alone.

"It didn't make any difference, Esther," he whispered to his long dead wife. "It didn't change a thing."

Gertie heard about the accident as soon as she returned from rounding up a small herd of horses on the Jagged R's south range. She didn't take time to wash off the trail dust. Something in her heart told her there wasn't time. She just turned her weary horse around and galloped toward Dead Horse.

Instinct caused her to rein in at the saloon. "Ah, Doc," she whispered as she swung down from the saddle and looped the reins over the hitching post. "Sure hope you haven't gone and done somethin' stupid."

But her instincts proved true. She found him slumped at a table in the far corner of the smoke-hazy room, an empty bottle of whiskey in front of him. His head was tilted forward, his chin nearly resting on his chest.

Gertie crossed the room with quick strides. At his table she stopped, turned a chair around, and straddled it, leaning her forearms on the chair back. She stared hard at the man she'd fallen for, hook, line, and sinker. "Why'd you do it, Doc? Gettin' all liquored up ain't gonna bring 'em back."

Rick glanced up, meeting her gaze with red-rimmed eyes glazed by alcohol. He made no reply.

"This town needs you, Doc. What if Faith's boy was t'get hurt? You wouldn't be able t'help none."

"I don't want to help," he mumbled. "It doesn't change a thing."

"'Course it does."

Rick straightened slightly and looked toward the bar. "Stretch, bring me another bottle."

"Doc . . ." She covered his hand with her own.

He yanked it away. "Thish isn't any o' your concern, Mish Duncan," he slurred. "Why don'tcha go back t'your horses, where ya belong?"

His words hurt, but she figured he had a right to hurt her if he wanted, what with James and Nancy being killed the way they had. She figured he had a right to strike out at anybody who tried to get close right now. She'd felt that way a time or two herself. She could take it 'cause she loved him.

"All right, Doc. You just sink down in the bottom of that bottle. I'll be here when you're done."

He slammed his palms down on the table and shouted, "I don't want you here!"

She tipped her hat back on her forehead. "It's a free country. I think I'll stay anyways."

"Go to hell," he muttered as he grabbed the bottle Stretch Barns had brought to the table.

"Looks like you beat me to it," she replied as she watched him pour another drink and toss it down without hardly a swallow.

The deaths of James and Nancy Telford shocked the tiny community. The young couple's bodies arrived two days later, but Rick didn't bother to leave the saloon to claim them or make arrangements for their burial in Dead Horse's cemetery. Gertie did it for him. Rick didn't attend the funeral, either. Nothing seemed important to him except the next drink. Nothing seemed important except escaping the pain.

As for Faith, she was greatly saddened, not just by the tragic deaths of James and Nancy, but also by what their deaths had done to Rick Telford. And to Gertie, too. When she saw her friend at the funeral, she wanted to weep for her as much as for Rick. She was reminded how very suddenly life could end. She was reminded how brief a person's time on earth was, how quickly it could all be over. Selfishly she kept remembering Drake's kisses and her response to them. She kept thinking that her time with him could end suddenly. She knew it mustn't end before he knew she loved him.

Drake was one of the few people not personally touched by the deaths of the young couple. Although sorry for the sudden loss of life, he hadn't known James and Nancy and thus was spared the grief himself. However, he knew James Telford's journey to Cheyenne had been important to the townsfolk of Dead Horse, and he made it his business to find out whether James had convinced railroad officials to authorize a spur through Dead Horse. He knew, once the time of mourning had passed, that others would be wondering the same thing.

The day after the funeral, Drake was going over some correspondence received from the territorial capital when Gertie knocked on the open library door.

"Come in." He leaned back on his chair.

Her expression was grim as she walked toward his desk. "Mr. Rutledge, you're gonna have to hire yourself a new wrangler."

He raised an eyebrow. "Why is that, Gertie?"

"Well, sir . . . " She paused as she removed her dusty Stetson. "Truth is, I haven't been tendin' to my duties. Not since what happened to the Telfords."

"Sit down, Gertie." He motioned to a chair off to one side of his desk.

She hesitated a moment, then did as he'd bade her.

Drake swiveled his chair to face her, then leaned forward, his forearms braced on his thighs. He searched her face with his gaze. With a note of compassion in his voice, he said, "I think this has more to do with the doctor than with his son's death. Am I right?"

"Yes, sir, you are."

"I hear he's taking it rather hard."

Gertie nodded, and her gaze fell to the floor between them.

"What is it you think you can do for him?"

She looked up again. This time there was a spark of determination in her blue eyes. "I'm gonna help him dry out again."

"You can't help unless he wants you to. I've seen this before, Gertie."

"He'll want me to," she answered stubbornly.

Drake leaned back on his chair. He knew there was no changing her mind. He could see it in the set of her shoulders, hear it in the tone of her voice.

He hated to see her get hurt. He'd come to like the outspoken wrangler in her trousers and boots. She had befriended Faith and taken young Alex under her wing. Besides, she was good at her job. Nobody knew horses the way Gertie Duncan did.

After a few moments of silence, Drake said, "I won't accept your resignation, Gertie, but you can take off whatever time you need. Your job will be waiting for you when you get back."

"Mr. Rutledge, I can't—"

He stopped her with a raised hand. "If you can help out a friend, so can I."

He saw her surprise and understood it. Only in the past couple of weeks had he participated in the management of the ranch. Only recently had he become a familiar sight in the yard or out on the range. Gertie Duncan had no reason to believe that her employer was also her friend.

He rose and stepped toward her, holding out his hand. She stood, too, and clasped his hand with her own, giving it a hard shake.

"I mean what I said," he told her. "Your job will be here when you're ready to come back."

"Thanks, Mr. Rutledge. I . . . I don't know what to say."

"You don't have to say anything."

She nodded and sniffed, then turned and walked toward the door.

"Good luck, Gertie," he added as she disappeared into the hallway. He knew she was going to need all the luck she could find.

After a moment, he returned to his desk and looked once again at the papers spread across the surface. He'd already read the documents twice, but he kept hoping he'd missed something. He hadn't, of course. That was one thing that had made him a good lawyer: he was observant of details. Right now he wished he wasn't so blasted observant. He'd like to think a divorce would be easy for Faith.

He went over to the window, as he was frequently wont to do these days. He stared out at the yard. It was Monday—wash day—and he hoped he would find Faith hanging clothes on the line. He was disappointed. She was nowhere in sight.

With a sigh, he turned and leaned against the sill. He pushed his patch up onto his forehead, then rubbed both eyes with his fingertips, swearing softly beneath his breath as he did so.

Ever since the passage of the Comstock Law, divorce had become more difficult to obtain throughout the country, states and territories alike. Adultery remained the strongest case for winning a suit of divorce, but without proof of that adultery, Faith could not hope to obtain release from her marriage to George.

Desertion was also a possibility. But her husband hadn't been absent for three years, and Drake was unwilling to wait until that amount of time had passed.

There was no other choice. He would have to locate George Butler and obtain the proof they needed. That could, of course, take months to accomplish.

Already Drake felt his frustration grow.

He heard the rear porch door close and turned once again to look out the window. Faith and Gertie appeared a moment later near the corner of the house.

Faith balanced a basket of clean clothes on her hip. Her fiery hair was caught at the nape in a net, but red gold strands had pulled free to curl against her neck. His fingers itched to brush the hair away so he could kiss the pale flesh beneath her ear.

He shook his head to drive off the image, at the same time shifting his gaze to Gertie.

The wrangler still held her Stetson in her left hand, as she had when she'd left Drake's library minutes before. She bounced the hat against her thigh, speaking to Faith, her eyes downcast.

A few moments later Faith set down the clothes basket and hugged the taller woman, standing on her tiptoes to do so. Even from here he could feel Faith's love and concern for her friend.

Would she be able to love him just as much? he wondered.

He remembered the way she had responded to him the night she'd found him playing the piano. He remembered the swirl of emotions in her eyes. She didn't judge him as others had. She didn't see him as a wretched man or a monster, the way

Larissa and his own father had seen him. She
responded as a woman to his touch, without shrink-
ing away.

But would she be able to love him?

Old doubts surged suddenly to life.

Maybe he was only fooling himself. Maybe she
cared for him only in friendship, the way she cared
for Gertie. Maybe Larissa was right.

Maybe no woman could love him.

*"I cannot marry you, Drake," Larissa said as she
paced restlessly from one side of his bedchamber to
the other.*

*It hurt to watch her. His head pounded, and his
remaining vision was blurry. He closed his left eye.
"We'll put the wedding off for a year," he said. "By
that time—"*

*"You don't understand me. I said I cannot marry
you. Not in a year. Not ever."*

*The pain behind his right eye intensified as he
tried to look at her once again. "Why not?"*

*"Why not?" Her echoing words were edged with
disbelief. "Dear heavens, look at you."*

*They had been the glittering couple of the season,
the darlings of every party. Everyone had known
Drake Rutledge and Larissa Dearborne—the darkly
handsome lawyer and the golden-haired beauty.
Everyone said they'd been destined to marry. He'd
heard it said time and again, and he'd believed it.
After all, Larissa had told him how much she loved
him. She'd told him so the night she'd slipped into
his room and shared the delights of her perfect body
with him. He'd given up his dreams of the West for
her. He'd been willing to stay at Rutledge and*

Seever for the rest of his life for her. And he'd wanted her with a passion that threatened to consume him.

"You can't expect me to be shackled to half a man for the rest of my life," she went on, unaware of his thoughts.

He wasn't surprised by her words. Actually he'd been expecting them. "I've lost the sight in one eye, Larissa," he stated flatly. "I'm blind. Not emasculated."

She gasped. "Really, Drake. You needn't be crude."

He closed his eye again. "Sorry." Maybe she was right. Maybe he was only half a man. "What will you tell people? After all, they knew how much we loved each other. They'll expect you to stand by me."

"I'll simply say we called off the wedding because of your mother's death. After a while, it will be apparent we have no intention of setting another date." She paused a moment, then added, "I know you love me, Drake. I hope you'll get over the pain in time."

He laughed softly, bitterly. "That's very kind of you, Larissa, to be so caring."

He hated her. Hated her and all she stood for. Even half blind, he saw her more clearly in that moment than he'd ever seen her before. He wondered what he had once found to love. She was shallow and vain and selfish.

And he was no better. Larissa hadn't changed because of his accident, because of his scars or his blindness. She was just who she'd always been. He had loved her because she was beautiful, because she'd made his blood boil with desire.

"It's not my fault," Larissa said petulantly, interrupting his thoughts once again. *"No woman wants to . . . no woman could . . ."*

"Love me?" he finished for her, staring at her blurred image.

"Well, you aren't exactly the man I accepted the proposal from, now, are you?"

"No, Larissa, I'm not." He sighed and let his head fall back against the pillows. *"Consider the engagement broken. You needn't come to see me again."*

He heard the door open.

"This is for the best, Drake."

"Yes."

"You'll get over me in time."

I'm already over you, *he wanted to say, but the words wouldn't form. They were strangled by a bitter fury at life, at fate, at the world, at God.*

But most particularly, at beautiful women who lied with ease, who said they loved when there was no love in them. . . .

Drake blinked away the unhappy memory and watched as Faith walked toward the line and began the task of hanging sheets and clothes to dry. Across the distance he heard her singing softly to herself, and the melody brought a smile to his lips.

Faith was beautiful. Perhaps even more beautiful than Larissa. But there was far more to her than mere comeliness. She had a heart full of love, and she showered it upon those around her with a pure honesty of spirit.

One day he hoped she would shower her love upon him. There was a chance she loved him already. It was that chance he clung to as he returned to his desk and drafted a letter to William Driscoe, an investigator residing in California.

*   *   *

A summer storm blew in during the night. Roiling clouds filled the heavens, hiding the full moon from view, turning the night as black as pitch. Tall trees bent before the wind, leaves crackling and clapping, branches snapping. Minutes later spikes of lightning, jumping from cloud to cloud, flashed brightly. Thunder pounded like an Indian's drum, rolling before the wind until it faded in the distance. In the yard, one of the dogs bayed. The horses whinnied and snorted as they circled the corral, the sound of their hooves on the hard-packed earth adding to the din of the storm. From somewhere in the mountains came the shriek of a mountain lion.

Faith observed nature's dramatic display from her bedroom window, feeling as strangely tossed and restless as the storm itself. Feeling akin to the shrieking mountain lion.

Something was about to happen. Something was about to change. She could feel it as distinctly as she could feel the summer wind upon her cheeks. It was as electrifying as the lightning. Her skin tingled with it.

"'For now, these hot days, is the mad blood stirring,'" she whispered.

She felt as wild, as mad, as any of Shakespeare's characters had ever been. For wasn't it madness to love Drake? Wasn't it madness to dream, even a little, that she might have a future in this place?

Lovers and madmen have such seething brains,
Such shaping fantasies, that apprehend
More than cool reason ever comprehends.

As the lines played through her mind, she laughed

aloud. Never before had she understood the truth of them as she did now.

Lovers and madmen indeed! To risk one's heart. To risk one's all. It was truly an act of madness.

Sheets of rain began to fall on the heat-parched earth, soaking the ground and freshening the air. The wind grew cool as it whipped her nightgown and tossed her hair.

"I don't care if it's madness," she shouted, leaning out her window and looking up at the heavens. "Let me be mad! Let me love!"

As if in reply, lightning flashed directly overhead, followed immediately by a deafening clap of thunder.

"Let me love," she repeated, whispering, this time the words a prayer.

Got to get away . . .

Got to get away . . .

They're behind me. I can hear them.

Got to get away.

In here. I can hide in here. Quiet, Butler. Don't let them hear you panting for breath. Stay quiet.

I wonder if they can smell me sweat? I stink with fear. My clothes are ruined. Damn them.

Quiet. That was close. I thought for a moment it was over for me.

Looks like they're gone. Yeah, I think they're gone.

What time is it? Not long until dark. I'll wait here, just to make sure. Can't afford to make any more mistakes. No more mistakes.

I've got to get out of San Francisco. I can't stay here. No money. Not even a plug nickel. I can pawn my watch. At least I've got it back. It'll get me enough for train fare out of here.

Never liked this city. Always was bad luck for me. I should have stayed in New York. It's Jane's fault I'm here. Lying, rutting whore. This is all her fault.

Got to get out of San Francisco. Got to find someplace safe.

14

The morning sky was silvered by clouds, the temperature cooled by the previous night's storm. Everything seemed fresh and new.

A good day for new beginnings.

Drake looked for Faith in the kitchen and found her standing at the stove, turning bacon in the frying pan. Wisps of fiery red hair curled along her nape like tiny fishhooks. Her dress was simple, her body uncorseted. She moved with the ease of someone who was comfortable in her surroundings. The thought pleased him immensely.

As he stepped up behind her, he noticed the batter in the stone crock, waiting to be poured onto the hot skillet. "Smells good. I love hotcakes."

She gasped at the sound of his voice, whirling around to face him, fork in hand, wielded like a sword. "Drake!" Her free hand flew up to smooth her hair.

He grinned, thinking that he'd like to kiss her. "Good morning."

"I didn't hear you come in." Her eyes were wide, her cheeks flushed.

"Quite a storm we had last night," he said conversationally, remaining close even though he could see she was flustered by his nearness. It made him want to kiss her even more, but now wasn't quite the time. "Did it wake you?"

"Yes." The flush in her cheeks grew more pronounced.

He loved the way more wisps of her hair curled around her face. He enjoyed the gentle arch of her dark brows, the lush fullness of her mouth, the perfection of her small, shell-shaped ears. He caught a faint whiff of her cologne, a clean, sweet scent that would forever remind him of Faith.

She broke the connection between them by turning back to the stove, saying, "It's almost chilly today."

"A good day for a ride." He waited for a response. When none came, he asked, "Would you go for a ride with me after breakfast? I'd like to show you more of the ranch."

Her hand stilled above the frying pan, then continued to lift crisp slices of bacon onto a plate.

"Faith?"

The silence lengthened before she replied, "Yes, Drake." She still didn't look at him. "I'll go for a ride with you."

"Maybe you could pack us a picnic lunch."

This time she glanced over her shoulder. "I shouldn't be gone so long. The children—"

"Parker will keep an eye on Alex and Becca while we're gone."

"The ironing—"

"Can wait."

She looked away a second time. "All right. I'll pack us a lunch."

Drake felt a lightness in his heart such as he hadn't felt in years. "Good. You see to the food. I'll get the horses ready." He headed for the back door.

"Horses?"

The note of surprise in her voice caused him to stop and turn. She was looking at him with wide eyes.

"Drake, I'm not much of a horsewoman. I thought . . . I thought you meant in the buggy."

He stared at her in wonder, hardly noticing what she'd said. How miraculous it was that she'd come to live in this house. She'd let in so much light and laughter in the short time she'd been at the Jagged R. Gently she'd forced him to face life again. Incredibly, unexpectedly, he'd grown to love her.

"Maybe we shouldn't—" she began.

"I think a woman who makes her home on my ranch should learn to ride horseback. Don't you?"

It was her turn to be silent and stare. He saw how she weighed his words and knew she was wondering if he meant them the way they sounded.

I do, Faith. I mean them exactly as they sounded.

"I suppose you're right," she said softly.

"We won't go too fast."

There was something fragile about the look in her eyes. "No, not too fast."

Drake didn't think they were talking about horses any longer. "I promise." He wished he could hold her in his arms and promise her more. Much more. Instead he turned and left the kitchen.

Additional promises would have to wait until he was sure he could keep them.

*   *   *

With a surreptitious gaze, Faith studied Drake from beneath the brim of her straw bonnet. Even though she knew little about riding herself, she could tell a man who was comfortable in the saddle. He looked like someone who belonged where he was.

"This is the westernmost border of the Jagged R," he said, interrupting her musings. "I thought we'd eat our lunch up on the ridge there. Above the line shack."

"What's a line shack?"

He pointed. "There."

She saw it then, a dismal-looking dwelling hewed out of the side of the hill. "Who lives there?"

"The men when they're riding line."

"The men? You mean Parker and Swede and the others?"

Drake laughed. "All the comforts of home. Come on. I'll show you."

He had a wonderful laugh, she thought as she followed him. And a beautiful smile.

She wondered at the change in him. Only a few short weeks ago he had been a man consumed by rage. She had thought it impossible for him to smile.

He glanced over his shoulder. "I lived in a shack like this one winter up in Montana. That's where Parker and I got to be friends. You learn a lot about a person when you've got to live with them in a place no bigger than this. Especially when you're snowed in for weeks at a time."

In front of the shack, they reined in. Drake dismounted, then stepped over to her horse. His hands spanned her waist as he helped her to the ground. Her heart tapped a riotous beat in response to his touch, but Drake seemed completely unaware of the affect his nearness had on her. He released her almost at once, then opened the door of the shack, motioning for her to look inside. Faith stepped forward and glanced around, glad for a moment to calm her raging senses.

The dugout had been scratched out of the side of the hill. The back wall and part of the two side walls were formed by the rich brown earth. The remainder was made of logs chinked with mud. A flat roof made of dirt-covered logs butted up against the hillside. A couple of cots stood against opposite walls, and a small wood stove, for cooking and heating, was nestled in the front right corner.

Faith had stayed in some undesirable places in her life, but this was more miserable than anything she could even imagine.

Drake knocked on the door. "All the Jagged R line shacks have wooden doors. Usually there's just a blanket or an old cowhide." There was a note of pride in his voice.

Faith didn't find much comfort in a wooden door. Quickly she stepped outside and drew in a breath of fresh, clean air. "You didn't mind living like this?"

"It *is* a bit different from the ranch house." He chuckled as he raked his fingers through his long black hair, then resettled his Stetson on his head. His smile faded as he answered her question. "No, I really didn't mind it. I always brought along plenty of books to read. Of course, summer was a better time to draw line duty. A man could learn a lot, spending time out in this country. You learn to read the signs of the seasons. You appreciate sunsets and flowers. You enjoy a serenade by an old hoot owl or a howling coyote. And you get to know your horse mighty well."

He paused, looking slightly embarrassed at having admitted so much. With a shrug he added, "I guess I was born to be a cowboy. I dreamed about coming west from the time I was a boy. It was all I ever wanted to do." He frowned. "My parents didn't approve."

More questions swirled in her head—about his parents, about his schooling, about Larissa. Most of all, about Larissa. But she held her tongue. She wanted him to tell her what he wanted her to know. She had no right to more than that.

He took hold of her arm. "Come on. We'll lead the horses from here."

She smiled, relieved not to have to get back in the saddle just yet. "Thank you."

"You'll get used to it." He looked down at her. "You'll be able to ride as well as anyone on the ranch in no time at all."

How long will I be here? Will it be long enough?

As quickly as the questions formed in her mind, she drove them away. She wasn't going to let this day be spoiled with doubts and fears. There would be plenty of doubts to deal with later.

Once up the hillside, Drake spread a blanket on the ground beneath some tall pines. Then he tethered the horses while Faith set out the sandwiches she'd wrapped in cloth napkins. Moments later he sat down beside her, and both of them turned their gazes upon the pastoral scene below.

"It's beautiful here," Faith said reverently.

"Yes, it is." He turned and met her gaze. "But I'd forgotten it until you came."

Her heart beat madly in her chest. She felt the

strange curling sensation in her stomach that always happened when he was near. She felt as if she'd always known him. Why was that?

Tentatively she reached out and touched the scar on his cheek. "Does it hurt you still?"

His jaw tightened. "No."

"Except for the memories," she whispered.

"Except for the memories." He took hold of her hand, drew it slowly away from his face. Then he turned it and kissed her palm.

"Would you tell me about it?"

He stared into her eyes for a long time, and she knew he was remembering, knew he was deciding whether or not to trust her with that part of himself. Her heart ached for him, for she felt the unseen scars as if they were her own. She knew they went deeper than the visible scar on his face.

"I was living in Philadelphia then," he began, his decision obviously made. "I was practicing law in my father's firm."

Faith listened as he recalled the day that had changed the course of his life. She relived the accident with him and then each moment, each hurt, that had followed. The guilt he'd borne over his mother's death and the added weight of his father's blame. The physical pain of his injuries. The rejection from Larissa. The frustration that had come with his partial blindness. She understood his doubts, his rage, his bitterness, and she longed to be able to make him forget them all.

As if he knew what she was thinking, he tightened his hold on her hand. "I don't know what would have become of me if you hadn't come to the Jagged R."

"I haven't done anything."

"But you have, Faith. You brought light into my

house." He leaned toward her. "Then you brought it into me."

She couldn't breathe, couldn't move, couldn't think. She simply waited for the moment their lips would meet. Waited, knowing that his kiss would be both sweet and furious at the same time.

It began with a feather-light touch. After a breathless moment, his lips parted and his tongue teased her mouth until she gave him entrance. She'd never been kissed like this before, and she felt afire with it. Heat surged through her, along with a yearning for more. Her skin tingled. There was an ache at the juncture of her thighs and another in her breasts. She knew only his touch could soothe her raging desires.

He could have taken her there, on the blanket, beneath the cloudy skies. It would have been against everything she believed was morally right, but she wouldn't have stopped him. He could have removed her clothes and made love to her. She wouldn't have denied him. She *couldn't* have denied him.

And they both knew it.

Drake's arms encircled her, drew her close against him. His mouth released hers, and he pressed his face, his lips, against the sensitive curve of her neck. A groan echoed in her ears, and she wondered where it had come from, then realized she had made the sound.

"Marry me, Faith," he whispered.

It took a moment for the words to sneak past the fever clouding her brain, took a moment for her to understand what he'd said. When she did, she drew back from him, staring at him in complete and total surprise. "But I . . . I'm already married."

"Divorce him."

"Divorce him?"

"Yes."

Divorce George? Marry Drake?

"I love you, Faith."

She gasped. Her hand flew up to cover her mouth. Her eyes widened in amazement. Doubt immediately darkened his face, and she knew he'd misunderstood her surprised silence.

He opened his mouth to speak, but before he could take back his declaration, she silenced him with her finger against his lips.

"'Speak low, if you speak love,'" she whispered in warning.

"Faith—"

"Are you sure that's what you want, Drake? To marry a divorced woman? There's bound to be a scandal. I'm an actress. You're an important man. There will be people who—"

"To the devil with them." He pulled her back into his arms, pressing her close against his chest. "It's only you who matters. Do *you* want to marry *me*?"

She still couldn't believe this was happening. It was impossible, incredible. She should not even have met this man, let alone fallen in love with him. And that he should love her was nothing short of a miracle.

Did she *want* to marry him?

She'd never wanted anything more in her life. From the moment she'd met him, she had felt a bond between them. She had tried to deny it. She had tried to withstand it. But that bond had remained, an invisible cord drawing her to him. Closer, ever closer.

It was against all wisdom that she should give her heart to him. But only last night she'd prayed she would be allowed to love. Now that prayer had been answered. Now Drake had offered the chance to her. She couldn't run from it.

He cupped her chin between his fingers, tilting her head so their eyes could meet. "I've written to a man I know in California. I've asked him to find your husband."

"You want to find George?" A knot formed in her stomach.

"Well, not to find *him* necessarily. But we must learn if he's obtained a divorce."

She drew back, felt the separation from him like a cool breeze on her skin. "And if he hasn't . . . "

"Then we'll prove his adultery and file our own suit."

She felt ill. "You did this without asking me?"

"I didn't want to make any promises until—"

"Didn't you think I might have a reason for not doing so myself?" Panic made her voice sharp. "You're an attorney, Drake Rutledge. Don't you know why I haven't sought to be free of him?"

But, of course, he didn't. He didn't know George Butler as she did. He didn't know what her husband might do out of pure spite. He couldn't understand the fear that dwelled in her heart, knowing that George could take her children on a whim, knowing that the courts gave him the right to do so, knowing that Alex and Becca could be kept from their mother forever, as she had been from her own when she was a child. Drake didn't understand. He couldn't understand.

She had been a fool to think, even for a moment, that she might be able to marry Drake Rutledge. She couldn't take the risk of losing her children, not even for love. She had to make him understand that marriage for them was impossible.

She got to her feet, her hands balled into fists at her sides. "Did you think I was so eager to find myself another husband?"

"Wait a minute. That's not why—"

"I didn't come to Dead Horse looking for anyone to take care of me, Mr. Rutledge." *What are you doing?* her mind screamed, but she couldn't stop herself. She *had* to do this. "The children and I have gotten along just fine without anyone else around. Who do you think supported us all these years? It certainly wasn't the children's father."

"Faith, I only wanted to help."

She knew that. In her heart she knew that.

But she also knew she was afraid. Afraid of losing her children to George. And, if she were honest, she was afraid of what it meant to give herself completely, to give her heart, to give her trust, to someone. Afraid of what it would do to her if she should be betrayed once again.

If she stopped what was happening between them now, if she never admitted she loved him more with every breath she took, then she couldn't be hurt. If she held very tight to her heart, then she wouldn't know the pain of having it broken when they were forced to part.

At least, that's what she wanted to believe.

An old memory taunted Drake as he looked at Faith, saw her drawing farther away from him.

You can't expect me to be shackled to half a man for the rest of my life. . . .

He rose from the blanket, wondering if half a man was what Faith thought him, too.

No. He would indeed be blind if he failed to see that she cared for him. He believed she returned his love. And he guessed it was because she loved him that she was afraid. He could almost see the shield of fear she was trying to raise between them, and he understood it. He'd raised one just like it many years before.

"It won't work, Faith."

She tilted her chin in a challenging manner. "What do you mean?"

"I love you, and I'm not going to let you push me away. Maybe I was wrong to try to find George without talking to you first. If so, I'm sorry. At least I did it for the right reasons." He held out his hand toward her. "I promise you this, Faith. I'll take care of you and the children. You'll never have cause to regret loving me."

She shook her head. Tears shimmered in her eyes. "I never said I love you." Her denial was a mere whisper.

He wanted to hold her. He wanted to crush her to him and drive away the last shred of doubt from her heart—and his, too, if any doubt remained. He wanted to brush away her tears. He wanted to shelter her and care for her. He wanted to kiss her until he drove both of them mad. He wanted to caress her and learn each curve of her body. He wanted to make her his.

"No," he admitted, "you haven't said you love me. For now, I hope it's enough that I love you."

Her gaze dropped to the ground between them as she shook her head again. "You don't understand."

He closed the distance she'd put between them with a few quick strides. He didn't touch her, and she didn't look up. "You're wrong, Faith. I do under-stand."

"You can't."

"Dearest Faith."

He saw a tear trickle down her cheek.

Softer this time, "Darling Faith."

She raised her head. Her blue green eyes were luminous and, he knew, revealed far more than she wanted them to.

"What do you think the chances were that you would end up in Dead Horse, working for me? You're an actress. Why are you employed as a house-keeper? *My* housekeeper? Out of all the cities and towns in this country, what were the odds that we would find each other?"

She gave a small shrug.

"A hundred? A thousand?"

Again she shrugged.

"A million?" It took all his resolve not to hold her and kiss her and force her to admit she loved him. "I quit praying a long time ago. I stopped believing in a God who cares what happens to we small humans on this earth. But something brought us together. Maybe I could believe again, now that you are here."

A flicker of hope shone briefly in her gaze.

"I know this much. I believe in you. I believe we were meant to be together. I don't believe there is any power on earth that can keep us apart, that can keep us from being a family."

"Oh, Drake." Her words came out on a sigh. "If only . . . "

This time he did take hold of her, drawing her ten-derly into his arms. He pressed her head against his chest and stroked her hair. He let his hands tell her what his words could not.

He loved her. He would always love her.

And he believed in miracles. He had to. What else besides a miracle could have brought Faith Butler to Wyoming and into his dark and lonely world?

15

Gertie took Rick to her hunting shack, high in the mountains.

After the word had come about James and Nancy, Gertie had spent several days sitting with Rick in the saloon, trying to convince him to stop his drinking. In the end, he'd been too drunk to argue with her anymore. He'd simply passed out cold, and she'd dragged him from the saloon, tossed him over the back of a spare horse, and brought him into the mountains, far from the nearest bottle of whiskey.

More than once in the hours that followed their arrival at the shack, Gertie wondered if she'd made a mistake and was afraid. She'd never seen anybody talk to folks who weren't there. But Rick did plenty of talking. Occasionally he made sense. Most of the time he didn't. When he finally drifted into sleep, she was afraid again. Afraid he wouldn't ever wake up.

Just after dawn of their third day in the mountains, she sat watching Rick sleep. She'd spent a good portion of the night wondering whether or not she'd done the right thing in bringing him there. Who was she, after all, to try to keep a man from drinking himself to death? He sure as heck hadn't asked her to help him.

With a sigh, she closed her eyes and leaned back in the rickety, spindle-backed chair, her legs stretched out in front of her, crossed at the ankles.

You've done some dang fool things in your life, Gertie Duncan, she thought, *but this surefire takes the cake. A hell of a way to catch a man. Truss him up like some calf ready for branding and make sure he can't get away. Shoot. He's more like t'hate you now.*

"Pitiful," she added with an unladylike snort. "Dang sure pitiful."

"Gertie?"

She sat up with a start. Braced on his elbows, Rick had risen up in bed and was watching her with blurry eyes.

"Where are we?" he asked, his voice weak and scratchy.

"My cabin." She let her gaze sweep the one room. "This is where I come to get away when I've had enough of them cowpokes at the ranch. Nobody knows about it but me. And now you." She looked at Rick again. "How you feelin'?"

He groaned as he lay back against the pillow and closed his eyes.

"Can't say that I'm surprised." She walked over to him, her voice softening as she said, "You dang near killed yourself, Doc."

"You should have let me."

She sat on the edge of the bed. "Yeah, maybe I shoulda, but I didn't. Listen here, Doc. I'm real sorry about what happened to James and Nancy. Just like I'm real sorry about the way you lost your wife a while back. But drownin' yourself in whiskey ain't gonna bring any of 'em back."

"I need a drink," he grumbled.

"Sure thing." Gertie went over to the bucket on the table, where she filled a tin cup with fresh water from the creek. Then she carried it back to the bed. "Here ya go, Doc."

He raised his head, covered her hand with his own quivering fingers, and took a swallow. He gagged and spit it out. "Good Lord, woman! What are you trying to do to me?" He stared at her with accusing eyes.

"Givin' you a drink, just like you asked for."

"I meant whiskey."

"Well, you're outta luck. There ain't any."

He sat up, dropping his legs over the side of the bed. He looked down at himself, dressed only in his woolen drawers. He blinked his eyes several times, then glanced around the cabin. "Where are my clothes?"

"I don't recall where I put 'em right at the moment."

He stood, weaving slightly on unsteady legs. His eyes flashed with anger. "Listen, Miss Duncan, you can't keep me prisoner here. Now get me my clothes."

His breath was foul and he was in dire need of a bath. She didn't suppose there was much about him to love at the moment, but love him she did.

"Sorry, Doc. I can't."

"Then I'll just go as I am." He headed for the door.

"It shouldn't take you more'n about five or six days t'walk back to Dead Horse. You'd best take care of your feet. They're likely t'get mighty sore 'fore you get there. Oh, and you oughta keep an eye out for bears. I've seen some signs of a grizzly 'round these parts."

He turned back with a scowl. "Where's my horse?"

She shrugged, a sheepish grin slipping into the corners of her mouth.

Rick swore at her, then yanked open the door and stormed outside.

She let him go. She figured he wouldn't go far. He hadn't eaten anything solid for more than a week now, not since he'd received word about his son. Gertie knew there wasn't a lot of strength left in his legs. He'd been hard-pressed to stand up long enough to relieve himself since coming to the cabin. She'd just give him some time to work off steam, then go looking for him. She knew he didn't have a prayer of finding the horses on his own.

"Like it or not, Doc, we're gonna see this through," she said as she turned to stoke the fire in the stove. She wanted to have a good meal waiting for him when he returned. He would need his strength back before he could concentrate on getting well.

On her hands and knees, Faith attacked the kitchen floor with scrub brush and soapy water. It was as if she were trying to rub Drake from her thoughts with elbow grease and soap suds. But it was a useless effort. He was firmly entrenched in her mind. She'd thought of nothing else but him since the moment he'd told her he loved her, since the moment he'd said he wanted to marry her.

What's wrong with me?

She'd asked God to let her love Drake, and when her prayer was answered, she'd run like a scared jackrabbit.

But what if I'm wrong? What if it isn't love I feel?

She'd loved George once, but she couldn't remember a time she'd felt for him what she felt for Drake. Maybe this terrible, burning wanting was nothing more than lust. Maybe it had nothing to do with love.

She sloshed more water onto the floor and scrubbed with extra vigor.

And what if he doesn't really love me?

She'd been left before. There had been something missing in her. She'd been unable to keep her husband. She'd failed as George's wife. What if she failed again with Drake?

"I don't need a man," she whispered, scrubbing faster. "I've done just fine on my own."

Just fine.

She'd done just fine.

A sob was torn, unwillingly, from her throat. Tears fell onto the floor to mingle with the soapy water.

"I'm afraid," she whispered. "I'm so afraid."

A divorcée. An actress *and* a divorcée. Whether Drake wanted to admit it or not, there would be talk. Ugly talk. Even in Dead Horse, Wyoming—where she'd felt such acceptance—there would be talk. Would he really want her then? He'd only begun to come out of hiding. When people shunned him because of her, would he still want her? Marriage was difficult enough without adding such troubles.

On the other hand, Faith had never let people's gossip stop her before. She'd been an actress all her life, like her parents before her, and she knew she wasn't immoral or corrupt or any of the other things actors and actresses were supposed to be. She'd always been rather proud of who she was. She'd never taken handouts or charity. She'd always worked to support herself. She'd raised her children to believe in God, to know right from wrong. She'd . . .

Faith brought her raging thoughts to an abrupt halt as she straightened and sat on her heels. With the back of her wrist, she swept loose strands of hair away from her face.

"Admit it," she told herself aloud. This wasn't about being divorced or being an actress or facing a scandal. This was about trust, about risk, about taking chances. She could be hurt again, hurt more deeply than ever before.

Or she could find more love and happiness than she'd ever dreamed of finding.

The question now was, would she take the chance? Would she allow herself to trust Drake, not just with her heart but with the safety of her children?

As if summoned by her tumultuous thoughts, Drake appeared in the kitchen doorway, looking strikingly handsome. He wore black trousers, vest, and suit coat, with a white shirt beneath. He carried a black Stetson in his right hand. A gold watch chain disappeared into a watch pocket.

Her breath caught in her chest at the sight of him. She'd scarcely seen him yesterday. She'd known he'd intentionally left her alone to work through her thoughts and doubts—which were legion. Now he was there before her, and all she could think of was throwing herself into his arms.

"I'm going to be gone for a few days," he said without preamble.

"Gone?"

"Parker and I are going to meet with a man from the railroad."

She stared at him, her mind harkening back to the

day—not so very long ago—that she'd determined to help Drake start living again. And now it had happened. He was going to help bring the railroad into Dead Horse. She'd succeeded in what she'd set out to do. Maybe she'd succeeded in all she was supposed to do. Maybe it was time for her and the children to move on.

Her gaze fell to the floor between them.

Or could it be that Drake was right? Could it be that this was where God wanted her to be? And how could she be sure?

"Faith?" The gentle timbre of his voice drew her gaze to his. "You're making this much harder than it needs to be."

"I know."

He crossed the room with slow, deliberate strides. She thought for a moment he might reach out and draw her to her feet. Instead he knelt, bringing his gaze level with hers, unmindful of the soapy water dampening his trousers.

"I won't allow anything to happen to Alex and Becca," he said softly. "I promise you that no matter what your husband tries to do, I won't let him take your children from you."

"But the law—"

"There are ways. Times change. Laws change. Judges can be reasoned with."

Was it possible? she wondered. Could he be right?

Drake lifted his hand as if to touch her, then let it fall again to rest upon his thigh. "What else are you afraid of, Faith?"

Surprisingly, she didn't hesitate to answer. "I'm afraid your love for me isn't real, or if it is, that it won't last. I'm afraid I'll take a chance on loving you and only get hurt. How can you possibly know if you love me or not? I've been here such a short time. You don't really know me, Drake. You don't know who I am."

"I know you, Faith," he answered softly. "I know you love your children. I've seen your patience, your joy, your tenderness, your concern. I know you're kind and generous with both friends and strangers and that you give more than anyone ever asks you to give. I know you're talented and hard-working." He reached out again, this time fingering a strand of her hair. "I know you're beautiful but never vain . . . because you have even more beauty in your soul."

His image blurred as tears filled her eyes.

"I know when I hear your voice my heart comes alive. I know when I hear you singing I feel like singing, too. I know that even when you're afraid, you do whatever you need to do, whatever must be done." He moved his hand to the side of her face, pressing his palm against her cheek, cupping it gently. She leaned into it and closed her eyes.

Always his touch had been gentle, she thought, even when he'd been filled with bitterness and rage.

He continued in a whisper, "I know that when you kiss me you make me feel whole again instead of like half a man. I know that when you look at me you don't see a monster."

Faith felt the words pierce her heart before she understood them in her mind. Then she lifted her head from his hand and opened her eyes to stare at him.

Half a man? A monster? Is that what Larissa had seen? If so, then she'd been the one who was blinded in Drake's accident. When Faith looked at him, she saw a man who took her breath away. She saw a virile male who stirred untapped reservoirs of desire with a single glance, a solitary caress.

"I know I want you, Faith. I know I love you. And I'll love your children as if they were my own. We could be a family, if you'll only take the chance."

Take the chance. . . .

Her heart beat like a tom-tom.

Take the chance. . . . Take the chance. . . . Take the chance. . . .

Drake rose from the floor, towering above her, tall and strong and splendid. "Please think about what I've said while I'm away."

After he'd walked out of the kitchen, she released a humorless laugh. Think about what he'd said? She knew she would think of little else but Drake Rutledge.

How could she do otherwise, loving him as she did?

"I've asked Faith to marry me," Drake told Parker after they'd been riding in silence for about an hour.

His friend reined in his horse, coming to a dead stop. "You've asked . . ." Eyebrows raised, he stared at Drake in obvious surprise. "Well, I'll be." He chuckled and gave his head a shake. "When you got back to livin', Drake, you did it up right and in a hurry."

"She hasn't said yes yet."

"You think she won't?"

Drake stared off toward the horizon. "I don't know."

He remembered the way she'd looked at him, her pretty eyes brimming with unshed tears. She loved him. He was sure of it. What he wasn't so sure of was whether or not she would ever risk admitting it, to herself or to him.

"Wait a minute—" Parker intruded on Drake's thoughts. "Isn't there the matter of a husband somewhere?"

Drake scowled. "Afraid so. I've written to an old friend of mine. He used to work for the Pinkertons. He's living out in California—or at least he was seven years ago. I'm hoping he'll be able to find Mr. Butler." He touched his heels to his pinto's sides and started forward at a walk. Parker's horse followed suit.

"What are you going to do if this friend of yours finds Faith's husband?"

"Prove his adultery. Get her a divorce."

Parker let out a low whistle. "And if you don't find him?"

Drake didn't have an answer to that question. He didn't even want to think about it. Divorce on the grounds of desertion was possible, of course, but it could take much longer to prove. As he understood it, George Butler had walked out on Faith just over two years ago, so they couldn't even begin proceedings until next winter.

"What if she can't get a divorce?"

Drake slanted a dark gaze at his ranch foreman. "She'll get one."

But what *would* he do if Faith couldn't get a divorce? He couldn't take her as his mistress. She might think he didn't know her, but he knew her well enough to understand it would break her spirit to live with him without the blessing of marriage. She might love him enough that he could seduce her into sharing his bed, but it would eventually destroy the precious bond between them. He could never let that happen.

"She'll get a divorce," he said again, more to himself than to Parker.

She must, he added silently, knowing that to lose Faith now would be a hundred times worse than the blindness that had changed his life seven years ago.

Faith went for a stroll with the children after supper. She refused to admit that the house seemed unpleasantly quiet and empty without Drake there.

They walked down from the ridge to the river below and sat in the shade of the tall cottonwoods, pines, and aspens. Alex recounted the day Mr. Rutledge had taken him fishing there, pointing out the place where he'd caught his very first fish.

Becca was suitably impressed with her brother's adventure. "Do you think Mr. Rutledge will take me fishing, Mama?"

Before Faith could open her mouth, Alex said, "'Course not. You're a girl."

Becca's eyes filled with tears of disappointment as she looked at her mother for confirmation.

"Alexander Butler," Faith said sternly, "I've never heard such nonsense. Where did you get such an idea? Becca is perfectly capable of going fishing."

"Well, she wouldn't catch nothin'."

"Perhaps not. But perhaps you won't catch anything the next time you go, either."

"Becca couldn't toss in her line the way Mr. Rutledge showed me. She's not strong enough."

"Then maybe you'll have to help her a little."

Becca rubbed her eyes, then sniffed noisily as she said, "I wish Mr. Rutledge was here right now."

"So do I," Faith admitted softly. She drew up her

legs, hugging them to her chest as she rested her chin on her knees. "So do I."

"Ma?"

"What is it, Alex?"

"Are we gonna stay here forever?"

Marry me, Faith.

"I don't know," she answered.

"Won't Mr. Rutledge let you keep workin' as his housekeeper?"

She glanced at her son. "Don't you miss traveling? Think of all the cities we've seen. And remember all our friends in Mr. Drew's company. Don't you miss them, at least a little?"

"I'd rather stay here with Mr. Rutledge."

Marry me, Faith.

"So would I, Mama," Becca chimed in.

Marry me, Faith.

She reached out and stroked Becca's strawberry blond hair, then glanced toward her towheaded son. It had been just the three of them against the world for so long now. They hadn't needed anyone else. They'd taken care of each other.

What had changed in these past weeks?

Wife and child,

Those precious motives, those strong knots of love.

That's what had changed. She wanted to be Drake's wife. She had fallen in love with him—and so had her children.

She turned her gaze once more upon the swift-running river, but it was Drake she envisioned standing before her.

We could be a family, if you'll only take the chance. . . .

"All right, Drake," she whispered. "I'll take the chance."

*   *   *

Mighty strange, reading my own obituary. I wonder who the poor fellow was. Sure as hell didn't have any more money than I do. Look at these clothes I'm wearing. Disgusting. Thank God he was about the same height as me.

At least the police are off my trail. George Butler is officially dead. Nobody'll be looking for him now.

Wish I didn't have to leave my watch on the body, but there was no getting around it. Not if I wanted to throw 'em off my trail.

At least I managed to scrape together enough train fare to get to Sacramento. Maybe my luck will turn once I'm there. Hell, it had better turn. Nothing's gone right since I came to California.

Wish I could've killed Jane, too. Wouldn't make any difference if I was caught. I've done it twice now already. The whore and the derelict. Didn't know it was so easy to do. I'd have enjoyed doing it to Jane. Besides, what would one more have mattered? It couldn't get much worse than it is. If they catch me, I'd rather hang for killing that bitch than a couple of strangers.

This isn't any way for a man like me to live. Always watching over my shoulder. Always wondering if someone'll recognize me. No way to live. I was supposed to get rich. I was supposed to live like the damned railroad barons in their fancy mansions in San Francisco.

Not like this. I wasn't supposed to live like this.

I remember when I was traveling with the company. Those were the good days. Always had nice clothes and a good place to stay. Always had the women, too.

Lord, the women. I could use one right now. Even that cold fish I married would be better than nothing. At least Faith was pretty to look at.

I wonder where she is?

16

Gregory Shoemaker, the railroad's representative, was a corpulent man in his late fifties, fastidiously dressed in a tweed suit, white shirt, and stiff collar. What hair was left to him had turned yellow gray and was trimmed close to his scalp. Smoking a fat cigar, he leaned back on his leather-upholstered chair with the air of a man used to commanding the attention and immediate agreement of those around him.

Drake disliked Gregory Shoemaker from the first moment they met.

"As I told Mr. Telford a few weeks ago, I'm afraid I can promise nothing for Dead Horse." Shoemaker's nose wrinkled, as if the very name of the town caused a bad taste in his mouth. He tapped the ashes from the cigar into the ashtray on the table that separated him from Drake. His gaze drifted to the window of the opulently decorated hotel room that served as his office. It was a deliberate dismissal.

Drake wasn't so easily dismissed. "It's my understanding James Telford went to Cheyenne to meet with other people in your company. It sounded as if there might have been another opinion expressed there."

Shoemaker's round face turned red, and his eyes narrowed as he directed them toward Drake again. "I can assure you, you're mistaken, Mr. Rutledge. I make these decisions."

Drake rose from his chair, his gaze never wavering. He set his Stetson on his head, then leaned forward, resting his knuckles on the table. "Let me help you understand a few things. I am not some cowpoke just off the Chisholm Trail with only two bits in his pocket to show for it. I have enough money to buy and sell you, and if you want me to prove it, I'll be happy to get myself a ticket to Cheyenne so I can have a talk with your superiors. Maybe they'll be interested in the number of cattle I'd be shipping out of Dead Horse."

Shoemaker's Adam's apple bobbed as he swallowed nervously.

Drake straightened. He tugged the brim of his black hat, settling it more securely on his head, shading his eyes from view. "Now, why don't you check into this a little more thoroughly and find out just what it will take to get that line up to Dead Horse. I'll come back tomorrow. Shall we say about nine o'clock?"

"Now see here—"

"Or shall I simply send a telegram to arrange a meeting in Cheyenne?"

Shoemaker scowled, but Drake was unaffected.

"All right," the other man grumbled. "Be here at nine. I'll look into it for you."

Drake left without another word. When he stepped onto the boardwalk outside the hotel, he paused and drew a deep breath. And, suddenly, he smiled.

It felt good, he realized, to be doing something concrete. It felt good to care about something. He might not yet know the townfolk of Dead Horse, but he was going to do his damnedest to help them save their town. It was his town, too, even if he had realized it late.

He wondered if he would ever have realized it without Faith's help. He thought not.

Then he wondered what Faith was doing at that same moment. Breakfast would be over by this time and the dishes already washed and put away. What had she fixed the cowboys to eat this morning? Hotcakes? Eggs? Porridge?

She'd never been confident of her cooking abilities. He'd seen her reading that cookbook, poring over the recipes, then watching the men as they ate, trying to judge if she'd succeeded or failed. Early on, when she used to bring him his meals in the library, he'd been aware of how anxious she was about the food she'd prepared.

But she'd done her best. Faith always did her best. She deserved the best in return.

He glanced across the street at the row of shops. Before he went back, he meant to find Faith the perfect gift. Something that would prove how much he loved her.

Whistling beneath his breath, he stepped off the boardwalk and headed toward the shop marked "Millinery." It seemed like a good place to start.

*   *   *

In the afternoon, Johnny Coltrain hitched the horses to the wagon and took Faith into Dead Horse. The young cowboy never said a word from the moment they set out, but Faith probably wouldn't have heard him if he had. Her thoughts were on Drake, as usual.

It was four days since Drake had proposed to her, two days since she'd decided to accept. But she couldn't tell him her decision because he was in Green River City and she was at the Jagged R Ranch. Almost a hundred miles separated them. It was a little like Christmas, having a present and being told she couldn't open it just yet.

"Mrs. Butler?"

"Mmm?"

"You speak them Shakespeare lines so pretty an' all. I was wonderin' if you might be able to help me with somethin'."

She gave herself a mental shake and brought her attention to the young man beside her. "I'd be happy to try, Johnny. What is it?"

His face was flushed, his gaze glued to the broad rumps of the draft horses. "Well, you see, I got this girl over in Idaho Territory that I'm hopin' t'marry."

"You've got a girl, Johnny?" She couldn't help showing her surprise. She was certain he was only sixteen, seventeen at the most. How could he possibly be thinking of marriage at his age? He was only about nine years older than Alex.

His blush brightened, but he sat up straighter and turned to meet her gaze head on. "Yes, ma'am, I do."

Realizing she'd insulted him without meaning to, Faith touched his arm lightly and offered a warm smile. "She's a very lucky girl if you care for her enough to think of marriage."

"Thank you, ma'am." He grinned suddenly. "But

I'm the lucky one. Ilsa's just about the sweetest thing on earth."

"How did you meet her?"

"Her pa worked at the Jagged R for a while as the cook. But then he bought a farm last summer over in Idaho and moved his family there. I wrote to Ilsa a time or two, but I ain't much good at it."

"And just what can I do to help you, Johnny?"

The cowboy removed his hat and raked his fingers through his shaggy brown hair, then set the battered headgear back in place. He was silent for so long—his gaze once again turned upon the team—that she wondered if he'd heard her.

"Johnny?"

"I was hopin' you might help me write a letter to her." Again he blushed, his expression solemn. "You know. Maybe use some of that Shakespeare fella's words. Somethin' that'll let her know how I feel." He glanced at Faith, then quickly away. "You think you might be able t'do that?"

She wondered if there was something about this town, with its unhappy-sounding name, that just naturally brought love to people who lived in it or nearby. First Gertie and Rick, then Faith and Drake, and now young Johnny Coltrain and his Ilsa. How could Faith not help Johnny when she was so happy to have found love herself?

"I'd be honored to help you. Why not tonight, right after supper?"

"Yes, ma'am. Tonight'd be just fine." He slapped the reins against the horses' backsides. "Giddup there!" he shouted, grinning once again from ear to ear.

When Faith entered the general store ten minutes later, she was welcomed by Sadie and several of the other women she'd met at the Fourth of July celebration, and then again at the funeral service for James and Nancy Telford.

"Afternoon, Faith," Sadie called as the door closed behind her. "You remember Mrs. Ashley and Mrs. O'Connell."

"Of course. Good afternoon."

Sadie motioned her forward. "You haven't been into town for a spell. How're the children?"

"They're fine. It's hard to believe Becca was ever sick. I'm worn out just trying to see she gets her proper rest."

The other women all smiled and nodded in understanding.

"And Mr. Rutledge?" Sadie continued.

Made breathless simply by the sound of his name, Faith smiled gently. "He's gone down to Green River City."

That got everyone's attention. Looks of surprise were exchanged. Expressions of disbelief were evident.

"He's seeing what he can do about the railroad. He's going to finish what James Telford began."

Sadie shook her head slowly. "How on earth did you bring about that miracle, Faith Butler?"

"I had nothing to do with it. Mr. Rutledge is a very caring man. He's concerned about what will happen to Dead Horse without the railroad."

Claire O'Connell glanced at Sadie, then at Faith. "That's rather difficult to believe, given he's never even come into town. Not even so much as to go to church when the reverend is here for proper services."

"He came on the Fourth." The words were out of Faith's mouth before she could stop them.

"What?" Sadie exclaimed.

Faith looked down at her hands, which were clutching her reticule. "Not until after dark, and only for a short while."

"Well, I'll be," breathed the store's proprietress.

Faith lifted her gaze, moved it slowly from Claire to Madge to Sadie. "I know Mr. Rutledge seems quite a mystery to everyone in Dead Horse, but I assure you, he's a wonderful, kind, and caring man. He lost his parents quite tragically before moving here. He suffered an accident which cost him an eye and left his face scarred. He . . . " Was she saying too much? she wondered. Would Drake want her to speak on his behalf? But she couldn't stop herself from continuing. "He's thought himself . . . unpleasant to look upon. It isn't true, of course." Her voice softened. "He's actually quite . . . dashing."

Realizing what she'd just revealed, she felt heat rising in her cheeks. She lifted her chin and smiled, refusing to take back the words or what they'd implied.

Madge and Claire exchanged looks. Then each of them made hasty excuses and departed.

"Don't you worry about them," Sadie said into the awkward silence the other women had left behind. "They don't wish you ill. You've just caught us all by surprise with your news about Mr. Rutledge." She waved a hand toward the back of the store. "Come have a cup of coffee and tell me more about him. We'll want to give him a proper welcome when he returns from Green River City."

Faith swallowed the sudden lump in her throat. "Thank you, Sadie," she said softly, meaning much more than the simple words suggested.

*   *   *

Gertie continued to wonder if she was crazy for bringing Rick Telford into these hills to sober up. He surefire wasn't appreciative of what she was doing for him. She figured she'd rather bust fifty broncs in one day than knock heads with Rick for another ten minutes.

It wouldn't be so bad if she just knew what to expect from him half the time. But she didn't. One minute he was as docile as a newborn kitten. The next he was as cantankerous as a bronc with a burr stuck in his haunches.

That first day he was sober enough to know what she'd done, he'd set out walking, thinking he could find Dead Horse on his own. She'd let him wander around lost until an hour before sundown, then she'd gone for him. They'd ridden double on her dun-colored mare back to the hunting shack, but he hadn't been particularly grateful for the rescue.

Just like now.

Rick stared at the fried eggs and bacon on his plate as if they were poison. Much of the time "poison" was a fair description of Gertie's cooking, and she was the first to admit it. But even Gertie could fry up eggs and bacon without doing them too much damage.

"There's enough grease here to float a warship," Rick grumbled without looking up.

"Eat it anyway." Gertie sat down on a chair opposite him. "You need t'get your strength back."

"Why are you doing this, Gertie?" he asked, not for the first time.

"We been over that already."

"I'm not worth your time and trouble."

"I think you're wrong, Doc."

Rick sighed as he moved the food around his plate with his fork. "Take me back to Dead Horse."

"I don't think you're ready just yet."

He glanced up. His eyes were clearer today, but all that did was make it easier for Gertie to read the misery behind them.

"Doc, what're you punishin' yourself for?"

He ignored her question as he got up from the table and walked to the door. He opened it and stepped outside.

"Drinkin' won't bring 'em back." She followed him out. "Won't bring your wife back neither."

He let out a humorless laugh. "Don't you *ever* let up, woman?"

"Guess not."

"It must be why you're a good wrangler." He glanced over his shoulder, a mixture of resentment and admiration in his eyes. "You just hang on until you wear those wild horses down, don't you?"

"Yeah, I expect that's a fair description of what I do." She combed her unruly hair with her fingers, sweeping it off her forehead. "But you ain't no wild horse."

He sighed. "No. I'm not."

Lord almighty, she loved him. It near broke her heart to see him suffering this way. She didn't reckon it was going to make him love her in return, but she'd move heaven and earth to see him make it through this rough patch.

Thumbs hooked in the waistband of her trousers, Gertie walked away from the cabin, strolling out to the clearing that overlooked a high-mountain meadow. "Tell me about your wife," she instructed softly.

Her request was followed by a lengthy silence.

She waited. After all, she wasn't going anywhere. She was staying right here, stuck to Rick Telford like a tick on a hound dog, just like he expected. And that was where she meant to stay until he'd come to terms with himself and what life had handed him.

"Her name was Esther."

Gertie smiled sadly but didn't look at him. She just kept staring down at the meadow, quiet in the midafternoon sunshine.

"She was the daughter of a doctor and the grand-daughter of a doctor. I suppose that was one reason she agreed to marry me. I studied under her father. That was how we first met." He paused a moment. When he continued, his voice had softened percep-tibly. "Esther was pretty in a gentle sort of way. James looked a lot like her. She was a very caring woman. Worked beside me throughout our mar-riage, helping me with my patients. Even after James was born, she still found ways to help." He fell silent again.

"You loved her a lot."

"Yes, I did."

Gertie turned, unable to keep from it this time. Rick was leaning against the wall of the cabin, his head bent forward, his arms crossed over his chest.

Gertie wondered if her heart might break, right here and now. "She was mighty lucky."

Rick glanced up. "Lucky?" He let out a sharp laugh. "Not hardly."

She stepped toward him. "Why not?"

"Because I couldn't stay away from my liquor. Not even when I could see how unhappy it made her. Not even when my drinking affected my work. Not even when she became ill and needed me more than ever." He swore. "I made her life a living hell."

"My guess is she loved you anyway."

"Why are you doing this?" he asked again, this time with a note of real confusion in his voice.

Gertie decided it was time for some honesty of her own. "It's simple, Doc. You see, I understand why your Esther fell in love with you 'cause I feel the same way."

He opened his mouth to protest, but she stopped him with a raised hand.

"Don't say nothin', Doc, 'cause you ain't gonna change what I feel just by tellin' me I don't really feel it." She took a step forward. "Now I know you think you're too old for me, but you're wrong there, too. You ain't too old. 'Sides, age ain't got nothin' t'do with love. Nothin' at all. Feelin's are just feelin's. They just are what they are. See?"

"I've lived a good deal longer than you, Gertie, and I—"

"There you go again, talkin' about how old you are."

"I'm a drunk," he stated loudly. "An old drunk."

She shortened the distance between them with a few quick strides. She didn't stop until their noses were mere inches apart. "Is that what you *want* to be?" she shot back, suddenly furious with him.

She waited for an answer, but he didn't give her one.

"Ah, hell," she muttered, so angry now that she thought she might haul off and punch him. To keep from it, she spun around and marched off into the trees.

Let him stew in his own juices, she thought, and fry his own damned eggs.

*   *   *

Waiting for Drake's return from Green River City was torturous. Minutes seemed like hours, hours like days.

Faith gave the house another thorough cleaning, washing and dusting, polishing and scrubbing. She helped Johnny write his love letter to Ilsa. She went riding with Alex and found that her son was now the teacher and she the pupil. She made a new rag doll for Becca, sewing it at night by lamplight.

She avoided her bedroom until forced there by exhaustion. She knew when she closed her eyes it would be Drake she saw. He haunted her dreams, made her restless with yearnings that had lain dormant for years.

With each new day she greeted the rising sun with a prayer that Drake would return soon. She prayed he would meet with success. She prayed he would still love her, still want her, when he came home. Then she prayed he would return soon, before his absence alone broke her heart in two.

A full week passed before her prayers were answered.

Faith wasn't certain what had drawn her to the corner of the barn, but there she stood, staring toward the road that ran south to Green River City. She'd stood there for a good ten minutes before she caught a glimpse of something. Nothing more than a blur at first, and then she could make out two riders. They were cantering their horses.

Was one a black-and-white pinto?

She strained to see more clearly, walking forward, hardly mindful that she was moving at all.

Yes! Yes, one was a pinto.

She pressed the palm of one hand against her chest, as if to still the racing of her heart. She felt a wave of weakness wash over her and feared for a moment that she might faint from joy.

He's home.

Home. What a wonderful word it was! She'd never understood what it meant to have a home. She'd always thought it meant nothing more than having a house of one's own. But it didn't. A home was a place where people loved one another. Home was here, with Drake.

Hurry!

She saw the pinto break into a gallop, pulling away from the other horse. She knew Drake had seen her, felt it in her heart. She wanted to lift her arm and wave. She wanted to pick up her skirts and run to meet him. She did neither, feeling suddenly shy and unsure of herself.

I love you.

She waited, scarcely breathing, for him to arrive. She strained to see his face, to read his expression, wondering if she would discover her own feelings in his gaze.

And then he was there, sliding his horse to a stop, vaulting from the saddle. She saw his smile as he stepped toward her. She laughed, joy gurgling up in her throat, unable to be contained. A moment later she was in his arms, and he was whirling her around in a circle, his laughter joining hers.

"I love you, Drake." The words came out with ease, as if she'd been speaking them for years.

He stopped, set her feet on the ground, cradled her head between his hands, stared deep into her eyes. "What?"

"I love you."

"Say it again."

"I . . . love . . . you." She rose on tiptoe and kissed him.

When their lips parted, he whispered, "Say it one more time."

"You first," she returned softly.

He kissed her forehead. "I . . . "

He kissed her earlobe. "Love . . . "

He kissed the tip of her nose. "You."

He kissed her lips, hungrily this time, teasing her with his tongue, nibbling the fleshy part of her mouth with his teeth. Desire flared within her, white hot and instant. She leaned into him, longing for more than kisses.

It was the sound of Parker clearing his throat that finally pulled them apart. Faith flushed as she glanced up to meet the foreman's gaze, then looked at Drake.

"Well?" Drake asked.

She merely stared at him.

"Wasn't there something else you wanted to say?"

"I already told you." She smiled, despite her embarrassment over Parker's presence. "I love you, Mr. Rutledge."

"And?"

With mock innocence she echoed, "And?"

"And what else?"

Teasing humor vanished, and she answered him in earnest. "And I'll marry you, once we know I'm free to do so."

He drew her to him with an agonizing tenderness. "You'll never regret it, Faith," he whispered. "I swear, you'll never regret it for a moment."

"I know." She pressed her head against his chest and closed her eyes.

This time Parker coughed. "Why don't I take care of your horse while you tell Faith about the railroad?" Without waiting for a reply, he led the pinto away.

Faith gasped as she drew back and looked up at Drake. "The railroad. What happened?"

He grinned. "It looks good."

"Truly?"

"Truly."

She threw her arms around his neck. "We must go into town. We must tell everyone."

"Nothing's confirmed," he cautioned her.

"But it looks good. You said so. It will at least give people hope." Her smile faded. "You must do this, Drake. They've been waiting so long for good news. You should be the one to take the news to them."

He stared down at her. She felt his gaze like the caress of his fingertips. It warmed the skin, quickened her pulse. With sudden insight she understood his hesitation. It had been one thing to go to Green River City and meet with strangers. It was something else entirely to face the people who were his neighbors, the people he'd avoided for so many years.

"I'll be with you," she said softly, tightening her arms around his neck. "I'll be with you always."

17

Word about the railroad spread like a prairie fire through the town and neighboring ranches and farms. No one needed confirmation of the decision to justify a celebration. It was enough that it looked as though the railroad might come to Dead Horse.

It warmed Faith's heart to see Drake standing with the other men of the community. In a matter of minutes he'd become a leader, someone to look up to, a man of authority.

What had happened, she wondered, to the person who had locked himself away, a prisoner of his own anger and bitterness? She could scarcely remember what Drake had been like when she'd arrived at the Jagged R. Perhaps it was because she'd known instinctively that this man was there, waiting to be set free.

The women of Dead Horse, for the most part, seemed in awe of the mysterious Drake Rutledge. Faith was glad she had told Sadie, Madge, and Claire about his accident. She suspected they had told others. Therefore none seemed surprised by either his scar or his partial blindness.

But that didn't lessen the impact of Drake's overall appearance—his long black hair, his broad shoulders, his height, and what Faith had always thought of as his pirate's patch. The impact was especially strong upon women. There was something dangerously appealing about Drake that no female could avoid noticing.

I'm jealous, Faith realized with surprise. Every time Drake looked or smiled at another woman, she wanted to object, to stand between them and let it be known he belonged to her. It wasn't a particularly pleasant feeling, and she was glad when they finally returned to the ranch.

Throughout the afternoon and early evening, neither of them had spoken of Faith's proclamation of love or her acceptance of Drake's proposal of marriage. While in town, they had stayed apart. Faith hoped no one had realized the strength of emotions that existed between Drake and his housekeeper. With any luck, Madge Ashley and Claire O'Connell had been able to put their suspicions to rest, at least for now.

But once they were home, the children fed and put to bed, and the cowboys gone to the bunkhouse for the night, there was nothing to separate them any longer.

Drake led Faith into the parlor. Soft light spilled from a single lamp, lending a golden glow to everything within its reach. A gentle breeze caused the window curtains to ripple. Outside, crickets chirped, and in the distance, the hoot of a night owl could be heard.

Drake turned and drew Faith into the circle of his arms. He pulled her close, then rested his cheek on the crown of her head.

"Was I imagining it," he asked, "or did you tell me earlier today that you'd marry me?"

She laughed softly as she nestled more closely against him. "You weren't imagining it."

"Say it one more time."

"I'll marry you, Drake."

He tipped her head back and kissed her sweetly. When their mouths parted, he stared down into her eyes. "It may take time. There's no telling how long. It could be months. Maybe even a year or more."

"I'll wait."

"There's bound to be talk. You said so yourself."

"I can take it if you can. I can bear anything as long as you're with me."

His thumb brushed lightly over her temple and cheek. "Have you forgiven me?"

She didn't have to ask him what for. She knew what he meant. "Yes, even though you shouldn't have started looking for George without talking to me first."

"We'll discuss everything from here on out," he promised. "You'll have a part in every decision I make."

They kissed again. Kissed until Faith was left limp and breathless. Then Drake guided her to the sofa and settled her there.

"I have something for you," he said as he stepped back from her. "Wait here." He strode from the room.

Was this really happening to her? she wondered as she stared at the empty doorway. Was any of it truly possible?

I must be mad.

How could she accept a marriage proposal when she might still have a husband? It was wrong. She couldn't promise anything until she was free.

But it doesn't feel wrong. Nothing has ever felt so right to me as this does.

What would she do if they couldn't find George? What would she do if they failed to find grounds for a divorce? Worse still, what if George fought the divorce? What if he did try to take the children from her? What if he regretted leaving them with her?

But that was ridiculous. George had mentioned getting a divorce himself. He had left the children with her by choice, had said he didn't want them. For all Faith knew, she was already a free woman. George had probably divorced her and married that blonde he'd left with. Jane. Jane was probably the new Mrs. George Butler by this time, and all of Faith's fears had been for naught.

Would God have brought Drake and me together if our marriage wasn't meant to be?

The thought comforted her, bringing with it a new peace and assurance. There must be a way. She would be patient. She would not become a prisoner to fear again.

Drake stepped back into the parlor doorway, his arms laden with packages. "I brought you a few things from Green River City."

Faith laughed aloud, her worries and doubts fleeing like darkness before a flame. "A *few* things?"

"You think I got carried away?"

"Perhaps a little."

He knelt on the floor in front of the sofa and set the packages beside him. All signs of teasing disappeared as he met her gaze. "I've never done this before," he confessed.

She leaned forward at the waist, wanting to be closer to him. "No one has ever done this *for* me."

Drake heard volumes of truth in that simple statement. He wanted to cradle her in his arms and promise her that nothing would ever hurt her again. He wanted to find George Butler and break his neck.

He picked up one of the packages and handed it to her. "Open it."

Faith's eyes sparkled as she untied the string and tore back the tissue paper that wrapped the first gift. It was a dress, the same blue green color as her eyes. She lifted the bodice and held it against her, gazing down at it as she rubbed the palm of one hand over the fabric. "It's beautiful," she whispered.

"*You're* beautiful." He set the next package on her lap, eager for her to continue.

She raised her eyes to meet his. Warm color infused her cheeks, making her even more beautiful.

"Go on. Open it," he encouraged.

She looked down at the package as she loosened the string and lifted the lid off the hat box. She drew out a straw bonnet, decorated with ribbons that matched her new dress. "Drake," she breathed, "it's lovely." She rose from the sofa and went to a gilded mirror on the opposite side of the room.

He watched as she set the bonnet on her head at a jaunty angle, tying the ribbons beneath her chin in a perfect bow. When she turned, she gave him a saucy smile. "What do you think?" Her eyes sparkled merrily.

"I think you'd better open the rest of your gifts."

He couldn't recall anything he'd ever enjoyed more than watching Faith open one package after another.

There was a second dress in one, matching shoes, gloves, and pocketbook in another. There were petticoats and frilly undergarments; when Faith opened that package, she blushed and refused to meet his eyes.

He wanted to kiss her. Wanted more than anything to lift her into his arms and carry her up the stairs to his bedchamber, remove her clothes, and make slow, passionate love to her. He would move mountains in order to hasten the day he had the right to do so.

Finally he placed a small box in her upturned hands and waited anxiously as she lifted the lid and pushed aside the tissue paper. He heard her sudden intake of breath.

Her gaze darted up to meet his. "Oh, Drake."

"Does it fit?"

She shook her head, seemingly unable to speak.

He took the narrow, solid gold ring—filigreed and set with three sparkling diamonds—from the box and slipped it onto her finger. "It does fit."

"You shouldn't have."

"Why not? I want my wife to have a beautiful wedding ring. This was the finest I could buy in Green River City."

"But I'm not your wife."

"Yet."

Tears glittered in her eyes, and he longed to kiss them away.

"Yet," she whispered as she removed the ring and handed it back to him.

"I'll keep it safe for our wedding day."

She nodded wordlessly as two tears trailed down her cheeks.

Drake dropped the ring into his pocket, then drew

her from the sofa and into his arms. "What is it, Faith? What's wrong?"

"What if I'm never free to marry you?" she asked softly. "What if we've tempted fate by pretending I had the right to accept your proposal?"

He removed the straw bonnet and tossed it aside before kissing her forehead. Then he pressed her head to his chest as he stroked her hair. "You *will* be free. You *will* be my wife."

Against his shirt she whispered, "'Our wills and fates do so contrary run / That our devices still are overthrown; / Our thoughts are ours, their ends none of our own.'"

"*Hamlet?*"

She nodded.

With his finger beneath her chin, he tilted her head, forcing her to look at him. "'Men at some time are masters of their fates.'"

A hesitant smile curved her mouth. *"Julius Caesar."*

"Trust me, Faith. Not even fate will keep us apart." He tightened his arms around her. "You have my promise."

By moonlight, Gertie walked to the hot springs. The small, warm-water pool wasn't far from the cabin. It was one of the reasons she'd selected this site on which to build her hunting shack. She hadn't told Rick about the springs. Perversely, she'd forced him to make do with heating his water on the stove and filling the small washtub whenever he wanted to bathe.

As she sank into the hot water, her tension eased and the taut muscles in her shoulders relaxed. She let out a long sigh, closed her eyes, then sank beneath the water. When she resurfaced, she rested the back of her head on a smooth stone and stared up through the trees and rising steam at the star-studded heavens.

What now? she wondered. What was she supposed to do next?

She hadn't returned to the cabin since she'd stalked off in anger earlier in the day. She'd gone to where she'd hidden the horses and taken her mare out for a long ride, trying to settle her thoughts. It hadn't worked, of course.

"This lovin' stuff sure is a problem," she muttered.

She'd been better off when she'd just had her work to tend to. She wasn't any good at bein' a woman, never had been, never would be. She should have known that and kept herself away from Rick Telford from the start.

At least he was sober again. He might not stay that way, once he was back to town, but for now he was sober.

"Maybe I oughta just keep him here. Never let him go back at all."

She shook her head. Even she didn't want a man by making a prisoner out of him. She'd rather dry up inside than get him that way, no matter how much she loved him.

She would have to take Rick back to Dead Horse soon. He'd have to make the decision about what he did when he got back there. He would have to make his choice to stay sober or go back to drinking until he killed himself.

She swore softly as she straightened and reached for the soap sitting on the ground. She lathered her hair and skin, then rinsed herself clean. Next she pulled her dirty clothes into the water for a thorough scrubbing. When she was finished, she got out of the pool and dried herself off, then dressed in clean, dry clothing before laying the just washed items on two large boulders not far from the water's edge. She would come for them tomorrow afternoon once they'd had a chance to dry in the sun.

She took her time walking back to the cabin. Rick would probably be asleep by now. He'd spent a great deal of time sleeping since she'd brought him here. She didn't know whether or not that was good for him. She wished she knew she was doing the right thing, keeping him here even this long.

She combed her fingers through her short, damp hair as she let out a long sigh.

She guessed she didn't know much about anything except horses. She most always knew what a horse was going to do. She could read things by the twitch of an ear or the flick of a tail. But folks were different. It was hard to know what they were thinking or feeling.

Hell, she didn't know much about her own thoughts or feelings, if truth be known. She'd never wasted time on them. She was a wrangler, had been a wrangler for years. She hadn't needed to know anything except how to best break a bronc and make a good saddle horse out of it. Horses had been all that mattered to her for as long as she could remember.

The cabin came into view, and Gertie stopped to stare at it.

Something else mattered to her now. Rick mattered. She wanted him well. She wanted him to look at her and see that she was a woman.

She swore softly at her own foolishness as she started forward again. She might as well wish to be the queen of England. It was just about as likely to come true.

The cabin door creaked softly as she opened it and stepped inside. Pale moonlight spilled in with her, falling across Rick's bed. He was sitting on the edge, staring at her.

"I wondered if you were coming back," he said as he stood.

"You oughta know I wouldn't just leave you here."

"Yes, I guess I ought to know that."

She pushed the door closed. "I thought you'd be asleep."

"I've been doing some thinking."

She heard him step toward her, felt herself grow tense at his sudden nearness.

"You were right about me, Gertie. You were right about a lot of things."

She wasn't quite certain how to reply, so she remained silent.

"I owe you a debt of gratitude."

Gratitude? That wasn't what she wanted from him. "You don't owe me nothin', Doc," she said as she moved away from the door, slipping away from him, too.

Behind her she heard a match strike, saw the flicker of light intrude on the darkness, followed by the glow of the lantern as the wick caught fire. A moment later Rick's shadow joined hers on the wall of the cabin.

"Gertie?"

"What?"

"Will you look at me?"

She drew in a deep breath, then did as he'd asked.

He touched her cheek. "I apologize."

"Don't want your apologies, Doc, or your grati-tude."

"Nonetheless, you have them both."

Then he did something surprising. He kissed her.

Kissing was a whole lot different when the other party was willing, she discovered as the pressure on her mouth increased. Her stomach bounced and tumbled like a bronc rider hitting the ground after being thrown free of the saddle. Her arms circled his neck.

She pressed her body close to his and thought how foolish Rick was for calling himself old. There wasn't anything old about the feel of him against her. He was built lean and muscular. Most of all, she felt his desire for her, pressing against her belly through the clothes they wore.

She felt scared, uncertain, uncharacteristically shy. She knew what she wanted, knew he wanted it, too, but she'd never let a man this close before and wasn't sure what she was supposed to do next.

But you do know, Gertie Duncan, her mind argued. *Heckfire, you been listenin' to cowboys braggin' about their womanizin' for most o' your life.*

Feeling clumsy and awkward, she claimed Rick's mouth in another kiss. If anything was going to happen between them, this was the time, and she was going to have to get it started. She removed his shirt, then ran her unsteady fingers over his chest and abdomen, exploring and discovering. She kept her eyes tightly closed, a little bit afraid of what she might see if she opened them.

Rick broke the kiss. "Gertie," he whispered tightly, "you shouldn't—"

"Yes, I should, Doc."

She swallowed her doubts and fears, then forced herself to trail her fingers down his chest to the bulge in his trousers.

He groaned, and she wondered if she'd hurt him.

She tried to remember what she'd heard in the bunkhouse when the cowpokes were talking about the women they'd bedded.

But it seemed she didn't have to remember anything, because Rick's hands took over now. Within moments there were two piles of clothes on the floor, hers and his.

"Open your eyes, Gertie."

Reluctantly, she did. Feeling his gaze upon her, she wasn't certain whether she was glad he'd lit the lantern or sorry for it. She was afraid he would find her body lacking all the things a woman should possess. She knew she was scrawny, built like a pole, with small breasts and few curves. She didn't look anything like the soiled doves she'd seen in the saloons from here to Texas. What if Doc looked at her and discovered he didn't want her after all?

It didn't happen that way.

He drew her with him to her bed, where he laid her back on the tick mattress, then joined her there. As he kissed her again, his hands began to explore her body, and she forgot to feel self-conscious about her flaws and her ignorance. He made her feel beautiful and perfect in a thousand different ways.

By the time he rose above her, she was more than ready to discover what it meant to be joined with a man in such an intimate act. She knew he would either do it or she'd be driven stark-raving mad.

There was a moment of pain, but it was soon forgotten as their passion rose and ebbed and rose again. Finally, when she began to believe she could stand it no more, there was an explosion of sensations inside her that caused her to arch against him. She heard guttural sounds in his throat as he drove more deeply inside her.

Pleasure warmed her as they lay in the silent after-glow of lovemaking. Gertie couldn't ever remember a time when she'd felt so complete, so extraordinary. She knew she'd never felt so much like a woman as she did right now.

And glad of it, she thought. For this particular moment, perhaps for the first time in her life, she was glad to be female.

Rick pulled her close against him and whispered in her ear, "Thank you, Gertie."

For some reason, she found his thanks disturbing. But she pushed away any doubts. She might have to face them come morning, but she didn't have to do it now.

In the morning would be soon enough.

18

August arrived, ushered in by another heat wave. The sun burned the grasslands to the color of sand and shrank the streams and rivers from their banks. The house on the bluff above Dead Horse blistered in the summer sun. Late afternoon thunderstorms blew through nearly every day, exploding with spectacular displays of lightning but no rain.

Short-tempered cowboys snapped at each other. Even the ever-affable Gertie scarcely had a good word to say to anyone after she returned to the ranch. Alex and Becca were no better than the others; they fought with each other constantly.

Only Faith and Drake seemed immune to the effects of the high temperatures that blasted the valley like a furnace. Each moment they were together was a joy, and they made an unspoken pact not to allow anything to mar the newly discovered pleasure of loving one another.

When each day was done, they rendezvoused in

the parlor. Drake frequently played the piano, and Faith would sing, her sweet voice drifting out the window in the still of an evening. They talked about their childhoods, acquainting each other with the pasts that had shaped them. Drake told Faith about his parents, about his schooling, about his years of travel. He even told her about Larissa. And Faith talked about the cities she'd visited and lived in, about the life of an actress, about her dreams and aspirations.

They had covered nearly everything imaginable, had come to know each other better than either had thought possible, when Drake broached the one topic they'd been avoiding. "Tell me about George."

She looked up and met his gaze. "What would you like to know?"

"How you met. Start there."

"The company was in Boston," she said softly, looking back in time as she returned her head to his shoulder. "We were performing *The Taming of the Shrew*, and I had the role of Bianca. I was seventeen. I don't know how George came to be backstage that night." She gave her head a slight shake, realizing she'd never asked him and wondering why she hadn't. "I don't even remember who introduced us. Just suddenly there he was, telling me how marvelous my performance had been, that I should have had the lead part, that I would be famous and wealthy one day, that I was a great beauty."

"You *are* a great beauty."

Again she shook her head. "No, he was the beautiful one. I always thought he looked like an archangel with his golden hair and blue eyes. He had the most disarming smile. I remember thinking he had the whitest, straightest teeth of anyone I'd ever known.

I'd never met anyone else like him. His tongue was so glib. I often said he could make a river run upstream with just a little sweet talk."

"You loved him."

"Yes. At least I thought I did." She stopped and considered her answer, then said, "No, I know I loved him. But it was the man I thought he was whom I loved, not George himself. I just didn't discover it in time. We were married a few months after that first meeting, just after my eighteenth birthday."

She paused again, wondering what to say next. She couldn't tell Drake how unhappy and disappointing her marriage bed had been, that she had never enjoyed George's lovemaking, that she had tried to avoid him whenever possible, that she had feared there was something wrong with her because of it. She couldn't tell him about her dashed expectations or about the cruel words George had so often hurled at her. She couldn't tell him about the time George had hit her with the back of his hand. She'd been pregnant with Alex and unable to work. They'd had little money left, and George had flown into a rage, blaming her for all the things they'd lacked. It was the one and only time he'd struck her physically, but not the last or only time she was in pain because of him.

Drake's fingertips stroked slowly over her hair. "He hurt you."

"George expected life to be easy. He expected everything to be given to him on a silver platter. It often was. But not by me. I failed to do what I was supposed to do. I was supposed to make him rich or, at the very least, to support him while he pursued other pleasures." She pressed her mouth closed, not wanting to hear the bitterness that had crept into her voice.

"But he gave you Alex and Becca."

Drake amazed her sometimes, the way he knew just the right thing to say.

"Yes, he gave me Alex and Becca."

He tilted her head, forcing her to look up. "If they'll let me, I'll be a father to them. I'll love them as if they were my own."

Her heart felt as if it would burst. She'd never thought she would be able to trust again. She'd never thought she would be willing to risk her heart, her love, again. But she trusted Drake. She'd risk anything for him.

"I'll love them as much as the children I hope we'll create together." He placed the flat of his hand against her stomach as he kissed her temple. "I hope we'll give Alex and Becca many brothers and sisters."

With gentle guidance, he turned her until she was lying across his lap, cradled in his arms, her hands clasped behind his neck. A firestorm ignited within her as his mouth claimed hers in a kiss made more furious by controlled passions. She ached with wanting and knew that only Drake could soothe that ache with his touch, with his body.

He lifted his mouth a hairbreadth from hers. She opened her eyes, her vision glazed by desire.

"How long before we hear anything from California?" she whispered. "How long before we can marry?"

His laugh was low, seductive. "Not soon enough," he replied softly.

She ran her fingers through his hair, loving the feel of it, loving the look of it. Loving the look of him—rugged, dangerous, not quite civilized.

"You make me feel things I never . . . " She caught her breath as he cupped her breast, tracing his thumb over her taut nipple. She wished she could remove her clothing, wished she could feel his skin against hers. "Oh, Drake, I . . . I want you," she confessed, then blushed like a virgin.

She saw the storm of his own desire, which only increased the ache in her loins. She could sense how tightly he held himself in check, knew that his wanting was as great as hers.

"I think," he said, his voice low and strained, "it's time you retired for the night, before we do something we might both regret."

"No one would know," she whispered desperately.

He smoothed her hair. "*We* would know."

"But—"

He silenced her with his finger over her lips. "I want you as my wife, Faith. Not my mistress."

She felt the heat increase in her cheeks, and she lowered her gaze from his. All her life she'd seen the looks, heard the whispers that said simply because she was an actress, she was a woman of low morals. She had known it wasn't true, had known that it would never be true. There had been plenty of opportunities, had she been willing, but she'd never been tempted.

Never, until now.

She glanced up again, stared at the man she loved beyond reason. She would do anything for him, be anything for him. She would forget everything she held to be true, turn her back on the values to which she'd adhered throughout her life, if he asked her to. She saw that he knew it and loved him even more because he refused to take advantage of her weakness.

He kissed her again, tenderly this time, then rose from the couch with her in his arms. He carried her to the stairs, then set her on her feet, one step above him.

"Good night, Faith."

She remembered the first time he'd kissed her, then bade her good night. It was a pattern she longed to break. She wanted him to carry her to his bedroom and—

"Go to bed, Faith. I'm a man, not a saint." His smile was tense.

Oddly, she felt like laughing. Joy bubbled up inside her, joy and a sense of power in her womanhood. "Good night," she said again, and this time she turned and hurried up the stairs.

Gertie scrambled out of bed and darted outside, where she emptied her stomach. It was the fifth time this week that she'd been sick, and she was beginning to get worried. Not so much about what might be wrong with her, but because she might have to see Doc about it.

Leaning against the side of the barn, she slid to the ground. She drew up her legs and rested her forehead on her knees as she let out a low moan.

She didn't figure she'd ever been so miserable in her whole life as she'd been this past month. And it was all her own blamed fault, too. Throwing herself at a man like she had up in them hills.

The morning after she'd lain with Rick and discovered all the pleasures she'd never known existed, she'd brought him back to Dead Horse. When the town had come into view, he'd stopped his horse, then told her he wanted to ride on in alone. He'd thanked her again for all she'd done. Told her she had a kind heart. Then he'd ridden away from her. As far as she knew, he hadn't gone back to the saloon in the following weeks, hadn't drunk so much as a single drop of whiskey.

Nor had he come to see her.

Gertie was beginning to think that loving a man was more trouble than a cow stuck in a bog. Leastwise a dumb animal she could lasso and pull out of the fix it got itself into. There wasn't nothing she could do about loving Rick Telford or making him love her.

Her stomach rolled, and she thought she might be sick again. She swallowed the bitter taste of bile and dragged in several long, deep breaths until the queasy feeling went away. When she felt a little more steady, she pushed herself up and headed for the well.

She felt better once she'd rinsed her mouth with water, but not much. The light-headedness lingered as it had, off and on, for days. That wasn't a good way for a wrangler to feel, especially if she was busting a bronc when it happened, like she'd been doing yesterday. Parker had seen the fall she'd taken and had asked her if she was feeling all right. She wouldn't have a job for long if the foreman thought she wasn't able to do what she'd been hired to do.

"You're gonna have t'face him sooner or later," she told herself aloud as she scooped up a handful of water and splashed her face with it. "Might as well be sooner."

Maybe when she saw Doc she'd find out she didn't care so much anymore. Maybe when she saw him she'd discover all she'd wanted was one night. Maybe her itch had got scratched, and she'd find what she felt wasn't love after all.

Maybe . . . but she doubted it.

*   *   *

Rick stared at his reflection in the mirror. The face of a forty-three-year-old man stared back at him. A forty-three-year-old man who had no business thinking about a girl of twenty-five the way he kept thinking about Gertie Duncan.

He swirled the brush in his shaving mug, then applied the soap lather to his face and began the morning ritual of scraping away the dark gray bristles.

Gertie hadn't come into Dead Horse since the day they'd returned from the mountains. For all he knew, she'd left the Jagged R Ranch. For all he knew, he'd never see her again.

Was that so bad? Wasn't that what he'd wanted?

But he hadn't had the chance to thank her properly for all she'd done for him. He wasn't fool enough not to realize she'd saved his life when he'd thought it wasn't worth saving. He'd had plenty of time in recent weeks to take a long hard look at his past and the mistakes he'd made. He'd had plenty of time to think about what he meant to do differently from now on.

Finished shaving, he splashed his face with water and dried it with a towel, glancing one last time in the mirror.

"You made love to her," he accused his reflection.

What weakness in his character had allowed him to take such advantage of her? Gertie might be a tough, no-nonsense wrangler around her horses, but she was an innocent when it came to men. She had a girl's infatuation for him, and he'd used it to have his way with her, letting his sexual hunger rule his head.

He closed his eyes, remembering how she'd looked

in the lamplight. Surprised even now that he'd found her lovely, perfect, desirable. That tenderness and affection had shared equal parts with desire in his lovemaking. He hadn't felt like that in years.

"You're an old fool," he muttered, turning away from the mirror.

He put on his white shirt, tucked it into his trousers, and drew the suspenders into place. Then he sat on the edge of his bed and put on his boots.

He should go up to the Jagged R, quit hiding in this house and face what he'd done. He should try to make some kind of amends. He ought to find some way to show Gertie his appreciation.

He was halfway down the hall, headed for the kitchen, when a knock sounded at the front door. He turned and went to answer it.

Gertie Duncan stood on the other side.

"Mornin', Doc," she said quickly, a proud defiance sparking in her dark blue eyes.

"Gertie."

"Sorry t'come by so early."

"It's all right. I've been meaning to come up to see you." He motioned her inside. "Do you want some coffee?"

She shook her head. "This ain't no social call. I . . . I ain't been feelin' well and . . . and I thought maybe I oughta see a doctor."

Now that she mentioned it, he noticed she was pale and drawn. Frowning, he took hold of her arm. "Tell me what seems to be the problem," he said. He steered her toward his office. Once there, she sat on the examination table, and he sat on the chair behind his desk.

Haltingly she described her symptoms, and as he listened he realized how much he'd missed the sound of her voice, the sight of her crooked, gap-toothed smile, the twinkle in her eyes. He'd missed her stubborn refusal to admit defeat. He'd missed listening to the unusual opinions she expressed so freely. Come to think of it, he'd missed everything about Gertie.

Then, when she fell silent, her words finally penetrated his thoughts. He stared at her as first shock and then a crazy kind of pleasure swept through him.

Gertie was pregnant.

He rose suddenly from his chair and strode to the window, needing a moment to collect himself before informing her about the nature of her illness. He wasn't sure exactly how Gertie would take the news.

"Doc?" She sounded scared.

He drew a deep breath, then turned to face her.

Her eyes were wide, her face white. Her chin quivered slightly. "You think I'm gonna die, Doc? Have I got a cancer or somethin'? Is that what's makin' me so sick?"

"No, Gertie, I don't think so."

"How you gonna find out?"

"I don't believe it's even necessary to examine you." He took a step toward her. "I believe I know what's causing your illness."

He watched as she drew herself up straighter and tilted her chin bravely. "Well? You may as well tell me, then."

"Gertie, I think it's quite likely that you are with child."

She stared at him blankly.

"I believe you're pregnant with *my* child."

She shook her head slowly.

"Have you had your monthly flow?"

She blinked, looking as if she didn't understand

what he was asking. After a few moments, her cheeks aflame with color, she shook her head again.

He closed the final distance between them and placed a hand on her shoulder. "I think it would be wise if we took a trip down to Green River and found us a minister."

Gertie's mouth fell open, and now she looked at him as if he'd gone mad. Maybe he had. He certainly hadn't expected to be proposing marriage to her, especially not under these circumstances. Even more surprising was the pleasure he felt at the notion of being married to Gertie.

"I think we should go today. Right now, in fact."

"You want to marry me?" she finally managed to say.

He did a quick mental calculation. "You're only four weeks along. We might be able to create at least a modicum of doubt in people's minds, especially since first babies often arrive late."

"I see. You want to marry me to protect our reputations?"

"If we leave at once, we can be to Green River City by—"

"I don't aim t'go to Green River, Doc." She slid off the examining table. "And I don't aim t'marry you."

"But—"

She jabbed him in the chest with her index finger. "If I was one bit concerned 'bout what folks thought of me, I sure as heck wouldn't be a wrangler, livin' on the range with a bunch of cowboys. If I'd cared, I wouldn't've hauled you off into them mountains and kept you there till you dried out. After all that, I don't reckon I'm gonna start carin' what folks say 'bout me now."

"But, Gertie—"

She jabbed him again, pushing him back a step. Anger flashed in her eyes, along with a glimmer of tears. "If you think I'm gonna marry you just 'cause you're feelin' guilty 'bout this baby, you can just have yourself another think. I'll be hanged if I'm gonna strap myself to a man just so's he won't hafta feel guilty."

"Wait. You don't understand—"

"Oh, I understand all right." She pushed him back another step. "You're still tryin' t'thank me for helpin' you. Well, I've helped plenty of dumb animals in my time, but I didn't ever go off half cracked an' marry one of 'em. And I sure as heck ain't gonna marry you." One final shove bumped him up against the wall. "And that's my final word on the subject." She whirled around and marched out of his office.

Rick remained there, staring at the empty doorway. She'd refused him? That wildcat of a girl had done her best to win his affections, and now that she had them, she'd refused his proposal?

Suddenly he laughed aloud. He felt younger, stronger, and lighter than he'd felt in years. And he wasn't about to let the best thing that had ever happened to him walk out of his life.

Miss Gertie Duncan might think she'd had the last word on the subject, but she—as she'd so aptly put it herself—could just have herself another think.

Hotter than hell. August in Sacramento. And only a few dollars to see me through the week. I shouldn't spend it on booze. The landlady will be wanting her rent. Maybe I'll pay her in another way. Widows are usually willing. They know what it is they're missing, and they're glad to see me.

Hot. Hotter than hell.

Hot like Jane.

I wish I'd killed her when I had the chance. I can't seem to stop thinking about it. She deserved to die. So did that whore. And that sick bastard I switched clothes with, too, more than likely.

But Jane deserves it more. Wish I could have . . .

I don't believe it. Look at that poster. The Raymond Drew Company presents The Taming of the Shrew. *Well, I'll be. Maybe my luck's changing after all. Maybe I'd better go inside and have a look.*

Could she still be with this company after all this time? Faith would have to take me in. Faith is my wife, all legal and proper like. She'd have to do what I tell her to do. No more worrying about money. I could get myself some decent clothes, a bath, a shave.

A woman. I could use a woman. Faith was pretty. She wasn't much fun in bed. She wasn't particularly willing. But she was pretty, and she's my wife. She'd have to take care of me. She'd have to make room for me in her bed.

Her bed. Lord, what I wouldn't like to do if I was in her bed right now.

I never cared much for theaters. Fake opulence with dim lighting disguising how shabby things really are. But look, there's Drew now, making himself look important.

Pompous jackass.

Well, look who's here. Raymond Drew. How have you been? Is Faith with you?

Dead Horse? Where the hell is Dead Horse?

Becca? Who's Becca? Oh yeah, the little one. Sick, you say?

Funny, I'd forgotten about her and the boy, but I'm not about to tell Drew that.

Just a loan. Just enough to get me back with my family. A man's got a right to be with his wife when his child is sick. I know it's been hard on her, me being away so long. I was only trying to make a living. Surely she told you that.

You're a good sort, Mr. Drew. I'll pay you back as soon as I'm able.

The old skinflint. Barely gave me enough to get to Wyoming. But at least I can get out of this town. And if anyone's still looking for me, they won't be looking in some godforsaken place called Dead Horse.

I wonder what Faith will say when she sees me again after all this time.

19

Drake tore open the envelope from William Driscoe and quickly scanned the letter. He cared nothing for the words of greeting, personal reminiscences, and good wishes. He looked for only one thing: George Butler's whereabouts.

In the middle of the second page, he stopped and reread Driscoe's nearly illegible scribbles: "Mr. Butler was found dead a month ago in San Francisco, apparently murdered by thieves. He was buried there and left no belongings. . . ." The letter continued with more particulars, but none of them seemed important at the moment. Only one thing mattered: George Butler was dead.

He wasn't sorry for the thrill he felt when reading those words. How could he be? The man's demise meant a divorce wasn't necessary for Faith. It meant no more delays. It meant they could be married at once.

Letter in hand, he rushed out of his office. He

checked the kitchen, the parlor, and the upstairs before he remembered it was Monday. Wash day. He descended the back staircase, three steps at a time, then dashed out the back door.

"Faith!" he shouted as he rounded the corner.

Holding a sheet to the clothesline with both hands, clothespins in her mouth, she turned toward the sound of his voice.

He held up the letter. "I've heard from Driscoe. He's got news about Butler."

She blanched. The pins fell from her mouth, the sheet from the line, but she didn't seem to notice. "What does he say?" she asked breathlessly, her gaze locked with his.

"He says you've been widowed. Your husband died last month in San Francisco." He grasped her shoulders. "Faith, we can be married at once."

"George is dead?"

That wasn't the reaction he'd been expecting. "Yes. It appears he was murdered by robbers."

"George is dead," she repeated softly. Tears glimmered in her eyes.

Drake regretted not being more tactful about how he'd told her the news. He'd been thinking only of himself, of what it meant to him. All it meant to him was that she was free. Apparently that wasn't all it meant to Faith.

"I should feel something, shouldn't I?" She walked away from the clothesline and the basket of clean laundry, over to the bluff, where she stood staring out at the valley below.

Drake followed her.

"I was his wife for ten years, and I didn't even know when he died." She glanced over at Drake. "That's rather pathetic, don't you think?"

He had no response.

"I wonder if he suffered or if he went quickly."

"Faith." He touched her shoulder.

Her expression was sad, slightly tragic. "I think I must be a terrible person not to mourn him, at least a little."

"You're not terrible." He drew her into his arms.

"I'll have to tell the children. Becca doesn't remember her father at all, but Alex does."

"Would you like me to tell them?"

She shook her head against his chest. "No. It's something I must do."

"Then I'll go with you."

She was silent for a moment, then said, "Yes. I'd like that."

Quiet doubts slipped past his defenses, causing Drake to wonder if she didn't feel more for George Butler than she'd admitted. If she might not have changed her mind about marrying Drake, about loving him. If perhaps her memories of the handsome "archangel," as she'd described George Butler, hadn't made the idea of marriage to Drake unbearable.

"Drake?"

He looked down as she looked up.

She smiled tenderly. "Reverend Arnold will be in Dead Horse this Sunday for services. Perhaps he could marry us then?"

"You're sure?"

"You said yourself we could be married at once."

He pulled her closer to him, lowering his mouth toward hers. "I'll be a good husband, Faith."

"I know you will," she managed to reply before he kissed her, long and hard.

Later that day, after telling the children about their father's death and about her plans to marry again,

Faith took the little mare Drake had given her and went for a ride, following the winding river. After about an hour she dismounted and sat in the shade of some trees growing along the river's bank. She stared at the water as it swept by, glimmering in the sunlight of late afternoon.

It felt odd, knowing George was dead, knowing she was no longer tied to him by the bonds of marriage. She was certain she should feel saddened by his passing, but it was like trying to feel sad over the death of someone she'd never known. George seemed little more than a stranger to her now.

Strange, to be made sad because she wasn't already sad.

She closed her eyes and leaned her head against the tree at her back, memories flitting through her mind with surprising swiftness. The girl of seventeen who'd fallen in love with the dashing young George seemed a stranger to her as well. Sometimes she wondered if that girl had ever existed or if she were merely someone Faith had imagined, like a character from a play or a storybook.

She tried to remember if there had been a time when she'd been happy with George, when her heart had trilled in her chest at the mere sight of him, when each day had begun with a feeling of anticipation because she would be spending time with him. She must have felt that way once, but she couldn't remember. It seemed she had always loved Drake. Even before she'd met him, it seemed as if she'd loved him and only been awaiting his arrival into her life.

And now they were to be wed. There was nothing and no one to keep them apart. There would be no delay while she awaited the granting of a divorce. There would be no danger of losing her children to a man who would neglect them. There would be no scandal, no mean-spirited gossip. By Sunday night she would be Drake's wife. He wouldn't kiss her in the parlor and then send her to her own, lonely bed. She felt a quiver of excitement at the images her train of thought brought to mind.

Somehow she knew Drake's lovemaking would be wonderful. She didn't know how or why she knew it, but she did. Her body yearned for his touch. She had yearned for him for many weeks now. Come Sunday, she would have to yearn no more.

Come Sunday, she would be Mrs. Drake Rutledge.

Gertie leaned on the corral gate, staring dismally at the horse inside. She hadn't worked the gelding today like she'd been supposed to. She hadn't felt like it. All she wanted to do was lie down someplace cool— wherever the heck that might be—and sleep.

"Gertie?"

She glanced over her shoulder and watched Faith's approach.

"I haven't seen much of you since your return. How is Dr. Telford?"

"He's okay."

"And what about you?"

"I'm okay, too." She returned her gaze to the horse in the corral, hoping Faith hadn't seen the truth in her eyes. She was anything *but* okay.

"You haven't forgotten your reading lessons, have you? You were doing so well."

"Ain't had the time for it."

"Well, maybe you'll have the time again soon." Faith touched Gertie's arm. "Have you heard the news about us? About Drake and me?"

"Yeah, I heard. I'm real glad for you." She tried to put on her best smile. She really was happy for Faith. From what she'd seen, the two of them were good for each other. *Like Doc and me.* She nearly laughed aloud at that thought.

"I was hoping you would do me a favor, Gertie."

"If I can, you know I'd be glad to."

"I'd like you to stand up with me."

Gertie gaped at Faith. "You want me t'be part of your weddin'?"

Faith's smile was serene. "Yes."

"Shoot, I'm no good at stuff like that. I proved that back on Independence Day. I got me no business in a dress. I look plumb foolish."

"You don't have to wear a dress."

This time the laughter ripped right out of her chest. "You want me there in my Sunday best buckskins?" she asked with a dash of sarcasm.

"If that's what you want to wear."

Her laughter died abruptly. "You're serious."

"Gertie, you were kind to me from the first day I came to the Jagged R. You've taken an interest in Alex, helped occupy his time while I did my work, taught him all about horses."

"Wasn't nothing."

"You've been my friend. I want you to be my witness when I marry Drake."

Her friend. A lump formed in Gertie's throat, making it hard to reply. She could use a friend right about now. She wondered what Faith would think if she knew her *friend* was in the family way. Not that it mattered to her what folks thought, but all the same . . .

"Gertie? Are you certain you're all right?"

She shoved away from the corral. "'Course I am,"

she snapped, suddenly irritable. "What do you think's wrong with me?"

Faith raised an eyebrow but said nothing.

Gertie wished she could confide in her, but she didn't know how. She'd always been tight-lipped about her own business. Always had thought it best to keep her private matters to herself.

As if understanding Gertie's dilemma, Faith said, "You can talk to me any time about anything. Just remember that."

She shrugged, as if Faith's offer didn't mean the world to her.

"We're planning the wedding for Sunday, immediately following services. You'll be there?"

"I'll be there."

"Thank you." Faith stepped forward and kissed Gertie's cheek, then hurried back to the house.

I coulda been married by Sunday myself, she thought as she watched Faith disappear through the back door.

It had been three days since Rick had told her she was expecting his baby. Three days since he'd said they should get married right away. Three days, and she hadn't seen hide nor hair of him.

Her mood darkened.

Hang it all. What was going to happen to her now? A pregnant wrangler. Wasn't that going to go over big with Mr. Rutledge? He'd been right fair to let her have some time off to take care of Rick, but he wasn't bound to be as generous when she couldn't do her work because she was increasing. And what was she going to do with the baby after it was born? Who was going to take care of it while she was working? In the past few days she'd mulled over those same questions many times, but she'd never had an answer for them. Still didn't.

A vision of herself, holding a tiny baby in her arms, popped suddenly into her head. She felt an odd warmth in her heart. My baby, she thought with a sense of wonder. I'm gonna have a baby all my own.

For the first time since hearing the news, she smiled. Really smiled.

"Little one," she whispered, "I don't reckon I know how I'm gonna do it, but I'm gonna take care of you. You'll see. We'll get on just fine, the two of us."

Whether by design or by chance, none of the hands were present for supper that evening. Faith and Drake sat at opposite ends of the table, with the children on either side.

Like a family, Faith thought as she passed a serving bowl to Alex.

It still didn't seem real to her. Only yesterday she'd thought there was a long wait before her. She had prepared herself for it. She had even feared tempting fate by wanting Drake so badly, had wondered if she would ever be able to marry him. And now she'd been given her greatest wish. She was going to be Drake's bride on Sunday, only six precious days away. Her future lay before her like a great banquet table full of choice delights.

Suddenly she realized she was staring off into space. She brought her gaze back into focus. That's when she saw Drake had been watching her.

"Whatever you were thinking must have been good." His tone was teasing, his voice low and suggestive.

She smiled. "It was."

"Ma?"

"What is it, Alex?" she asked, pulling her gaze reluctantly from her future husband's.

"I was wondering something." Her son frowned down at his plate.

"Yes?"

"Well, you said if we want, we can call Mr. Rutledge 'Pa' after you're married." He glanced quickly at Drake, then back at his plate.

More softly she said, "Yes," and waited for him to tell her what was troubling him.

His frown darkened. "Well, if he's my pa"—he looked at her again—"how can I work for him as his wrangler?"

Relieved, she might have laughed except for the seriousness of her son's expression. "I think you should ask Mr. Rutledge."

There was no amusement on Drake's face. He was as serious as Alex himself. "Come over here, Alex."

Her son rose and went over to stand beside Drake's chair.

Drake put his hands on Alex's shoulders and leaned toward him. "It takes a lot of work to run a ranch like the Jagged R. From everybody, whether family or hired hand."

Faith saw Drake's fingers tighten.

"You're going to be my son, come Sunday. We're going to be a family. You, your ma, Becca, and me. And the Jagged R will be your home. You don't need to worry about anybody hiring you. You'll do the work because it will be your ranch. Your home. Yours and your brothers and sisters."

"I don't have any brothers."

Drake's smile was patient. "I hope you will someday."

Alex shrugged, as if that question were settled. "So, I can work as your wrangler when I get older?"

"Yes, son. You can work as my wrangler when you get older."

Warm contentment spread through Faith. She'd just seen a glimpse of her future.

And the future looked good.

20

Faith awoke with a start. She sat up, placing one hand over her rapidly beating heart. The details of the nightmare had already been swallowed into some dark place in her mind, leaving only remnants of terror. Sweat trickled down the back of her neck and between her breasts.

She rose and went to the window, hoping for a cool breeze to soothe her, but the night was still. A sliver of moon was directly overhead, halfway on its trek across the sky.

It was just the heat, she told herself. She was feeling oppressed by too many hot days in a row. That was what had caused the nightmare. There was nothing to fear.

She had a sudden, desperate urge to go to Drake's bedroom, to lie down beside him and ask him to hold her, much as Becca did with her mother when she'd had a bad dream. There was a strange ache in Faith's heart that made her want to keen.

Panic ignited, forcing her from her bedroom. She ran down the flight of stairs, not stopping until she reached Drake's door. She raised her hand as if to knock, then thought better of it. Instead she hurried down the last flight and stepped out onto the porch. Finally she descended the front steps and walked across the swath of lawn toward the bluff.

Here at last she found a light breeze, rising up from the valley below. She forced her breathing to slow, forced her jangled nerves to calm.

The nightmare was the result of exhaustion, she told herself. It was all the work and planning for the wedding and not enough sleep. That was all. Nothing more.

The days since Drake had received William Driscoe's letter had been happy, contented ones. Alex idolized Drake, and Becca was completely under his spell, too. Sadie Gold had once again organized the women of Dead Horse, this time to help with Faith's wedding. She had them all baking and sewing and heaven only knew what else.

At the ranch, there had been plenty of good-natured ribbing to go hand in hand with the congratulations. Faith had enjoyed every moment of it. They were all her family, she'd realized—Parker, Gertie, Swede, Johnny, Dan, Will, and Roy. She'd grown to care for each and every one of them. This was her home. She had everything she would ever need or want right here.

In truth, her life on the stage seemed far away and long ago. It seemed to have happened to someone else entirely. Her new life was harder in many ways, the work never-ending. But it was infinitely more satisfying to her at the end of the day when she tucked her

children into their beds and saw the healthy glow on
their cheeks, heard the laughter in their voices.

And evenings with Drake were always pure bliss.
She'd never been kissed so thoroughly, never felt
such urgency for time to pass. Her love for Drake
increased by the minute, as did her happiness.

As those thoughts filled her head, the effects of
the nightmare drained away and she felt once again
the rightness of what lay before her. She let out a
long sigh as she combed back her long hair with her
fingers. Night air cooled her scalp, and she was
thankful for a slight respite from the heat. She
turned and looked at the house, the roof rising
above the treetops. She could see the window to her
room—only it wouldn't be hers for much longer. In
a few short days she would move her things down
one floor and into the master bedchamber. In a few
short days she would be Drake's bride. In a few
short days . . .

She shivered again, but not from a nightmare or
from the cooler air. This time it was her imagination,
toying with the idea of Drake's lovemaking.

"Just a few more days," she whispered, smiling in
anticipation. "Just a few."

There was no doubt about it, Rick thought as he
slapped the reins against the horse's rump. Gertie
Duncan was a stubborn woman. Otherwise she
would have come to her senses by now and returned
to town to see him.

He grinned, almost looking forward to the coming
confrontation. He felt surprisingly lighthearted and
sure of himself. Of course, he knew it wasn't going to
be easy, changing Gertie's mind about marrying him.

He doubted anything would ever be easy when it came to Gertie.

He glanced up at the clear blue sky. An eagle soared overhead, winging its way toward the mountains to the west. The sun, still early in its daily trek, had already evaporated the morning dew from the range, and the summer air smelled fresh and clean. From up on the ridge, he heard a young boy's shout of pleasure.

Not long ago, he wouldn't have taken note of any of these simple things, not even when he'd been sober. He'd always been too busy wishing he could drink again, resenting the pull the bottle had on him. But no more.

He had Gertie to thank for so much, but his thanks wouldn't be welcomed. Gertie didn't understand he could still be grateful for the help and support she'd given without confusing it with the love that had taken hold of his heart.

And now she was carrying his child. It seemed an impossibility, a miracle. Only a few short months ago he'd been hoping James and Nancy would give him a grandchild sometime soon. Instead they were buried in the Dead Horse cemetery. Perhaps Gertie's pregnancy was simply the opening of a window after a door had been closed.

His horse and buggy topped the rise, and the Jagged R came into view. A moment later he saw Gertie on horseback in the field just beyond the barn. She called something to Alex as the boy guided his mount through a maze of poles stuck in the ground.

He steered the buggy in her direction. He still didn't know what he was going to say. Whatever he came up with, she would probably dismiss it. He'd hurt her, and for that he was immensely sorry.

Somehow he had to make her see that she'd been right and he'd been wrong.

She turned her head and saw him. The smile left her face, replaced by a frown.

When he drew near to Gertie, he reined in, then got out of the buggy. "Morning." He waved at the boy and called, "Good morning, Alex."

Alex waved back but didn't stop riding.

Rick returned his gaze to Gertie. Her hat hung from its leather string against her back. Her chestnut hair gleamed in the morning sunlight. Her complexion was tanned, but even so, he could see the splash of pink in her cheeks as he walked toward her. He loved it when she blushed like that.

"You haven't been back to town, Gertie."

She glanced toward Alex. "Been busy."

"Too busy to see me?"

She ignored him.

"I've missed you."

That caused her to look over.

"I'd like to talk with you."

"Don't know that we have anything more t'say to each other, Doc. I think maybe we said it all."

"I wish you'd call me Rick."

She cocked an eyebrow.

"Would you mind dismounting? Just for a moment? I'm going to get a crick in my neck from looking up at you."

She shrugged, then did as he'd asked.

Rick took a deep breath, searching his mind for the right words to say. He felt as tongue-tied as a boy just out of short pants. "Gertie," he began hesitantly, "I've made a lot of mistakes in my life. Through the years, I failed my wife, my son, my patients. I don't want to make another mistake with you."

Hurt flashed in her eyes.

He took hold of her hand, squeezing tightly so she wouldn't pull away. "No. You've misunderstood. The mistake I mean would be losing you." His grip tightened even more. "Common sense says I'm too old for you, and maybe I am. But I don't care. I want you with me, Gertie."

"Why?"

"Not because of guilt, although I shouldn't have taken advantage of your innocence when we were alone. I am guilty of that."

He lifted his free hand to run his fingers over her hair.

"Not because you're pregnant, although I want the baby to have a father."

He moved closer to her, saw her eyes widen.

"Not because I'm grateful for what you've done for me, for saving my life when I didn't think it was worth anything, although I'm glad you did."

He brought his mouth close to hers, close enough to feel her breath mingle with his own.

"Not because of any of those things."

"Then why, Doc?" she whispered hoarsely.

He kissed her, long and slow, cradling her head between his hands, and when he released her he answered, "Because I've come to care for you."

She swore softly.

"That wasn't quite the response I was hoping for," he confessed, his voice teasing.

Her heart thumping loudly, Gertie took a step back. She jammed her thumbs into the waistband of her trousers and turned her head, staring off at Alex. The boy was still riding through the training course she'd set up for him, oblivious of her turmoil.

Hell's bells! What was she supposed to do? She'd

already convinced herself she didn't need Rick
Telford in her life, that she could get along just fine
without him, that she wasn't cut out to be a wife.
What was she supposed to say to him now?

As if he'd heard her unspoken question, he said,
"Marry me, Gertie. Not because of the baby or for any
other reason except that you care for me, too."

"What if there wasn't no baby, Doc?"

"I'd want to marry you anyway."

She wished she could believe him. She wanted to
believe him.

Rick took hold of her arm and drew her back
around, forcing her to face him once again. "*Do* you
care for me?"

"Look at me, Doc. I ain't wife material. I wear
trousers an' I smoke tobacco an' I bust broncs an' live
in a bunkhouse with a bunch of sweaty, smelly cowpokes. I don't speak proper. I can't read no better
than Alex over there, even though his ma's been
helpin' me some. I'd make a mighty poor doctor's
wife."

His smile was patient and understanding. "Then
you shouldn't have set out to make a doctor fall in
love with you."

She felt like crying, something she tried never to
do, even on the worst of days. Wranglers didn't cry.
Not if they were going to be accepted by the other
cowpokes on a ranch. She'd learned that a long time
ago.

"I'm all confused," she mumbled, speaking the
truth before she could stop herself.

"I know." He drew her close. "So was I for a while.
But I'm not any longer." He kissed her. "Marry me,
Gertie."

Her heart pounded so hard, she could scarcely

hear herself think. She went all weak in the knees, and her throat was choked with tears. Somehow she managed to say, "I reckon you'll be plenty sorry if I do."

Rick laughed. "I doubt it."

Then he kissed her again, and the last of her resistance went out of her.

"All right, Doc——" she began when the kiss ended.

"Rick," he interrupted.

She sighed. "All right, Rick, I'll marry you. But don't say I never warned you how sorry you'd be."

"I won't."

"And we won't say or do nothin' until all the hullabaloo for Faith and Mr. Rutledge is over. Agreed?"

"Agreed." He was grinning as though he'd just won first prize at the state fair.

"Nothin' fancy for us, neither. We just go down to Green River an' do it nice an' quiet like."

"If that's what you want."

She scowled at him. "Don't be so damned agreeable."

His smile only broadened. "Okay."

She cursed again, then spun around and strode to her horse. She ignored the stirrup and swung up onto the saddle using only the saddle horn. Gathering the reins in one hand, she returned her gaze to Rick one final time. "Don't think I'll be changin' for you. I am just who I am."

Something subtle altered his smile into a look of tenderness. "I wouldn't change a single hair on your head, Gertie Duncan," he answered softly. "Not one single strand."

She stared at him hard, hoping beyond hope he was telling her the truth and scared spitless he wasn't, that he was offering to marry her only because of the baby. She cursed the rainy day back at the start of summer when she'd realized she was falling for Rick Telford. She cursed the moment she'd asked Faith to help her look more like a woman. And she cursed the night she'd discovered the more intimate side of what being a woman meant. Her life had been a whole heck of a lot simpler when all she'd had to worry about was a bunch of cantankerous mustangs who needed busting.

With a sound of exasperation, she spun her horse around and raced away.

George Butler despised riding in the emigrant car among those too poor to buy a decent seat in the passenger car. When he'd come west with Jane, they had traveled in the *Silver Palace* with their own private berths hidden behind rich crimson curtains trimmed in gold that hung from the ceiling and trailed on the soft Axminster carpet.

In contrast with those earlier accommodations, the emigrant car had only a coal stove, a single convenience for both men and women, and rows of benches too short for anything but a young child. That was all. No berths. No curtains. No carpets. No comfort.

After leaving a sweltering Sacramento—a hundred and five degrees at midday—the train had arrived in Truckee near midnight. The temperature had fallen to nineteen degrees above zero, and George had thought he might freeze to death before they finally left.

Now, two days later, after departing the Mormon town of Ogden, the train was once again traversing the dusty plains of Utah, the land white and glaring. By mutual agreement among the passengers, the windows had been left closed to shut out the fine alkaline dust that irritated their eyes and nostrils.

Dust and heat. Heat and dust. Dust and heat.

There was little to see outside to break the monotony of travel, but George chose to stare out the window rather than respond to the chatter of the old crone with the two blackened front teeth who sat beside him. Hour after hour he watched as the train chugged its way through desolate country—muddy streams and rough, arid valleys that occasionally narrowed into canyons, sudden buttes and sagebrush, jackrabbits and antelope.

The only thing that improved his spirits was anticipation of the surprise he would see on Faith's face when he showed up in Dead Horse. Raymond Drew had said the little girl—what was the brat's name again?—was sick. She might even have died by this time, which could be a problem for him.

Not that he cared particularly one way or the other. He'd never wanted babies hanging around. But if the girl had died, Faith and the boy might have moved on. That wasn't a happy prospect. He needed Faith to be there.

Chances that she wouldn't be there were slim, however. Raymond Drew had been certain he'd have heard if Faith had joined another company.

No, she was still there. George just had a feeling about it.

He grinned at his reflection in the window glass. Faith was going to be surprised all right. She'd probably spent the past two or three years crying her eyes out, missing him. She'd be glad to see him after all this time, and he could think of a few interesting ways to celebrate.

Yes, sir. Faith was going to be surprised to see him.

21

August 29, 1886

 Today is my wedding day.
 It is early morning as I sit at the table in my room on the third floor of this house. The sun has yet to peek over the horizon. The sky is slate gray, in that half state between dark and light. Alex and Becca are asleep in the adjoining room. The house is quiet. It seems only I am awake and eager for this day to begin.
 It has been more than a year since my last entry into this journal. I don't know why I awakened this morning, wanting to put my thoughts down. Perhaps one day, when I am old and gray, I will read these words and smile in memory of the young woman, so in love, so happy. And that is what I am.
 So in love.
 So happy.
 Looking back over the days since I learned I have

been a widow for several months and, therefore, free to marry Drake, it seems both no time at all and as if it has been forever. Perhaps that's because George's memory has faded into near nothingness and because Drake is real and alive and here. Whatever the reason, I am ready to move forward with my life.

Sometimes I fear that so much happiness, built upon the death of another, must surely be a sin for which I'll be punished. There are moments when dread strikes my heart, and I await the moment when it will all be taken from me.

Do I, Faith Butler, deserve such a wealth of joy as Drake has given me?

There has been so much to do in preparation for the wedding, and I am impatient for it to be over, impatient for the moment to arrive when I am truly Drake's wife. In my heart, I am his wife already.

Yesterday we returned to the parlor when the day was done and the children in their beds, as has been our habit in recent weeks. It was not the first time he has held me in his arms and kissed me with passion, but it seemed so. I thought I might be driven mad with desire. I wonder if I should be ashamed for the things I feel and think. For the things I want him to do to me and I to him. Yet I cannot be ashamed, even if I should be. They seem so right, so natural.

Time goes on crutches till
Love have all his rites.

I did not understand the truth of those lines ever so much as I do now. I could scarcely sleep last night for thoughts of the night yet to come. Time crawls until I can be fully and completely his.

Never once had I thought to love again. Certainly never did I expect to give my heart so completely as I have given it now. This is, I think, simply another form of madness, but if so, I am willingly mad. It is tremendously freeing to be able to trust someone again, to not hold others at bay for fear of what hurt might be incurred later.

Today marks the beginning of a new life for all of us. Not just the children and me, but Drake too. I look at him now and cannot remember the angry man whom I met in his darkened library. I know he was once so, but I cannot remember him. And only within these pages can I confess that I am glad Larissa Dearborne was a stupid woman. If not, I would never have met Drake. If not, I would not know such bliss.

Yes, I am glad Larissa was a fool. Selfish of me, I know. Drake suffered because of her, but out of his hurt came the man I love, the man who loves me.

The day has arrived. The first rays of sunshine are spilling through my window onto the floor. The robins have begun to sing in the trees, as if rejoicing for me.

It is going to be a glorious day. I can feel it.

I altered my favorite dress, the gold-and-brown stripe with the silk polonaise. Sadie made me a gift of a felt hat with an aigrette in front that matches the gown perfectly. A new pair of tan suede gloves completes my wedding attire.

Will Drake think me beautiful?

Silly question. It has always meant nothing to me when people complimented my looks, yet I long for Drake's approval. I want him to think me beautiful, to desire me. As I desire him.

I hear sounds in the next room. The children must be waking. It is time for me to close this entry.

Today is my wedding day.

And tonight, my wedding night.

*   *   *

Drake mounted the stairs to the third floor, glad that after today it wouldn't be necessary to do so. After today, when he went looking for Faith, he would find her in his own bedchamber.

Pausing at her door, he rapped softly. "Faith?"

"Come in."

He twisted the knob and pushed the door open before him. His gaze immediately sought and found her. She was standing in front of the looking glass, her hands up near her head as she secured her hat into place. As he entered the room, her arms lowered and she turned slowly to face him.

He stopped abruptly, whispering her name like a prayer. Never had he seen her look more enchanting than she did at this moment. It wasn't her clothes, although they were lovely, the gold color flattering to her complexion. It was more the expression she wore and what it did to his heart. She was beautiful in countless ways, ways that mere words failed to define.

He held out the small box in his right hand. "I brought you something."

"Not another gift." She smiled as she shook her head. "You've spoiled me enough already."

He moved farther into the room. "I'll never spoil you enough." He stopped, took one of her hands, and placed the small box in it. "Go on. Open it."

She lifted the lid and a gasp slipped through her parted lips. "Drake . . . "

"It was my mother's."

She gave her head a slow shake. "I can't—"

"I want you to have it."

She lifted the gold necklace, set with teardrop-shaped topaz stones, from the box.

"It matches your dress," he said, stating the obvious.

She nodded. "As if it were planned," she whispered, more to herself than to him.

His hands on her shoulders, he turned her to face the mirror, then met her gaze in the reflection. "Maybe it *was* planned. Only not by us."

She covered his hand with her own. "You know I don't need gifts to make me happy."

"I know. That's one of the reasons I love giving them to you." He kissed the smooth curve of her neck, then took the necklace and fastened it in place. "I think it's time we got the children and went to town."

"Drake?" She turned, a sudden urgency in her voice. "You've made me so terribly, wonderfully happy. I didn't know I could feel this way." The words rushed out of her, like water bursting through an earthen dam. "I never dreamed, never hoped I would ever find a love like this. Sometimes, I'm afraid I'll wake up and find it's all been a dream and that you were only someone I imagined. Or that I'm too happy and you'll be taken from me." She swallowed hard. "I wasn't a good wife to George. I didn't know how to make him happy or to please him. He turned to other women for his pleasures. He said I was . . . cold."

His heart tightened in his chest as he drew her into his embrace. "Ah, Faith, you're anything but cold." He brushed his lips against her temple, lowering his voice. "You don't have to be afraid that I'll disappear. I won't ever leave you, no matter what." He was tempted to remove her hat and then her hairpins. He was tempted to remove her dress and make love to her right then and there. "You taught me how to trust again, Faith. You can trust me, too."

He heard her draw a deep, shaky breath, then she stepped back from him, offering a quivery smile. "Nerves," she explained with a tiny shrug of her shoulders.

"I know." He took hold of her arm. "Come along, Mrs. Butler. I want to change your name to match my own."

A true smile brightened her face. "I want that, too."

Everyone was there. Gertie Duncan and all the Jagged R cowboys. Sadie and Joseph Gold and their children. Rick Telford. The O'Rourkes and the Hornes. The widows O'Connell and Ashley. Jed Smith, wearing his false leg in honor of the occasion.

Benches had been placed in the shade of the trees near the river. Most people had come there directly from church services, but even those who had not attended church, like the Golds and Stretch Barns, were dressed in their Sunday best.

Standing nearest the river, talking to the reverend, was Drake. He looked dashing in his black coat and trousers, white shirt, and gloves. In all Faith's years in the theater, she'd never seen anyone she thought more handsome, anyone who commanded more respect or attention.

"Is it truly possible he wants to marry me?" she whispered to herself as she stared out the back door of the hotel.

"What?" Gertie asked.

Faith gave her head a slight shake as she turned to look at the woman beside her.

Gertie had indeed worn her fancy buckskins, and Faith thought she looked wonderful. The soft clothing had fringe along the outside seam of the trousers as well as across the back of the jacket. In honor of the special occasion, Gertie's dark curls were freshly washed, shiny clean. Her eyes sparkled with pleasure, and there was a look about her that made Faith wonder if Gertie were keeping some sort of secret.

She might have asked, but just then Becca skipped through the doorway. "Mama, Reverend Arnold says it's time to begin. You're to come out now."

Faith's stomach fluttered, and her mouth went dry. It was time. It was about to happen. It was real.

"Ready?" Gertie asked.

Faith reached for the bouquet of late summer wildflowers Becca had picked that morning on the way into town. "I'm ready."

Gertie and Becca led the way out of the hotel. Faith hesitated a moment, then followed them into the sunlight.

Her gaze was locked on Drake.

Drake . . .

Her future . . .

Her happiness . . .

Her all.

From the window of his hotel room, George watched as Faith came into view. He knew it was Faith, even though he couldn't see her face. No other woman he'd ever seen had hair quite that color.

So, she thinks she's going to marry another man, does she? He grunted. *Not likely.*

And to think he might have arrived in this two-bit town too late. When he'd registered last night, he'd asked the proprietress if she knew Faith Butler.

"Of course," the woman had answered. "Are you here for her wedding? Isn't it exciting? To think she's going to marry Mr. Rutledge tomorrow. They say he's very wealthy. He must be to own that big ranch of his. I'll confess to you, he frightens me just a little to look at him, but we can be thankful he's decided to help this town. Once the railroad comes up, we'll all prosper. I was afraid I would be forced out before too long. Thank heavens it won't happen now."

George had been going to sign his last name as Harvard, the alias he'd been using since leaving San Francisco, but then he thought better of it. Quickly he'd scrawled his real name across the registration book.

"Butler?" Mrs. O'Connell had asked upon seeing his signature. "Are you family?"

"Yes," he'd replied evenly, "but Faith isn't expecting me. I'd like to keep my presence a secret until tomorrow." He gave her one of his most charming smiles. "Will you help me do that, Mrs. O'Connell?"

He hadn't known for certain what he intended to do, but now, as he watched Faith walk down the aisle between the rough wooden benches, he made a quick decision. Mr. Rutledge might very well be his ticket to a life of ease. If he waited until after the two of them were married, the law just might become involved. George couldn't afford to have that happen.

And if things didn't go as he was beginning to hope, he would at the very least have a wife to support him and a town where he wasn't known.

He slipped his arms into the sleeves of his suit coat, then tried to brush the travel dust from it. Afterward he smoothed his hair back with a dab of water on the palms of his hands. A quick glance in the mirror told him he looked as presentable as possible.

"Good enough for a dead husband," he said, then smiled. "Actually, *remarkably* good for a dead husband."

"Dearly beloved . . . "

Faith was only vaguely aware of Reverend Arnold's exhortations regarding the union between man and wife. Her pulse was racing too fast for her to concentrate on anything except wishing it to be over. In a few minutes she would be transformed into Mrs. Drake Rutledge. It mattered little to her what the reverend said or how long or short the ceremony was. She just wished it to be over.

"If any man has just cause why these two . . . "

Her heart was happy, her soul content. Only a few months ago, if someone had told her what would be happening today, she would have scoffed. But look at her now. It was—

"I believe I have just cause."

There was a collective sucking in of breath from the wedding guests. For one terrible moment, Faith's gaze locked with Drake's. Then he turned around. But Faith couldn't seem to move. Even her heart threatened to cease its beating.

In a disapproving voice the reverend asked, "And just who are you, sir?"

"I am the bride's husband."

More gasps followed the statement, then a buzz of whispers began. Faith felt as if she were starving for air.

No! No, it can't be true. It can't be.

"Am I not your husband, Faith, my dear?"

She turned slowly, wanting to delay that terrible moment of truth a little longer. But it was true, and it couldn't be avoided.

He stood behind the wedding guests. He was thin, and his clothes looked worn. Yet he still had an air of assurance. Tall, golden-haired, handsome. George, the avenging archangel, returned from the dead.

How very like him, she thought, feeling the insane urge to laugh.

She became aware of Drake's fingers tightening on her arm. She glanced up, wanting nothing more than to take hold of him and never let go.

It had happened. This had been the nightmare she couldn't recall. To be this close to heaven only to find the gates closed and locked. To find Drake only to lose him.

Then she saw something in his gaze that calmed her fears. He was here. He was with her. Together they could face anything. She had planned to get a divorce from George. She still could. Drake would help her. She needn't be afraid. It would all work out. It had to. They—she and Drake—had been brought together for a purpose. He would see that this nightmare stopped. He would see that it turned out all right.

George strolled confidently down the break between the benches, drawing her gaze back to him. "It's fortunate I arrived when I did, my dear. It would have been rather messy to find yourself with two husbands. Don't you think?"

Drake stepped forward. "What do you want, Butler?"

"Ah, an enraged bridegroom." George smirked as he lifted an eyebrow. "How positively quaint."

"You were reported dead," Drake challenged.

"So I heard. However, as you can clearly see, the report was false. I am very much alive." He waved a hand at the onlookers. "But perhaps we should find someplace more private to continue this discussion."

Faith tried to think of something to say but came up blank.

George gave her a cheerless smile, then turned toward the front bench where Alex and Becca were sitting. "Are these my children? Look how they've grown." He hunkered down and motioned them to approach him. "Come here and give your loving father a welcome back."

True terror sluiced through Faith. This was what she'd feared most of all. She understood the workings of George's mind, and she knew exactly how he meant to hurt her.

She moved quickly to place herself between him and her children. "Leave them alone, George," she whispered urgently. "Please."

"I don't understand." He rose from the ground. "I'm simply returning to my family."

"Whatever it is you want, you may have."

He looked genuinely surprised. "Whatever I want? But, my dearest wife, it is you and the children I want. Nothing more. Just you."

Her eyes filled with tears, and her throat was tight. "You're lying," she said, but only George was close enough to hear the words.

"You wound me to the quick." He covered his heart with the palm of his hand. "To the quick, my love."

She felt herself being sucked into some horrible vortex from which there was no escape. She wondered if she were about to faint. Drake's hand on her elbow saved her from finding out.

"I believe Mr. Butler is right. We should talk in private." He glanced over his shoulder. "Sorry, Reverend Arnold, but the ceremony is over. Alex. Becca. Get in the buggy."

Faith felt a sense of relief as the children hurried to do as they'd been told. *Run!* she wanted to scream. *Run away!*

"Come along, Faith," Drake said more softly.

"I beg your pardon, but—" George began.

Drake stopped him with a glare. "You may follow us to my house."

"See here—"

"I said to follow us, Mr. Butler."

"I haven't a horse."

Drake swept a gaze over the rapt townsfolk. "Parker, see that Mr. Butler gets a horse." Then, with a firm grasp on her arm, he drew Faith toward the waiting buggy.

"Mama," Becca said when Faith was settled on the front seat, "is that really my papa, like Alex says?" She hesitated, then continued, "I thought Mr. Rutledge was going to be my papa?"

Faith choked on a sob.

"I am, Becca," Drake responded firmly. "Just not today." He slapped the reins, and the horse shot forward.

No one spoke during the ride home. Faith didn't know if George followed, didn't have the courage to glance behind her to find out.

He'll take my children. He'll take my children.

It wouldn't happen. Drake wouldn't allow it to happen.

But how could Drake stop George? He was the children's father. If he—

No, it wasn't going to happen that way. Surely this day would not end this way. Not today. Not today of all days.

Today was to have been her wedding day.

22

George Butler might never have performed on the stage, but Drake recognized immediately that he was a consummate actor. No doubt George had convinced the entire town—with the exception of Drake and Faith—of his earnest desire to return to the bosom of his family.

And his performance didn't end when he entered Drake's house.

"So, this is where you've been living," George said to Faith as his gaze swept the parlor. "My dear, I always thought you had the beauty and even the talent to make a name for yourself. I just never imagined that your talent lay outside the theater." His insinuation was clear in his expression and the inflection of his voice.

Drake would have struck him then and there, but Faith's hand on his arm stopped him. She stepped forward, her head held high, her shoulders rigid. "What is it you want, George?" She sounded calm, too, just as any great actress would.

Her husband offered a mocking smile. "I believe I explained quite clearly in front of your wedding guests. I want to be with my family. Thank God I arrived when I did. As I said earlier, two husbands would have been an embarrassment. Not to mention illegal." His gaze shifted to Drake. "I believe I heard you're an attorney, Mr. Rutledge. Isn't it illegal to marry another man's wife? Couldn't one of you go to jail?"

Faith didn't give Drake a chance to reply. "You said you were going to divorce me."

"I never got around to it. And I'm glad that I didn't. I have learned the error of my ways. I've come to beg your forgiveness."

"What about Jane?"

"Jane?" George's expression hardened, and a look of fury flashed in his eyes. A moment later the look was gone, replaced by a careless shrug. "Oh, Jane. She and I were never suited. We parted company a long time ago. I realized I'd made a tragic mistake in leaving you, Faith. You're my wife. My place is with you and the children." He glanced toward the hallway. "By the way, where *are* the children?"

Drake answered, "In their room. We thought it best if we spoke to you alone."

"*You* thought it was best?" George's voice showed his contempt. "You have no right to decide what's best for my children."

Sheer willpower kept Drake from tearing the man limb from limb.

Faith sank onto the sofa. Her gaze fell to her hands, folded in her lap. "I don't love you, George. I want a divorce."

Drake saw right through the other man's pained

expression. He'd met others like him through the years, petty dictators of their own little worlds who took joy in hurting those weaker than they. George Butler wasn't here because he cared about his family. He was here for himself and only for himself.

Faith looked up, tears swimming in her eyes. "I want a divorce," she repeated.

Her husband shook his head. "If I can't change your mind, I suppose you shall have one. But the children will miss you, I'm sure."

"George," she whispered hoarsely.

"I'm not going to be separated from them again. Not by my choice. I erred in leaving them once. I won't allow us to be parted again."

Drake couldn't bear it. He saw Faith's heart breaking and couldn't take it any longer. He stepped over to stand beside her, placing his hand on her shoulder. "I think it's time you left my house, Butler."

Without flinching, George answered, "As soon as the children are ready to go with me."

"You aren't taking Alex and Becca anywhere." Drake clenched and unclenched a fist.

"I *will* take them. You may be an important man in this town, Mr. Rutledge, but that won't stop me. Faith has been living with you. It's apparent to anyone what's been going on here. That won't sit well with a judge. He'll take those kids from her, and she'll never be allowed to see them again."

"Faith is my housekeeper."

George ignored Drake's interruption. "What sort of mother can she be, to live in sin with a man in sight of the whole town? There must be plenty of talk, especially after today." He sneered as his gaze shifted to Faith. "You may have your divorce, my dear wife, if that's what you insist upon, but you'll never see your children again. The law will see to that."

Faith was crying softly now, tears streaming down her face. "Why are you doing this, George? Why?"

His expression turned once again to innocent concern. "Why? Because I love you, of course. I love you and the children, and I want us to be together again. You promised before God to be my wife until death do us part. Didn't that pledge mean anything to you?"

"Get out," Drake growled, his patience snapping. "Now."

"The childr—"

Drake took a threatening step forward. "Get out!"

Some of George's arrogance drained from his face. "Very well. I'll go. But I'll be back tomorrow." He picked up his hat. "Make up your mind what you're going to do, Faith. If I must, I'll send for the marshal to take them from here. The children are going to be with me. If you want to be with them, you'll be ready to leave, too."

Drake followed George into the entry hall and watched as he left the house. His chest tightened. His mind raced. He dreaded returning to the parlor. He knew Faith would look up at him, tears streaking her cheeks, and expect him to tell her everything would be all right.

He couldn't do that.

The law was on George's side. According to a long established tenet of the American legal system, fathers were the natural guardians of children. Even with the changing times, there was still a danger that George would gain custody. Drake had told Faith once that a judge could be reasoned with. Perhaps the promise had come too easily.

He raked his fingers through his hair, still wanting to do bodily harm to George Butler. He knew he must discover something that would give Faith the edge, and he must find it soon. George had returned with a declaration before many witnesses that he wanted to be reunited with his family, but Drake was certain it was a lie. He suspected Faith's husband had little if any money left. Money—that was what he was truly after. Drake wasn't fooled for a moment that George simply wanted to return to his wife and children. But how could he keep George legally from taking Alex and Becca?

"Drake?"

He turned and found Faith standing in the parlor archway. "He's gone," he told her.

"He can take the children. There's nothing we can do to stop him, is there?"

He said nothing. He'd rather be silent than lie to her.

"God forgive me," she whispered as more tears fell from her eyes. "I wanted him dead."

Drake stepped forward and took her into his arms, holding her close, murmuring senseless sounds of comfort, all the while pondering murder in his heart.

Faith moved through the remainder of the day by rote. While Drake closeted himself in his library, searching for answers in his law books, she saw that her children changed out of their Sunday clothes and answered their questions with words that explained nothing but were the best she could do. She prepared the noon meal for the subdued ranch hands, ignoring their looks of concern. She felt numb—and was grateful for it.

At supper, where all pretended this was just a normal day, the conversation was nearly nonexistent. By the time it was over, Becca was close to tears and Alex was mutinous.

"Can I be excused, Mama?" Becca whispered in a choked voice.

"Yes, you may."

Her daughter slipped from the table and ran up the back staircase. After a rebellious look at Faith, Alex followed close behind his sister. One by one, the cowboys likewise excused themselves, and within moments only Faith and Drake remained at the table.

She felt a strange panic squeezing her chest. She didn't want to be alone with Drake. She didn't want to face what had to be faced. Not yet. She kept her gaze locked on her untouched supper plate, pretending he wasn't there.

"Faith?"

She shook her head.

"Faith, look at me."

Reluctantly she lifted her eyes.

"We can't ignore it any longer."

"The law will give him the children. It's what I feared most."

"It's up to us to show why he shouldn't be allowed—"

"But the law is still on his side, isn't it? Simply because he's their father."

Drake was silent for a long time, his gaze unwavering. She could see his own heartache, which only increased her panic. Finally, in a gentle voice he replied, "Yes." He paused, then added, "But he won't succeed in keeping them."

"We can't be sure of that, can we?"

"Faith—"

"Please, Drake." She rose from her chair. "I can't talk about it now. I need some time alone." She fled, leaving the house, swift footsteps carrying her quickly down the hillside and toward the river. She'd found comfort and answers there before. Surely she would find them again.

She followed the riverbank. She had no idea how long she walked. Time had no meaning to her. Finally, when she became tired, she sank to the ground, drew up her knees, and hugged them against her chest while she stared at the river.

Her thoughts slipped backward. Like faded photographs, memories flashed in her head. The first time she'd met George. Their courtship. The day he'd proposed to her. Their wedding day. The hopes that had filled her heart. The disappointments that had followed. Small apartments. Dingy hotel rooms. Fights, lots of fights. Alex's birth. Becca's birth. The night she'd found George with Jane. The hard and lonely times that had followed.

George didn't love the children. He'd scarcely known they were alive even when he'd lived with them. They had been an inconvenience to him. If he were to take them, he would neglect them. And if Becca should fall ill again . . .

She shivered as the sun sank behind the mountain peaks.

She remembered the first time she'd met Drake. She remembered the way her heart had been drawn to him. Had she begun to love him as early as that first meeting, when he'd snarled at her? She thought perhaps she had.

Memories of Drake filled her mind, and she pondered them more slowly than the ones that had gone before. She wanted to study these memories, to hold them close to her heart. Drake, turning up the lamp in his library, expecting her to run in horror from the room. Drake, standing on the porch in the moonlight, bitter and alone. Drake, carrying Becca down to the lawn, his touch so gentle. Drake, in town the night of her performance. Drake, holding Alex's hand.

Drake, holding her.

Drake, kissing her.

Drake, loving her.

Tears slipped silently down her cheeks. She didn't sob, not even when she realized she was bidding Drake farewell in her heart.

Like it or not, George was her husband and the father of her children. She could refuse to go back to him. She could probably obtain a divorce in time. But Alex and Becca would be awarded to George. His threat was not an idle one. She had seen it happen often enough among her acquaintances and fellow performers. She had seen it happen to her own parents. Actors and actresses were notorious for their disastrous marriages and their divorces, and the courts were not kind to them.

Dusk fell over the valley, turning the sky to pewter and the earth to ash. A short while later, Faith was surrounded by the earnest darkness of night. Stars

twinkled overhead in a moonless sky. The song of the
night creatures began—the chirruping of bullfrogs,
the howl of a timber wolf, the hoot of an owl—but
Faith was oblivious of it all.

She laid her cheek against her knees, closed her
eyes, and began to rock back and forth. Soft, whim-
pering sounds rose in her throat but were strangled
there.

That was how Drake found her, and if he lived forever, he would never forget the sight of her at that
moment.

He dismounted and went to stand behind her, then
sank to his knees. He drew her back against his chest
and buried his face in her hair. "Faith," he whispered.
"Don't. Don't cry, Faith."

It was a long time before her silent sobbing ceased,
a long time before she spoke. "I wish you'd made love
to me. I wish you'd taken me to your bed."

"Darling—"

She pulled away, came up onto her own knees,
turned to face him, clinging to his arms. Then she
took hold of his hands and placed them on her
breasts. She leaned into him, capturing his mouth in
a kiss. He tasted her tears—warm, salty, frantic—
as their lips parted, their tongues met. He felt
her nipples peak beneath his thumbs, felt his
own desire harden as she moved her body
against his. He would have to have been a saint
not to respond to her movements. And he was no
saint.

She lifted her mouth and whispered, "Make love to
me now, Drake. Make love to me here, now."

He'd never heard such discouragement in a person's voice before, and it was the recognition of
her hopelessness that stopped him from doing as

she commanded. "Faith, don't. It's going to be all right."

She released him and rose, turning her back to him once again. "No, it isn't going to be all right. It's never going to be all right. I've loved you with everything in me. I never wanted to fall in love again. It hurts too much when it fails. But I loved you. Loved you more than I thought possible. I wanted to become a part of you. I would have been your lover. I loved you so much I would have given myself to you, divorce or no divorce. And now I can't have you. Can't ever have you."

"You're giving up," he said as he stood.

"What else am I to do?"

He took hold of her shoulders, turned her around. He wished he could see her eyes clearly, wished he could read what was written on her face. "Listen to me, Faith. I quit living seven years ago. I gave up. I turned my back on the world and wallowed in my own bitterness." He cupped her chin with his right hand. "You didn't quit. You rose above everything. You went on, no matter what. You gave your children whatever they needed. You didn't give up when George left you." His voice softened. "You can't just give up now."

She pulled away from him. "I'm not giving up. I'm being practical."

"Faith—"

"I'm still his wife."

Impotent rage welled in his chest. "Do you think I don't know that?"

"He has the right to take my children."

"We'll fight him. He's not a fit father. He deserted you, all of you. We'll fight him in court and win."

"And in the meantime, he'll take Alex and Becca away."

"Faith, you've got to trust me."

Her reply was small, almost inaudible. "I can't take the risk."

23

Faith looked around the sparsely furnished room with a feeling of déjà vu. This hotel was where she and her children had begun their sojourn in Dead Horse. How appropriate that this would be where it ended.

"I don't wanna be here, Mama," Becca wailed plaintively. "I wanna go home."

Home. Faith's heart twisted as she mouthed the word. But she couldn't bring herself to say it aloud, knowing it would hurt too much. Besides, the Jagged R wasn't their home, merely a place where she'd worked. No different from the countless theaters and saloon halls in which she'd performed over the years.

No different at all.

Her shoulders slumped as she realized how untrue her mental argument was. She couldn't fool herself or her children with such lies. Alex and Becca knew the Jagged R was more than where their mother worked and a temporary place for them to live. In recent weeks it *had* become a home. *Their* home. Theirs and Drake's.

Drake.

She missed him. Missed him beyond even what she had imagined possible. A short time ago, he'd stood on the front porch and watched her drive away in the buggy. He hadn't argued with her this morning, hadn't tried to convince her to stay, but he hadn't made her leaving easy. He'd stood there and watched, his expression grim, his gaze unwavering.

Faith, you've got to trust me. . . .

I can't take the risk. . . .

You've got to trust me . . .

Can't take the risk . . .

Trust me . . .

I can't . . .

She sank onto the end of the bed, trying to rid herself of those terrible words playing over and over again in her head. She knew she'd struck Drake a cruel blow with her reply, but there'd been nothing else she could do, nothing else she could say.

"Is there anything else you'll be needing, Mrs. Butler?"

Faith heard the curiosity in Claire O'Connell's voice, knew that whatever she did or said would be fodder for today's gossip at the general store. She glanced toward the doorway where the other woman stood. "No, there's nothing."

"I've sent Quinlin O'Rourke to find your husband. He went out half an hour ago."

"Thank you."

"I gave you these adjoining rooms so you could have your privacy from the children. Under the circumstances, I thought you might like . . ." Claire's words drifted into oblivion.

"Thank you," Faith said again, more softly this time.

Claire hesitated a moment, looking as if she might say something more. Then, with a slight shake of her head, she hurried out of sight, not bothering to close the door.

Alex turned from his place at the window. "We oughta go back to the ranch, Ma."

"We can't."

"That's not true," her son argued. "Mr. Rutledge said we could stay."

Faith rubbed her eyes, wishing she could wipe away the headache behind them. "He was wrong."

"He wasn't wrong." Alex spoke with all the conviction of an almost-eight-year-old. "*You're* wrong."

"What's this? A tiff between mother and son?"

Faith looked up at the sound of George's voice. Her stomach twisted into a knot.

George closed the door behind him. "Mrs. O'Connell would dearly love to hear what we have to say to each other, but I think I'll leave it to her imagination."

As Faith rose from the bed, Becca hid her face in her mother's skirts. Faith stroked the little girl's head, both seeking and offering comfort.

Yesterday she had been too upset to notice many of the changes in her husband's appearance that had taken place since the last time she'd seen him. Now she saw them. He had the look of someone who drank too much and ate too little. His clothes, always a source of pride to him, appeared worn and shabby, and they hung loosely on his gaunt frame, as if made for someone else. His gold hair looked dull and lifeless. Gray half circles were etched beneath his eyes, and his complexion had turned sallow.

Golden, debonair, handsome George. Once upon a time she had loved him. She remembered it was true, but she couldn't recall the feeling itself. She found nothing appealing about him anymore. Perhaps because she'd learned how deceiving appearances could be. Perhaps because he was the one who had taught her that lesson.

"You look ill, George," she said for want of anything else to say.

His mouth tightened. "Sorry, Faith. I'm not going to keel over dead just so you can marry your lover."

"Don't. We're here. Isn't that what you wanted?"

He muttered a foul curse as he approached her.

"Mama," Becca whimpered.

"Stop it, George. You're frightening her." Faith sat on the bed again and hugged her daughter. "It's all right, Becca. There's nothing to be afraid of."

"I don't feel good."

"It's okay, sweetheart. You don't have to—"

Becca twisted away suddenly and threw up on the floor. The vomit splattered onto her father's shoes and trousers.

George cursed again, this time shouting a string of words that must have been heard all the way down to the general store. "Clean that up before it makes us all puke," he snapped before storming out of the room.

Becca sobbed softly.

"It doesn't matter, darling," Faith crooned as she helped her daughter onto the bed. "You didn't do anything wrong. You'll feel better in a minute."

"I hate him," Alex said with real venom.

Faith wondered if she might shatter into a thousand pieces. Her head pounded. Her nerves jangled. But somehow she managed to say calmly, "Alex, he's your father."

"He's not my father! He's not!" Then, just as George had done moments before, Alex slammed the door behind him as he left.

Gertie didn't actually need to pick up supplies at the general store today, but she hadn't felt much like staying up at the Jagged R, where the mood was as unhappy as a woodpecker in a petrified forest. Everybody was snapping at each other, from the boss to Parker to young Johnny. 'Course, she was as guilty as the rest. Seeing Faith and her kids riding off this morning was about the saddest sight she'd witnessed in years.

She glanced down the street toward the Telford house, wondering if Rick was inside or off on a doctor's visit somewheres. Tomorrow they were set to go down to Green River and tie the knot. That's what they'd agreed to on Sunday morning. She'd actually begun to feel a bit excited and happy about it, before George Butler showed up and ruined everything. She looked over at the hotel, wondering if Faith was all right. It didn't seem fair that Gertie was going to be married and happy while Faith's heart was breaking. No, it didn't seem fair at all.

Just then Gertie saw Alex come out of the hotel. He ran down the main street, short legs pumping. Gertie didn't know much about kids, but she could tell when somebody was hurting. She'd bet a month's wages that Alex was crying. She nudged her mare's ribs and followed the boy.

Alex veered off the road and headed toward the river, stumbling occasionally but never falling. He didn't stop until he reached the riverbank. Once there, he picked up a stick and threw it as hard as he could into the water. Then he picked up another and threw it, too.

Gertie dismounted. "Hey, Alex."

The boy spun around, then quickly rubbed his forearm across his cheeks, trying to erase all sign of tears. "What're you doin' here?"

"I thought you might need a friend."

"I don't need nobody." He turned his back to her and tossed another dried branch into the river.

"We all need somebody sometimes," she said as she stepped up beside him. She faced the rushing water but watched the boy out of the corner of her eye. "Want t'tell me what's got you all riled up?"

"I hate him!"

"Your pa?"

"Yes."

"Hatin' don't do you much good." She dragged the toe of her boot in a small circle, leaving a mark in the loose soil.

Alex looked up at her. "I hate him anyway. And I'm not gonna stay with him. I'm going back to the Jagged R. Mr. Rutledge said I could be a wrangler for him someday. Well, I'm not gonna wait. I can work with you, just like I've been doing."

Oh, Lord, what do I say now?

Gertie took a deep breath, then squatted beside Alex. As he'd done before her, she picked up a piece of wood and tossed it into the water. "Alex, I want you t'think long an' hard about this. I know things ain't easy for you, what with your pa showin' up and all. But things ain't easy for your ma, either. Don't you think she's gonna need you more'n ever?"

He sniffed and wiped his nose with his forearm.

"I know it'd just about break your ma's heart if you were t'go away."

"It isn't fair," he said with a choked sob.

"No, I don't reckon it is fair, but it's how it is."

Alex suddenly threw himself into her arms, knocking her off her heels and landing her backside in the dirt. She put her arms around him and hugged him close, letting him cry it out. At this point she was crying, too.

"It's gonna be all right, little wrangler," she whispered. "You'll see. It'll be all right. It's gonna work out. You'll see."

Gertie didn't know how long she held Alex, letting him weep against her shoulder. It didn't matter much. She just wanted to make the hurt go away. She also pondered a few choice things she'd like to do to that cur who called himself the boy's father. She might not know the whole story about him and Faith, but she knew enough to wish she could run him out of town and away from Faith, Alex, and Becca.

After a long spell, Alex cried himself out. He sniffed noisily as he pulled back. "Sorry, Gertie," he mumbled.

She wiped her eyes, not caring that he was supposed to call her Miss Duncan. "Nothin' t'be sorry for." She got to her feet. "Now I reckon you oughta be gettin' back to your ma 'fore she starts t'worry. You want me t'come along?"

"No." He shook his head. "I'll be okay."

"Sure you will, pardner."

"Gertie?"

"Hmm."

"You won't tell the other cowpokes about . . . about this, will you?"

She offered an understanding smile. "'Course not. Us wranglers've gotta stick together."

"Thanks."

She watched him walk away, saw the brave set of his shoulders, and she wanted to cry all over again. She wished she believed everything would be all right, like she'd promised him. Unfortunately she knew things often didn't work out the way she wanted, no matter what she did to try to change them.

Drake paced the length of his library, then turned. "I want you to go to San Francisco," he told Parker. "There's got to be something we can use against Butler. I only have to look at him to know he's in some kind of trouble. We need to know what. Driscoe will help you."

"I'll do my best."

"Parker?" He stopped pacing and faced his friend. He sought the right words as he handed Parker an envelope containing the necessary funds and all the information he'd managed to compile.

Parker laid a hand on Drake's shoulder. "Don't have to say it. I know how important this is. We won't let him take those kids from Faith."

Drake nodded.

"I'll send word as soon as I can."

He nodded again as Parker left the library. Then he went to the window and stared out at the lawn. He knew he was looking for Faith, wanted her to be sitting in the grass, reading to Becca, or standing beside the clothesline, wisps of hair curling around her face and neck.

I can't take the risk. . . .

He'd wanted her to trust him. She was supposed to

trust him. And now she was at the hotel, with her husband, with George Butler, and he couldn't do anything about it.

Drake leaned his forehead against the window frame. He tried not to imagine what was going on between them. He tried not to allow ugly doubts to surface, tried not to listen to the small voice in his head, whispering that Faith had returned to her husband by choice, that George was a whole man, not a blind one, that she had once loved her husband, lain with him, given birth to his children.

At last Drake was able to silence the doubts by remembering the look of defeat Faith had worn the night before and again this morning. She had done this to protect Alex and Becca. And could he blame her? Wouldn't he have given his own life to protect them all, if only he'd been given the chance?

He struck the window frame with his fist. *Damn!* He hated his own powerlessness. There had to be something he could do. He would never allow George Butler to take his family. Not as long as he could still draw breath.

It was nearly midnight before George returned from the saloon. Faith was in bed with the children, Alex on her left, Becca on her right.

Faith heard him enter the adjoining room, heard his footsteps on the bare board floor as he crossed to the connecting doorway, heard him twist the knob. She tensed, uncertain if she heard his curse or had only imagined it.

"Open the door," he ordered softly.

She pulled her arms from beneath the children's

heads, then slid out of bed and crossed to the locked door, her way lit by a low-burning lamp. Whispering, she replied, "Go to bed, George. The children are asleep."

"Unlock the damn door."

A moment's hesitation, then, "No."

This time she heard his curse and knew she hadn't imagined it.

"I'm staying in here with the children tonight. They're upset. I'm not leaving them."

"You're my wife, damn it! Now open this door." He pounded on it.

"Ma?" Alex called from the bed.

She pressed her hand against the door. "You're waking the children. Sleep it off, George, and we'll talk in the morning."

She heard a loud noise and barely had time to step back before the doorjamb splintered. The door burst open, swinging on its hinges until it struck the wall.

George strode through the doorway and grabbed her by the upper arms, hurting her with his tight grasp. "Next time I tell you to do something, you'll do it."

Even in the dim light, Faith saw something in his eyes she hadn't recognized earlier. Insanity.

Terror sluiced through her veins. What have I done? she wondered. What have I done?

His grip tightened. "You went to bed with him, didn't you?"

"No."

"Didn't you?"

She winced as if he'd hit her. "Not now, George. It's late." Her voice cracked, revealing her fear. She took a quick breath and continued, "You've had a long journey, and you're tired. Go to bed, and we'll talk tomorrow."

"Tell me." He gave her a shake. "Did you sleep with that ugly bastard?"

"Ma?"

"It's all right, Alex," she answered hastily, then to her husband, "Please. Let's talk about it in the morning. Please, George. You've been gone a long time. One more night can't matter so very much."

He drew her toward him, lowered his face close to hers. She could smell the cheap whiskey on his breath, but she sensed he wasn't drunk. "You can have your one night, Mrs. Butler, but this is the last time you'll stay in this room with them. You're my wife. Understand me? You'll sleep in my bed and you'll do whatever I tell you to do. Understand?"

"Yes, George." She shivered. "I understand you." She had to get away. She had to see that Alex and Becca were safe.

"Don't think of trying to run off with them," he whispered, reading her mind. "Those children are mine, and if you don't want the marshal taking them from you, you'll do as I say." He shoved her away. As he turned he added, "Don't try to lock me out again. You'll regret it if you do."

She stood, staring, as he went into the next room. She listened as he shed his clothes, dropping his shoes on the floor one at a time. She heard the squeak of the bed as he lay down.

It wasn't until Alex took hold of her hand that she realized she was shaking violently, enough to make her teeth chatter. Now it was her son's turn to say, "It's okay, Ma. I won't let him hurt you." Then he led her back to the bed.

Drake was halfway to Dead Horse the next morning—on his way to get Faith and the children and to hell with George Butler and any legal claims he might have—when he saw a young boy running along the road from town. He didn't have to get any nearer to know it was Alex. He nudged his pinto into a canter, closing the remaining distance between them. Then he reined in and dismounted.

"Alex, what are you doing out here?"

"I . . . was comin' . . . for you," the boy said between breaths.

Drake grabbed him by the arms and steadied him. "What's wrong?"

"It's *him*. He kicked in the door last night."

"Did he hurt your mother?"

Alex shook his head. "No, but he was going to. I could tell. He was mad 'cause she wouldn't go sleep in the other room. He was mad 'cause she locked the door." His blue eyes showed an understanding far beyond his years. "Don't let him hurt Ma, Mr. Rutledge. Don't let him take us away."

"I won't," Drake promised as he straightened. "Come on. We're going for your mother and Becca. I never should have let any of you leave the Jagged R."

They'd gone down to the hotel restaurant for breakfast. Faith had been thankful there were no other guests. It had been bad enough enduring Claire O'Connell's curious glances.

Only George had actually eaten what he'd ordered. The children and Faith had merely moved their food around on their plates. Finally George had stood and told the children to go outside and play while their parents had a talk.

Now, as she watched him moving around the hotel room, pausing at the window, then continuing his circuitous route, she shivered with dread. Instinct told her he didn't want to talk: he wanted to strike out and hurt her. She'd never feared him in the years they'd been together, despite the things he'd done. But something inside him had changed. There was an unholy look in his eyes that bespoke a soul well acquainted with perdition.

Now she feared him.

George stopped and turned toward her. "*You* are an adulteress." The words fell from his lips like venom.

She stilled her quaking heart. "I worked for Drake Rutledge as his housekeeper. Nothing more."

"His housekeeper, hmm? Then where is the money he paid you to *work* for him? Or are you still as worthless as you ever were?"

She was silent.

He took a threatening step toward her. "Where is it?"

"In my jewelry box."

She hadn't wanted to tell him, hadn't wanted him to have any money because she feared how he might use it. But at least her reply had diverted his attention for the moment.

George opened her jewelry box and removed the paper money and coins Faith had stashed away so carefully. She had intended to use it one day to leave Dead Horse, but of course that was before she'd accepted Drake's proposal of marriage.

Her breath caught in her chest when she saw George lift the topaz necklace, letting the gold chain slide through his fingers. "That isn't mine," she said quickly as she rose from her chair. "I must return it."

He cast her a sideways glance. "Not yours?"

"It was a wedding gift from Drake." Her chest hurt. "I must return it to him."

"Like hell you will."

"I must." Her throat tightened. "I can't marry him, so I must return it."

"Was this bauble payment for your favors, Faith?" he asked harshly. "Did you spread your legs for that ugly bastard? You must have done it only in the dark, when you wouldn't have to look at his scars."

"Don't, George. Don't be vile. I've already told you everything. I was never unfaithful to you. Now let me have the necklace."

"You're lying to me. You bedded him. I can see it in your face."

Caution flew to the wind, replaced by reckless anger. "No, I didn't. But I wish I had. I wanted to. I wanted him as I never wanted you. He's more man than you've ever been, and more handsome, too. You see his scars. I see only beauty. His kindness. His tenderness. I was more than willing to lie with him, but he wouldn't. I wanted him to make love to me long before I believed you were dead." She lifted her chin in defiance. "But he was too honorable to take advantage of my attempt at seduction. Does that surprise you? You can't understand what the word 'honor' means, can you?"

"Slut!"

His blow sent her crashing back against the wall. Before she could get her bearings, before the ringing in her ears could cease, he had pinned her there, his arm pressed against her throat.

"You belong to me, woman. You're mine. You'll do what I tell you to do." He pressed harder, cutting off her wind. "Do you know how easy it would be for me to kill you? I know. I know how easy it is. I've killed before. I could do it right now, and then I'd take the children away from here. You wouldn't be around to protect them, would you? The girl, she'll be pretty like you. There are men who would pay to—"

She kneed him in the groin as hard as she could. Hard enough to cause him to stumble back from her, which gave her a chance to draw a breath. He bowed over in pain, and she took advantage of the short reprieve. She grabbed a nearby ladder-back chair and swung it with all her might, landing a solid blow against the side of his head. He fell with a thump to the floor.

She stood shaking, staring at his inert form, and whispered, "You'll never hurt my children. Never."

The door flew open, and Faith lifted the chair, ready to strike again if necessary. Then she saw a commanding presence standing in the doorway.

Drake.

A tiny cry tore from her throat. A moment later she was in his arms.

"I'm taking you away from here," he said softly but firmly.

She nodded against his chest, unable to speak.

"It won't be easy."

I know.

"Will you trust me, Faith, to see that none of you come to harm?"

She lifted her head and looked up, meeting his gaze. "Yes."

His kiss was brief, urgent, and full of love. Then he said, "Let's get out of here."

"My things—"

"There isn't anything here you want. I'll get Becca and we'll go home."

24

Gertie leaned forward on the buggy seat, as if that would get them to the Jagged R sooner. Her stomach was tied in knots, and she wrung her hands anxiously.

She didn't know what had come over her day before yesterday. One minute she'd actually been looking forward to arriving in Green River City and becoming Mrs. Rick Telford, even though she still believed she was going to make one lousy wife. The next minute she'd been grabbing Rick's arm and telling him to turn the wagon around.

"Somethin's wrong, Doc. We gotta get back."

"What are you talking about? We're almost to Green River. We'll be married in an hour or two, and we can start back in the morning."

"No. That ain't soon enough. Turn back now."

"But, Gertie—"

"Now, Doc. We gotta go now."

All the way back, with Rick pushing the buggy horse to the limit of its endurance, Gertie had kept remembering the expression on Faith's face at the moment her husband had stopped the wedding. She'd kept remembering the gloom that had pervaded the ranch on the morning Faith and the children had driven away. Gertie was certain now that Faith needed her help, and she was intent on reaching the hotel as quickly as possible. But a short while before, she'd told Rick to turn off at the ranch instead. Something in her heart told her that was where they needed to be.

Gertie had never felt such relief as she did the moment the ranch house came into view. She glanced sideways at Rick.

Hurry, Doc.

As if he'd heard her, he clucked to the weary horse and slapped its rear with the reins. The animal broke into a reluctant trot.

Gertie reached over and covered one of Rick's hands with her own. "I've never been much good at words, Doc, but I want you t'know how much this means to me. I might be loco, comin' back 'fore we could see the parson. I just knew we had to."

He offered a tired smile. "You might be loco, Gertie, but if you are, then that's one of the things I love about you. I'll always try to do what you ask of me, if it's in my power to do so."

One of the things I love about you . . .

For a moment, as his words repeated themselves in her head, Gertie forgot about Faith and reveled instead in Rick's confession of love. He'd never actually used the word before, and she hadn't known how much she'd wanted him to until he did.

"Doc." She leaned toward him, her hand squeezing his. "We'll get us back down to Green River City just as soon as we can. That's a promise." She kissed him, the first kiss they'd shared since leaving Dead Horse several days before. Then she hopped out of the buggy as it rolled to a stop and hurried toward the house.

"Mr. Rutledge!" she called as she opened the front door. "You here?"

A moment later she heard footsteps upstairs. Just as she looked up, Faith leaned over the third-floor railing.

"Gertie. Thank God. Is Rick with you?"

"He's outside. What're you doin' here, Faith?"

"Get the doctor, please, Gertie. It's Becca."

Gertie didn't repeat her question. She just whirled around and rushed back through the open doorway. "Doc, git your bag and git in here quick. Becca's sick." She didn't wait to watch him follow her inside. Instead she ran up the stairs, taking them two at a time. She found both Faith and Drake in the children's bedroom.

Faith was bending over the bed, smoothing Becca's forehead with her fingertips. "It's all right, Rebecca Ann," she said softly. "Dr. Telford is here. He's going to make you feel better again."

Before Gertie could say anything or ask any questions, Rick entered the bedroom, his black leather bag in hand. His gaze met Drake's for the briefest of moments before he strode to the opposite side of the bed from Faith.

As Rick leaned down to examine the child, Drake spoke. "She took sick last night. We haven't been able to bring her fever down."

"She was doing so much better." Faith's eyes were wide and misty. "She was doing so much better. This is all my fault. She was upset by everything. If I hadn't . . ." She fell silent and glanced around her, as if she'd forgotten what she'd been about to say.

"Gertie," Rick said in a low voice, "take Faith down to the kitchen and see that she eats something."

"I can't leave," Faith protested.

"Gertie, take her now."

Understanding Rick's concern, Gertie took hold of Faith's arm. "Come with me. Let Doc see what he can do for Becca. She'll be all right now that he's here. You said so yourself." She glanced quickly at Rick, and he gave her a slight nod before returning his attention to his patient.

Gertie slipped her free arm around Faith's shoulders and drew her toward the door, murmuring platitudes and reassurances. She wished she knew if anything she said was true. She also wished she could ask what had brought Faith and her children back to the Jagged R.

And where, she couldn't help wondering, was Becca's father?

George paced back and forth across the length of the hotel room, his brows crinkled in an angry frown. He was caged, trapped in this cursed little town, and he didn't like the feeling one bit. He rubbed the side of his head where Faith had struck him with the chair, spewing obscenities about the woman he'd married and all the trouble she'd caused him.

Nothing had gone right for him lately, and this

time it was Faith's fault. Faith Butler, his faithful and loving wife. His *wife*, by God!

He paused and counted the remaining money in his pocket. The money he'd taken from Faith. Not much there. Not after several nights with Beatrice, the barmaid over at the Dead Horse Saloon. He still had the necklace Faith said belonged to Rutledge, but he'd be hanged if he was going to give it back. On the other hand, he couldn't go down to Green River and pawn it. Not yet, anyway. Now that there were people who knew he was still alive, he needed to stay in Dead Horse, hide out for a while longer, just in case.

With a sudden fierceness, he kicked over the small commode, breaking the porcelain pitcher and spilling water across the floor.

It wasn't fair! Why was he stuck here in this god-forsaken place? He should be living it high on the hog in the big city. He should have women at his beck and call, as he had in years past. Why was this happening to him? He didn't deserve this. Why were the fates against him? Wasn't he deserving of at least a little luck?

He strode to the window of the room and stared at the gray house on the ridge. It was an elegant place, built in the middle of nowhere. He could probably live for years on what Rutledge had paid for some of the oil paintings hanging on his walls or for that piano in the Jagged R parlor.

George cursed as he slammed his fist against the window frame. There had to be a way he could get his hands on enough money to take him out of this stinking backwater town and back to a city where he belonged. Back east, far from San Francisco and its accompanying ill fortune. Back to Boston or New

York City, where a man could live like a man was supposed to live. George was the one who should be living in luxury. Not Faith. Never Faith and those brats she'd raised.

The brats—that was it! That was how he was going to get out of here. Not with Faith, but with those kids. Those kids were his ticket to a life of comfort. The life he deserved.

Ah, yes. Those kids were the answer.

It was evening when Will Kidd delivered the envelope, addressed to Drake Rutledge at the Jagged R Ranch. Drake didn't have to open it to know the letter was from George Butler, and he knew Faith didn't have to be told. He could feel her apprehensive gaze upon him as he slid his finger beneath the envelope's flap and broke the seal. He removed the folded sheet of paper and read it in silence, his gaze flicking over the short missive several times.

"What is it?" she whispered.

Drake glanced up. "He wants to meet with me."

"Don't go." She grabbed his wrist. "It's a trap. You mustn't go. He's mad, Drake. I saw it in his eyes. He's insane."

"I have to go, Faith."

"No. No, you don't."

He cupped her chin, smoothing her skin with his thumb. "We have to settle things with him so we can marry. We belong together—you, me, and the children. We can't go forward until we come to terms with the past."

"But—"

"Shh." He kissed her, drawing her close against

him. He sought to comfort her with his tender caresses. He wanted only to dispel her fears.

Faith clung to him, as if afraid ever to let him go. Drake understood how she longed to continue pleading with him. He understood how much it cost her to refrain from it. Silently he swore to God that he wouldn't fail her. No matter what he had to do, he wouldn't fail her.

The two men met in the hotel restaurant late that night. No one else was present. Even Claire O'Connell had enough sense to remain out of sight.

Drake didn't speak as he took his seat on the chair opposite George. He deliberately kept his expression neutral, hiding the anger that burned in his heart. He didn't know exactly what George wanted, but he was certain it was about money. With a man like George Butler, it almost always was.

He read disdain in George's eyes as their gazes met across the table. It was a look Drake had seen before, but this time he was thankful for it. George was making a serious tactical error in underestimating his adversary. He saw Drake's blindness as a vulnerability, which was a mistake. But then, George had already proven himself a fool in other ways; Drake was not surprised to find his judgment flawed in this instance.

"You used to be a lawyer," George began, breaking the silence at last.

Drake gave a curt nod.

George cleared his throat. "Then you should know it won't go well for Faith in a divorce. She's an actress, and she's been living with you while married to me. No judge will allow her to keep the children. You know I'm right."

Drake did indeed know, but he didn't say so. He simply waited for the other man to continue.

George glanced quickly toward the doorway, then leaned forward, arms on the table, and spoke in a low voice. "Listen, I'm willing to make it easy on everyone. If I go away, there doesn't have to be a divorce. We'll just pretend I'm dead. You can marry Faith if you want or keep her as your mistress. Who cares?"

Drake's mouth thinned, but he held himself in check. Smashing his fist into George's face wouldn't solve a thing.

"Look, I'm a little short of travel funds right now," George continued. "And if I have to stay here, I want those kids with me, as is my right. But for, say, ten thousand dollars, I think I'd be able to leave Dead Horse and never trouble any of you again."

"Are you offering to sell Faith and the children to me?" Drake asked, then watched as George actually had the gall to smile.

"I wouldn't put it exactly that way."

Perhaps it would be worth ten thousand dollars to see the last of George Butler, but Drake knew it wouldn't be the last time they would see him. A man like George never stopped looking for an easy dollar. If Drake gave in to his blackmail this time, he would eventually return for more. Besides, even if no one else knew the truth, he couldn't pretend George was dead. Drake wouldn't be able to marry Faith until she was free of him once and for all.

"Listen, Rutledge." George's voice dropped to a whisper. "It's either this or I go for the marshal."

He's bluffing. The knowledge struck Drake with a

sudden certainty. George wasn't going to go for the marshal. He was in trouble, probably hiding from someone. He needed money to get away, far away. He was a desperate man, and desperate men usually made mistakes.

Drake rose from his chair. "Go ahead and send for him."

George's eyes widened in surprise.

"On second thought"—Drake leaned forward, knuckles on the table—"I think I'll send for the marshal myself."

The other man's chair tipped over, crashing to the floor as he jumped to his feet. "You son of a—"

Drake's hand around George's throat cut short his foul exclamation. "Come near Faith, Alex, or Becca again, and I'll personally validate your death notice once and for all! Understand me, Butler?"

"You can't do this," George croaked.

"Watch me." Drake gave him a shove, then strode from the room without a backward glance.

Faith awakened from the nightmare with a start, her heart racing. Becca! she thought, terror sluicing through her veins.

Tossing aside the sheet, she jumped out of bed and hurried into the adjoining room. A lamp, turn low, still burned on a table near the window, and the pale light revealed Drake sitting beside Becca's bed, holding the little girl's hand.

"Drake?"

He glanced up with a look of relief. "The fever's broken."

Her pulse slowed to a more normal rate. "How long ago?"

"Not long."

Faith moved to the opposite side of the bed and leaned over to see for herself. Becca's forehead was cool and dry to the touch. "Thank God," she breathed.

"You should go back to bed."

"I don't think I could fall asleep again."

Drake rose and came around the bed. He placed an arm around her shoulders, and together they watched Becca sleep. After several minutes Drake's arm tightened. "Let's go downstairs."

She didn't argue. She longed to be able to relax in his arms.

Carrying the lamp to light the way, he guided her out of the bedroom, down the stairs, and into the parlor. They settled on the sofa, Faith's cheek against Drake's chest. She felt his lips brush across the top of her head, and warm contentment spread through her.

After a long while she looked up. "What's going to happen now?"

He was silent for several heartbeats before answering. "We can't wait for George to try to take you or the children away again. When Becca's well enough, I want us to go down to Green River City to see the marshal. It's a chance I think we need to take. Will you go with me?"

Ever since George had interrupted the wedding a few days before, Faith had been trapped in a web of her own fears. She'd given up, just as Drake had said, and her lack of trust had almost cost her the only chance for real happiness she'd ever known. Now, as Drake held her in his arms, she felt the last of her apprehension melting away. His quiet confidence became her own. She believed in him. She trusted him. She loved him.

"Faith?"

"I'll go with you," she replied. "We all will."

"Like hell," came a snarl from the parlor doorway.

Faith gasped even as Drake rose from the sofa and shoved her behind him protectively.

George stepped into the room, his gun pointed directly at Drake's chest. "Never understood why a man'd want t'marry a whore. That's all she is, you know. Just another cold, unfeeling whore. That's all any of them are."

"Get out of here, Butler," Drake warned.

"You know what she wants from you, Rutledge? Your money."

"No," she whispered, wanting to shout the word but too frightened to do so.

"That's all they ever want," George continued. "You can buy 'em cheap in San Francisco. You don't need to marry them. Whores are a dime a dozen down there. Not worth the air they breathe, you know. None of them. Should have killed them all. Shouldn't have stopped with one. Should have killed Jane, too."

Faith knew she was listening to the ramblings of a madman and wondered if Drake knew it, too. Her fingers tightened on his arms in a silent warning for him to beware.

"Why don't we go outside and talk about this?" Drake suggested calmly.

George cocked and released the hammer of the gun several times. "Where're the brats?"

Drake replied, "Asleep."

"I should have killed her, you know. Nothing's

gone right for me. Nothing. Not since the day I met her. Let's go to California, she said. Let's go get rich. Faith there, she was supposed to become some great actress. She was supposed to make me rich, too. But all she ever wanted was a passel of brats and a house to raise 'em in. Now look at her. Just like Jane. Lying to me, just like Jane." He cocked the gun. "Well, it's not going to happen again."

"George, no!" Faith shouted. But she was too late to stop the scene from playing out to its horrifying end.

Drake lunged forward even as a deafening gunshot split the air. Faith saw him fall in midstride, saw the frightening red stain spread across his shirt. A silent scream echoed in her mind. She wanted to run to him but was unable to move.

"Now it's your turn." George cocked his weapon a second time and aimed it at her chest.

It didn't matter if he killed her. Not if Drake was dead. Nothing mattered if he was gone.

Faith heard the blast of the gun and waited to feel the bullet slam into her, waited to fall beside Drake. Instead she saw a look of surprise flash across George's face moments before he crumpled to the floor, his eyes frozen open in death. Faith drew a startled breath but remained unable to move.

Then Gertie stepped into view, her pistol in hand. Her eyes flicked from the two men on the floor to Faith. "I reckon we'd best see to the boss. There's no help for Butler now."

As if Gertie's words had released her from some invisible bonds, Faith rushed forward, then fell to her knees beside the man she loved.

25

Their wedding day arrived, a crisp autumn afternoon in late October. The leaves on the poplars and aspens had turned to gold; the ones that had already fallen crunched beneath the wheels of the wagons bringing their guests to the Jagged R. The purple mountain peaks had received a dusting of snow the night before, and the promise of winter hung in the air.

The marriage of Drake Rutledge and Faith Butler was to be a quiet affair, held in the parlor of the gray house on the ridge, with only a few witnesses—Alex and Becca, Rick and Gertie Telford, newlyweds themselves, Sadie and Joseph Gold and their children, and the Jagged R ranch hands. Faith had wanted to keep it small and intimate. After several weeks of caring for Drake as he recovered from the bullet wound in his shoulder and dealing with questions and suspicions from the Green River marshal, she longed for simplicity.

For a while, she had feared Drake would be accused of George Butler's murder. After all, the marshal had said, Drake wanted to marry the wife of the deceased. Perhaps this had been the easiest way to eliminate an inconvenient husband. Faith had responded to the implications with indignant denials. If anyone was to blame, it was she herself, she had declared. Drake had sought only to protect her and had been injured for it.

The marshal then turned his attention to his other suspect. There had been a time when Faith was certain Gertie would be arrested, especially after the wrangler admitted she'd seen George Butler enter the house and had followed him, gun in hand, with full intent to shoot if necessary. "I wasn't gonna let him hurt nobody agin," she'd confessed bluntly and without apology.

In the end, the marshal had ceased his search for someone to charge in George Butler's death and had ruled the shooting self-defense. Then he'd returned to Green River City, leaving the survivors to piece their lives back together again.

Now, with Drake recovered and Becca healthier than ever, the horror of that night seemed like a bad dream to Faith. There had been moments of guilt when she remembered that she'd wished George dead, moments when she'd blamed herself for what had happened to both George and Drake.

But those moments were few.

And today she'd put all such thoughts behind her. She faced the future with gladness and tingling anticipation. She was to be Drake's wife. She was to know what it meant to be loved by him. She would bear his name, and one day she would bear his children, too.

Faith knew she was most blessed among women.

Wearing her gold-and-brown-striped dress, a spray of dried flowers in her hair, Faith descended the front staircase. Her groom awaited her at the bottom. Her heart leapt at the sight of him—tall and handsome, his ebony hair tied back at the nape with a satin ribbon. She found the moment surreal, knowing she was bound to this man by a love still undreamed of only last spring.

With a look of adoration in his uncovered eye, Drake reached out and took hold of her hand, squeezing her fingers gently, drawing her toward him.

Toward Drake and all their tomorrows.

She went gladly.

Reverend Arnold smiled at the couple as they entered the parlor, and Faith heard one of the Gold girls whisper how handsome Drake was. Her heart swelled with pleasure, and she felt like laughing aloud.

"Dearly beloved . . . "

Yes, she was beloved. She felt it, like a soft wind caressing her skin. Dearly beloved, indeed.

O spirit of love, how quick and fresh art thou.

" . . . we are gathered here today, in the sight of God, to join this man and this woman . . . "

He is the half part of a blessed man,
Left to be finished by such as she,
And she a fair divided excellence,
Whose fullness of perfection lies in him.

" . . . in the state of holy matrimony . . . "

Honor, riches, marriage blessing,
Long continuance, and increasing,
Hourly joys be still upon you!

"I, Drake, take thee, Faith . . . "

Love . . . as sweet and musical
As bright Apollo's lute, strung with his hair.

And when Love speaks, the voice of all the gods
Make heaven drowsy with the harmony.

"I, Faith, take thee, Drake . . . "

Doubt thou the stars are fire,
Doubt that the sun doth move;
Doubt truth to be a liar,
But never doubt I love.

"'The Lord bless thee, and keep thee: The Lord make his face shine upon thee, and be gracious unto thee: The Lord lift up his countenance upon thee, and give thee peace.' Now and forevermore. Amen."

At the end of Reverend Arnold's benediction, Faith opened her eyes. Drake was watching her with a look so filled with love, it nearly stopped her heart.

"Drake, you may kiss your bride," the minister added.

"With pleasure." Drake drew her into his embrace, crushing her bouquet between them. Like a perfumed cloud, a sweet scent rose to tickle their nostrils. Drake smiled, then captured her lips in a kiss both tender and passionate.

I think there is not half a kiss to choose
Who loves another best.

Faith's heart soared with a joy too marvelous to be contained. When their mouths parted, she threw her arms around Drake's neck in reckless abandon and laughed as she exclaimed, "I love you!"

Applause broke out behind them, reminding Faith they were not alone, that there were guests to greet and food to be served and endless conversations to be held before the afternoon would be over.

Alex was the first to step forward. He held out his hand toward Drake. "*Now* can I call you Pa?" he asked with all due seriousness.

Drake responded in kind. "Yes, son. Now you can call me Pa."

Faith's heart fluttered.

"And me too!" Becca shouted, throwing herself exuberantly into Drake's arms, much as her mother had done only moments before.

Drake lifted the girl off the floor. "And you too." He planted a kiss on Becca's cheek, then met her mother's gaze.

My crown is in my heart, not on my head;
Not decked with diamonds and Indian stones,
Nor to be seen. My crown is called content.
A crown it is that seldom kings enjoy.

Standing side by side on the front porch, their arms around each other, Faith and Drake waved to their children as the Telford wagon rolled down the drive and into the glare of the setting sun.

"Alone at last." Drake drew her around to face him.

She felt the heat of his body, so close to her own. Unhurriedly he lowered his mouth toward hers, his gaze unwavering. In anticipation of what was to come, she moistened her lips with the tip of her tongue.

"Mrs. Rutledge . . ." He stretched out the words, making them a verbal caress. Then he kissed her. His mouth teased, tasted, and sampled, a sweet ending to a wonderful day. A sweet beginning to a wonderful night.

"Drake," she whispered, mingling breath for breath as his mouth still hovered above hers. Suddenly he scooped her into his arms and carried her into the house. She laughed aloud as she clasped her hands behind his neck. "Hold me like this forever. Never let me go."

"Never," he replied as he kicked the door closed with his foot, then carried her up the stairs and into his bedchamber.

At least two dozen candles flickered in holders throughout the room, and Faith knew that Gertie had placed them there before leaving with Rick and the children. The romantic gesture—so unexpected from the rough-and-tumble wrangler—touched Faith's heart, making tears spring to her eyes.

"Gertie's full of surprises, isn't she?"

Faith smiled as Drake lowered her feet to the floor. "Yes, she is."

"I'm glad." He tipped her chin with his finger. "This way I can look at you." His mouth lowered. "You're so beautiful, Faith Rutledge."

Her breath caught in her chest as she anticipated his kisses. She wondered, for the briefest of moments, if she could possibly be dreaming, if she might awaken and find herself in some dingy hotel, awaiting the next day's performance.

Drake plucked the spray of dried flowers from her hair, then removed her hairpins, one after another, each one clicking softly as he dropped them on the hardwood floor. When all such impediments were gone, he combed his fingers through her thick tresses, lifting her hair toward his face and breathing deeply.

"Do you know how often I've longed to do this?" he asked.

She shook her head in a sort of daze.

"Forever."

With gentle hands he turned her around and slowly freed the buttons of her bodice, pausing between each one to kiss the skin at the base of her neck. Gooseflesh rose on her arms. Her knees weakened. Her body felt weightless. She closed her eyes and allowed her head to fall back, reveling in the sensations he'd stirred within her.

Her bodice slipped downward, the fabric whispering over her skin on its way to the floor. It was followed a few moments later by her skirt, a puddle of gold fabric winking in the candlelight. Mere seconds after that, her corset and chemise were tossed into a corner.

Drake drew her against his chest as his hands explored her breasts. She closed her eyes, giving herself over to the pleasure his touch brought. His thumbs drew small circles around the aureoles. His hands gently kneaded and lifted, teasing her nipples until they grew taut and tingly.

She dropped her head back onto his shoulder and moaned. Then she heard a deep chuckle in his throat.

"Why do you laugh?" she asked, her voice—thick with emotion—no longer sounding like her own.

"Because I'm happy." He turned her toward him and kissed her, his mouth hot, his tongue probing. "Because I love you," he added when the kiss ended a long time later.

Feeling emboldened by desire, Faith slipped her hands inside his coat and forced it over his shoulders and down his arms. Her fingers fumbled as she hastened to remove his collar and shirt.

At last she was in his arms again, bare chest against bare chest. And still it wasn't enough. Not ever enough.

She stared up at him, yellow gold light flickering across his pirate's patch, wondering at the gentleness she'd discovered in a man she'd once thought dark and dangerous. She was no virgin, yet he made her feel innocent and shy. She knew what it meant to be joined with a man, yet she suspected she hadn't even begun to know what pleasures she would find in his arms.

She lifted a hand to caress his cheek, her fingers lingering on his scar. She felt him stiffen and knew a moment of truth had arrived. Without hesitation, she raised her other hand and untied the thongs that held the patch in place.

She knew he expected her to exclaim in horror or sigh in pity. She did neither. She felt neither. He was beautiful, wondrous, perfect in every way. Rising on tiptoes, she cradled his head between her hands and kissed him again with all the molten passion that flowed through her veins.

After a time, his mouth moved to the sensitive pulse point of her throat, then down to the cleft between her breasts, then over to one nipple, which he laved and teased with his tongue and teeth. Faith felt her insides grow as taut as a bowstring. She ached for more. Much more.

As if hearing her silent urging, Drake loosened the tie of her petticoats and let them fall to the floor, mingling with the other discarded clothing. Unexpectedly he knelt, his fingers tracing slowly down her arms, her side, her thighs. Faith shivered with pleasure as she hugged herself, the air suddenly too cool against her heated flesh.

With agonizing slowness, he unfastened her brown leather shoes with a buttonhook that seemed to have appeared out of thin air. Somewhere, in a place where rational thought still existed, she realized he had planned for this moment, and she smiled languidly. When Drake lifted her left foot to remove the first shoe, Faith balanced herself by weaving her fin-

gers through his thick, long hair. Moments—or perhaps an eternity—later, her right shoe followed the
left.

His hands on her thighs caused her to suck in a
breath of surprise. The ache of desire centered at the
juncture of her legs, and she thought for a moment he
might touch her there, that he might prepare her for
release. He didn't. Not yet. Instead he rolled off her
stockings, then removed the last of her undergarments, and finally rose to his full height once again.

Faith stood before him, in the glow of the candles,
completely naked. For an instant she felt dread cooling her passion. George had found her undesirable,
unsatisfactory, a failure as a woman, as a wife. What
if . . .

As she looked at Drake, felt his gaze upon her skin
like the caress of a warm chinook blowing down out
of the Rockies, her uncertainty vanished. She wasn't
cold. She was desirable. She stood before her husband, naked and unashamed, and she gloried in the
moment.

"You're so beautiful, my love." He fondled a sec-
tion of her hair, let it slide through his fingers like a
waterfall. "You're as warm and inviting as sunshine
on a summer day. Light and love. It's how I see you."
He paused once more, then whispered, "'O, she doth
teach the torches to burn bright! / It seems she hangs
upon the cheek of night / As a rich jewel in an
Ethiop's ear— / Beauty too rich for use, for earth too
dear!'"

Her mouth went dry, her heart beating hard in her
chest. He'd known. He'd understood, and with his
words he'd made certain her doubts could never
return again.

"Faith . . ."

There was an invitation in her whispered name, and she responded to it, reaching out to the waistband of his trousers. She felt the hardness of his desire beneath her knuckles as she worked the buttons free and fumbled with sudden nervousness. Or perhaps it was from anticipation.

As the last of Drake's clothing was abandoned to join the heap already on the bedroom floor, Faith allowed herself to look upon him as he had upon her only minutes before. He was wonderfully male and eager for her.

"Touch me," he whispered hoarsely.

Her eyes widened at the invitation. It was something new to her, this idea that she could explore and sample and enjoy.

"You're my wife. It's all right."

He guided her hand to his distended flesh. She felt her body responding, even as did his, as she closed her fingers around his tumescence and explored this heretofore unknown part of him. He groaned, a sound of both pleasure and pain.

Suddenly she was in his arms again. He carried her to the large four-poster bed and laid her in its center. When he joined her there, it was the most natural thing to twine her arms and legs with his, to join her mouth with his, to press her body close and feel the heat rush through her. His hands explored and petted and stroked. His fingers teased and taunted until she was slick and ready. She arched against him, wanting more, needing more, demanding more.

"Drake . . ."

He rose above her. She held her breath as their gazes met. The earth's own pulse seemed to pound a savage beat in her ears.

Then he entered her. A soft cry broke from her lips. A cry of joy.

Theirs was a wondrous joining. Time and again, he filled her and withdrew. She rose and fell with the ancient rhythm. Her senses thrummed, as did her heart. His harsh breathing echoed in her ears. His scent filled her nostrils, mingled with her own.

She quickened with him, felt herself rising to unexplored heights as his thrusts became swift and urgent. With a cry, she toppled over ecstasy's precipice, knew he'd followed when she heard his throaty groan.

They lay in a tangle of sheets, arms, and legs, Faith's head against Drake's shoulder. He stroked his thumb slowly up her spine, then down again.

Up . . . and down.

Up . . . and down.

Up . . . and down.

She was replete, too weary to do anything but moan. "Mmmmmm."

His arm tightened. He turned his head on the pillow and brushed his lips against her tousled hair. "Faith?"

"Mmmm?"

"I used to watch you on the lawn, practicing your Shakespeare."

"Mmm. I know."

"You're a fine actress. Will you miss the stage?"

She rose on one elbow, and her hair tumbled down over her face. She brushed it back so she could meet Drake's gaze. "Not as long as I'm with you."

A smile teased the corners of his mouth. "Perhaps we can rehearse together."

"Rehearse?"

With his hands on her upper arms, he drew her astride him. "Wasn't it your Shakespeare who said, 'All the world's a stage, And all the men and women merely players'?"

She felt his hardness beneath her, felt her own desire flare to life. "Yes," she breathed softly. "I believe it was."

"Then methinks, my dear lady"—he cupped her breasts, kneaded them with his palms, stroked them with his thumbs—"that we must rehearse this play again. Methinks it needs be practiced many, many times."

She lowered her mouth and brushed his lips with her own. She moved her body against him sensuously, felt his taut response. She laughed, a low, husky sound in her throat.

"As often as you like it, kind sir. As often as you like it."

Epilogue

It was a day of grand celebration in Dead Horse. The weekly train arrived just a few minutes past noon. There was a band on the platform, playing noisily and somewhat off key. There were plenty of speeches made by postulating politicians and other dignitaries. The women of Dead Horse laid out a picnic array that would do credit to a town twice its size. There were games and foot races for the children and horse races for the men. And finally, the day came to a close with a glorious display of fireworks.

Statehood! A grand occasion for one and all.

Mr. and Mrs. Drake Rutledge, with Alex and Becca asleep in the back of the wagon, were just pulling into the yard at the Jagged R when Faith suddenly grasped her husband's hand and let out a cry of surprise.

Drake yanked on the reins. "What is it?"

"The baby," she gasped. "I think it's coming."

"*Now?*"

She stared at him with wide eyes, unable to reply as the pain tightened like a band around her belly.

In an instant Drake was out of the wagon, shouting, "Parker! Will!" He lifted her off the wagon seat and carried her toward the house. "Somebody get out here!"

But no one came. The men were all in town, probably still tossing back drinks in the saloon.

"It's all right, Drake," she managed to say. "Don't panic."

"Don't panic," he muttered as he climbed the stairs. "Don't panic."

Faith would have laughed if she hadn't been in the grip of another strong pain. She should have realized she was in labor—after all, she'd given birth twice before—but she'd ignored the nagging, tiresome feeling in her back that had started early that morning. She'd thought it was only because she'd grown as large and ponderous as an elephant, despite having two more weeks to go before her confinement was due.

Drake set her gently on the bed, then stood back, looking helpless and useless.

This time she did laugh. She couldn't help being amused. She'd never, in the years they'd been married, seen him so at a loss as he was now. Drake, her dangerous pirate, her seductive lover, her husband, her champion. No matter what arose, he had always been there to see her through. Knowing she was the cause of his discomposure made her only love him more.

"Go and wake Alex and send him for Rick and Gertie," she instructed calmly. "Then bring in the clean sheets. Oh, and try not to alarm Becca. You know how she tends to fret over me, just as I used to fret over her."

Drake started to turn.

"Wait!" She drew a steadying breath. "You'd best help me out of this dress and into my nightgown before you go." She managed to rise, then doubled over as another pain wrapped its tentacles around her abdomen.

Drake grabbed hold of her. "I'm sorry. Darling, I'm so sorry. So help me God, I'll never let this happen again."

She straightened slowly and stared at the man she loved more than life itself. She managed a tight smile. "We're not through rehearsing just yet, kind sir. The play goes on, and I mean to enjoy it."

She caught his look of surprise just before she doubled over once again.

Drake paced the circumference of the house, oblivious of everything except the muffled sounds of labor coming from the upstairs bedchamber. He didn't notice the blanket of stars that spread across the heavens. He didn't notice the freshness of the night air or the attentive cowboys standing outside the bunkhouse. All he noticed were his wife's soft cries. Faith was in pain, and it was his fault.

Four years ago Faith's love had helped set him free from a prison of his own making, a prison of self-destruction, of blame and anger. Faith had taught him how to live again, how to love again, how to laugh again. She'd taught him how to believe again.

Now, at this dark moment, he found it hard to believe in anything. If he were to lose her—

350 ROBIN LEE HATCHER

Suddenly he stopped pacing and stared up at the window to their bedroom. His breath caught in his chest. Silence. That was all that met his ears. Only silence.

A moment later he was racing toward the front door. He burst through the opening just as a baby's wail split the silence. He ground to a halt at the base of the stairs. As if on cue, Gertie Telford stepped out of the bedroom, one flight up.

"Gertie? Is she all right?"

"Right as rain," she answered with a grin, "and ready t'see you." She motioned him up the stairs. "You go on in. I'm gonna check on the young'ns. My twins can be a handful, even in the middle o' the night. If they're not asleep by now, your Alex has gotta be plumb tuckered out."

Drake didn't hear if she said anything more. He was already up the stairs and into the bedroom.

He was vaguely aware of Rick standing beside the bed, wiping his hands and arms on a towel. He heard the doctor say something, was aware that Rick crossed the room, stepped past him, then closed the door as he left the bedroom.

But it was Faith who captured and held his attention. Faith and the squalling bundle in her arms.

"Hello," his wife whispered.

Her luxurious red hair clung damply to her scalp. There were circles beneath her eyes. A fine mist of perspiration covered her forehead and upper lip. But when she smiled at him, he knew he'd never seen her look more beautiful than she did at this moment.

"Come and meet your daughter, Mr. Rutledge."

His daughter.

Faith looked down as she parted the blankets, wrapped securely about the newborn. As if on cue, the baby quieted. "Come and see, Drake. She looks like you."

"Like me?" *God forbid.*

He moved across the room, never taking his gaze from the two of them, still not daring to believe that both were all right, that he hadn't lost the woman he loved or the child he had yet to meet.

Faith took hold of his hand without taking her eyes from the baby. "Here's your papa, little one."

He saw her then, a tiny scrap of humanity with a thatch of black hair on her head, a red face with a flat nose, and a double chin. Her eyes were squeezed tightly shut, and her mouth was puckered, as if she'd just sucked on an unripened persimmon.

"See," Faith prodded, her voice teasing. "She does look like you."

He let out the breath he hadn't realized he was holding. "Yeah, I guess she does."

His wife wore a secret, centuries-old smile, and he thought again how very beautiful she was.

Faith squeezed his hand. "I love you, Drake."

He knelt on the floor. "And I, you."

"There's so much joy in my heart. So many things I wish I could make you understand."

"I already do."

"You've given me so much. You taught me how to trust again, how to love without reserve."

He caressed her cheek with the back of his hand. "You taught me the same."

"And now you've given me this baby. Look at her. She's so perfect, so wonderful."

"She is perfect. Just like you." Drake leaned the side of his head against Faith's as both of them watched the now sleeping babe. "When I remember how alone I was, when I think how alone I'd still be if you'd never come to Dead Horse . . ." He let his voice drift into silence, not wanting to speak the possibilities out loud.

She drew back so she could look him in the eye, then said solemnly, "Chances are, we'd have found one another, Drake. Some things are simply meant to me."

He loved her, loved her beyond his imagination. He hoped he'd have an eternity to show her just how much that was.

He lay down on the bed beside his wife and child and pulled them both near to his heart. "Chances are, you're right, Faith," he whispered. "Chances are, you're right."

And this time, he truly believed.

Let HarperMonogram
Sweep You Away!

Chances Are by Robin Lee Hatcher

Over 3 million copies of Hatcher's books in print. Her young daughter's illness forces traveling actress Faith Butler to take a job at the Jagged R Ranch working for Drake Rutledge. Passions rise when the beautiful thespian is drawn to her rugged employer and the forbidden pleasure of his touch.

Mystic Moon by Patricia Simpson

"One of the premier writers of supernatural romance."—Romantic Times. A brush with death changes Carter Greyson's life and irrevocably links him to an endangered Indian tribe. Dr. Arielle Scott, who is intrigued by the mysterious Carter, shares this destiny—a destiny that will lead them both to the magic of lasting love.

Just a Miracle by Zita Christian

When dashing Jake Darrow brings his medicine show to Coventry, Montana, pharmacist Brenna McAuley wants nothing to do with him. But it's only a matter of time before Brenna discovers that romance is just what the doctor ordered.

Raven's Bride by Lynn Kerstan

When Glenys Shea robbed the reclusive Earl of Ravensby, she never expected to steal his heart instead of his gold. Now the earl's prisoner, the charming thief must prove her innocence—and her love.

And in case you missed last month's selections . . .

Once a Knight by Christina Dodd

Golden Heart and RITA Award–winning Author. Though slightly rusty, once great knight Sir David Radcliffe agrees to protect Lady Alisoun for a price. His mercenary heart betrayed by passion, Sir David proves to his lady that he is still a master of love—and his sword is as swift as ever.

Timberline by Deborah Bedford

Held captive in her mountain cabin by escaped convict Ben Pershall, Rebecca Woodburn realizes that the man's need for love mirrors her own. Even though Ben has taken her hostage, he ultimately sets her soul free.

Conor's Way by Laura Lee Guhrke

Desperate to save her plantation after the Civil War, beautiful Olivia Maitland takes in Irish ex-boxer Conor Branigan in exchange for help. Cynical Conor has no place for romance in his life, until the strong-willed belle shows him that the love of a lifetime is worth fighting for.

Lord of Misrule by Stephanie Maynard

Golden Heart Award Winner. Posing as a thief to avenge the destruction of her noble family, Catrienne Lyly must match wits with Nicholas D'Avenant, Queen Elizabeth's most mysterious agent. But Cat's bold ruse cannot protect her from the ecstasy of Nicholas's touch.